JACK

THE TRUE STORY OF
JACK & THE BEANSTALK

LIESL SHURTLIFF

ALFRED A. KNOPF
NEW YORK

THIS IS A BORZOI BOOK PUBLISHED BY ALFRED A. KNOPF

Visit us on the Web! randomhousekids.com

Educators and librarians, for a variety of teaching tools, visit us at RHTeachersLibrarians.com

Library of Congress Cataloging-in-Publication Data
Shurtliff, Liesl.
Jack : the true story of Jack and the beanstalk / Liesl Shurtliff. — First edition.
p. cm
Summary: Relates the tale of Jack who, after trading his mother's milk cow for magic beans, climbs a beanstalk to seek his missing father in the land of giants.
ISBN 978-0-385-75579-5 (trade) — ISBN 978-0-385-75580-1 (lib. bdg.) —
ISBN 978-0-385-75582-5 (pbk.) — ISBN 978-0-385-75581-8 (ebook)
[1. Fairy tales. 2. Adventure and adventurers—Fiction.
3. Missing persons—Fiction. 4. Giants—Fiction. 5. Humorous stories.] I. Title.
PZ8.S34525Jac 2015
[Fic]—dc23
2014013403

The text of this book is set in 12.5-point Goudy Old Style.

Printed in the United States of America
April 2015
10 9 8 7 6 5 4 3

First Edition

FOR my brother Patrick,
who was often told he was a naughty boy,
but grew up pretty great

CONTENTS

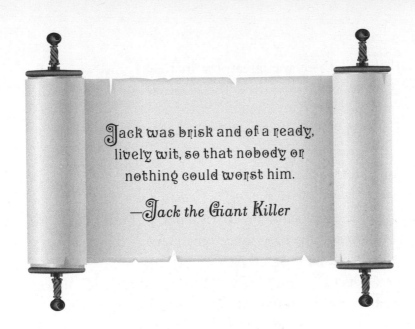

Jack was brisk and of a ready,
lively wit, so that nobody or
nothing could worst him.

—*Jack the Giant Killer*

CHAPTER ONE
A Sprinkling of Dirt

When I was born, Papa named me after my great-great-great-great-great-great-GREAT-grandfather, who, legend had it, conquered nine giants and married the daughter of a duke. Mama said this was all hogwash. Firstly, there was no such thing as giants. Wouldn't we see such large creatures if they really existed? And secondly, we had no relation to any duke—if we did, we'd be rich and living on a grand estate. Instead, we were poor as dirt and lived in a tiny house on a small farm in a little village. Nothing great or giant about it.

But Papa wasn't concerned with the details. He

believed there was greatness in that name, and if he gave it to me, somehow the greatness would sink into my bones.

"We'll name him Jack," Papa said. "He'll be great."

"If you say so," said Mama. She was a practical woman and not particular with names. All she needed was a word to call me to supper, or deliver a scolding. I got my first scolding before my first supper, just after birth, for as soon as Papa pronounced my name, I sprang a sharp tooth, and bit my mother.

"Ouch!" Mama cried. "You naughty boy!" It was something she would call me more often than Jack.

Papa had the nerve to laugh. "Oh, Alice, he's just a baby. He doesn't know any better."

But Mama believed I *did* know better. To her, that bite was a little omen of what was to come, like a sprinkle before the downpour, a buzz before the sting, or the onset of an itch before you realize you're covered in poison ivy.

Maybe I was born to be great, but great at what?

At five months old, I learned to crawl. I was fast as a cockroach, Papa said. One minute I was by Mama's skirts, and the next I was in the pigsty, rolling around in the muck and slops. Mama said she had to bathe me twice a day just to keep me from turning into a real pig.

I learned to walk before my first year, and by my second I took to climbing. I climbed chairs and tables, the woodpile, trees. Once Mama found me on the roof, and snatched me up before I slid down the chimney into a blazing fire.

"Such a naughty boy," said Mama.

"He's just a boy," said Papa.

But I didn't want to be "just a boy." I wanted to be great.

At night, Papa would tell stories of Grandpa Jack: how he'd chop off giants' heads and steal all their treasure and rescue the innocents. I knew if I was going to be great, I'd have to go on a noble quest and conquer a giant—or nine—just like my seven-greats-grandpa Jack.

There was only one problem. I'd never seen a giant in all my twelve years.

"**S**top staring at the sky, Jack," said Papa. "The work's down here."

It was harvesttime, same as every year. Work, work, work. Boring, boring, boring. And after the work was done, we were still poor as dirt.

Papa whistled a merry tune as he cut the wheat. I grumbled as I gathered it up in a bundle and tied it around the middle. We did this over and over, until we'd made a pile as tall as Papa. I thought we'd be nearly done, but when I looked up, I saw acres of uncut wheat. "Snakes and toads," I grumbled. How I hated the sight.

"Ain't she the prettiest sight you ever saw?" Papa called the land *she*, like a lady he was trying to woo. Most of the time it seemed like the land just spat in Papa's face, but he was ever faithful. Papa loved the land.

Me? I could live without it. I preferred a sword to a

scythe, and a noble steed to a cow. I'd go on a quest to fight giants and get gold and riches. Then I'd never have to milk another cow or harvest a crop on a hot day.

I looked toward the house, where Mama was hanging the wash on the line. Annabella was flitting around her like a butterfly, her braids bouncing on her shoulders, not a care in the world, until . . .

"*Eeeeaak!*" Annabella screamed, and frantically shook her apron. A fat grasshopper flew out and disappeared into the tall grass.

I stifled a laugh. Annabella is my sister, four years younger. I guess when I hit three or so, Mama decided I was a lost cause and tried again, taking every precaution to do things differently. So firstly, she had a girl, and secondly, she didn't allow Papa to name her or make any declarations of greatness. She was Mama's sweet girl.

I remember seeing Annabella for the first time after she was born, all pink and bald and toothless. Mama cooed at her like she'd finally gotten what she always wanted. A boring lump that didn't bite or even move.

"Back to work, Jack," said Papa.

I sighed. Papa cut and I gathered and tied. Work, work, work. Boring, boring, boring. I considered feigning illness so I could take a break.

But what luck! Someone else disrupted the work for me. Mama was walking toward us now. Annabella bounced at her side, and on the other side was our nearest neighbor, but certainly not our dearest friend, Miss Lettie Nettle.

She looked none too pleased at this moment. Her eyebrows were pushed together, and the folds around her mouth hung down around her chin like one of those sad-faced hounds, only she was an angry hound. She glared right at me. Mama anxiously twisted her apron in her hands.

I scratched my head and scoured my brain. Had I pulled any pranks on Miss Lettie lately? I didn't think so. . . .

Papa looked up and stopped whistling. He wiped his forehead with a handkerchief and glanced down at me, as if he knew what was coming.

"Good day, Miss Lettie," said Papa.

"Don't you 'Good day' me. It's a terrible day," said Miss Lettie.

"Oh? What's the trouble?"

"My cabbages have been stolen."

"Stolen?"

"Yes. Stolen. The whole lot of them!"

Miss Lettie Nettle's pride and joy was her field of cabbages. They always took first prize in vegetables at the harvest festival. If there was an early frost, Miss Lettie covered her cabbages with blankets. I'd even heard her singing lullabies to her fields.

"Well now, that is a tragedy," said Papa. "We always look forward to your big, beautiful cabbages."

"Tragedy? This was no tragedy, it was thievery!" Miss Lettie glared at me again. I blinked.

"She believes it was Jack who stole them," said Mama.

Annabella smirked a little. She always enjoyed watching me get in trouble. I searched for a beetle to put on her head.

"Now hold on a moment, Miss Lettie," said Papa. "What makes you think Jack had anything to do with your missing cabbages?"

Miss Lettie Nettle looked at Papa like he was brainless. "Because he *always* has something to do with it. Remember when he brought me a sack of sugar? I thought that was right sweet and neighborly, until it turned out to be *salt*!"

Ha! I forgot about the sugar-salt switch. Snakes and toads, the look on her face when she bit into a salty plum pudding was incredible! I never knew a face could twist in so many directions.

"I nearly choked to death!" said Miss Lettie. "And no one could ever forget the day he took my . . . my *underthings* and hung them out in public!" Miss Lettie turned as purple as a purple cabbage.

"I remember," said Papa solemnly, but I could tell he was biting his cheeks, holding back a smile. "I also remember that Jack confessed his crimes and paid penance. He's a truthful boy. So why don't we ask him? Jack, son, do you know anything about Miss Lettie's cabbages?"

I shook my head. "No, sir."

"You little liar!" said Miss Lettie. "This has your hand written all over it."

"I didn't set foot in your field! I don't even like cabbages."

"That much is true," said Papa. "Jack here doesn't

like anything remotely green. I remember trying to feed him some green beans as a baby, and he spat them all over my face." Papa chuckled. Miss Lettie did not.

"He's not a baby anymore," she said. "He's a great big lying, stealing, conniving, rotten—"

"If Jack says he didn't do it, then he didn't." This time it was Mama who spoke, her face solemn as an oath. I breathed out a sigh of relief. Mama didn't often defend me, but if she said I was innocent, then I was innocent. Her word was truth and law, and everyone knew it, even Miss Lettie Nettle.

Miss Lettie scrunched up her face. "Well then, *who* stole my cabbages?"

It was a mystery, and in a small village where mysteries are in short supply, word travels fast. By noon the whole village had gathered to inspect Miss Lettie's cabbage-less field. It was a mess, to say the least. There were great heaps of dirt in some areas, and giant holes in others. Some of the trees had fallen over, torn up by the roots. The Widow Francis's thirteen children turned it into a playground, sliding down the mounds of dirt and jumping into the newly formed ditches, unaware of any misfortune.

"My, my," said Baker Baker. Yes, his name was Baker Baker, firstly because his name was Baker, and secondly because he was an actual baker of breads and rolls and pies. He said his father named him that so he'd be twice the baker. It also had the effect of making him say a lot of words twice. "Who could have done such a terrible, terrible thing?"

A couple of suspicious glances drifted my way. They were probably remembering how I set fire to the blacksmith's shop a few weeks ago—but that wasn't on purpose. I was just trying to light a torch to go on a giant hunt.

"Jack didn't do it," said Papa. "I can vouch for my son."

"I heard some thunder last night," said Horace. "Kept Cindy tossing and turning." Cindy was Horace's pet pig. He carried her everywhere and talked to her like she was a real person. "Maybe it was lightning struck your field, fried all the cabbages."

"Do you see any fried cabbages here?" asked Miss Lettie. "They're gone! Uprooted! Stolen!"

"Wild animals, then?" offered Horace.

"Maybe it was your fat pigs," said Miss Lettie. "You're always letting those hogs get into my cabbages!"

"Cindy wouldn't eat your cabbages, would you, girl?"

Snort.

"See? Cindy's a good girl."

Miss Lettie snorted, too.

"I doubt a herd of cattle could have done this, let alone pigs," said Papa.

"I'm telling you, it was a storm," said Horace. "Didn't you hear it?"

There were murmurs of agreement. The harvest season brought with it plenty of storms—rainstorms and windstorms and lightning storms—any of which could destroy a whole village.

"But what kind of storm only tears up one field?" someone asked.

"It wasn't no storm," said another voice. "I know who stole your cabbages."

A hush fell as a man limped into the circle, pulling a creaky cart behind him. It was Jaber, the one-legged tinker. His other leg was a scratched-up chunk of wood from the knee down and it made a solid *thunk* with each step.

Thunk. Creak. *Thunk.* Creak. *Thunk.*

I'd only ever seen Jaber a few times before, but I remembered his wooden leg. He didn't live in the village, but traveled from place to place, fixing people's pots and bringing news from other villages. Some of his stories seemed a little too far-fetched—even for my imagination. Like the one about pigs living in houses, or the girl who arrived at the royal ball in a pumpkin pulled by mice and lizards.

Okay, so Jaber was probably a little nuts, but Miss Lettie Nettle, in her desperation, was willing to take answers from anyone, even a crazy, one-legged tinker.

"Who?" she asked. "Did you see who stole my cabbages?"

"Yes, ma'am, I did," said Jaber.

"Well? Who was it? Point out the thief!"

"It was giants," said Jaber. "Giants stole your cabbages."

Everyone froze.

Giants.

The word caught my attention like a crumb of cheese calling to a hungry mouse.

"Giants?" asked Miss Lettie. "Did you just say giants stole my cabbages?"

"Yes, ma'am," said Jaber. "Came in the night and ripped 'em right out of your field."

Mutters and whispers rose amongst the villagers.

"Could it be true?" someone asked.

"It isn't true."

"Hogwash," Mama murmured.

"Where are they?" Miss Lettie asked. "Which way did they go?" Giants or not, she looked ready to track them down and beat them with a hoe until they gave her back her precious cabbages.

Jaber pointed straight up. "In the sky. The giants live in the sky."

Then the village erupted with laughter. Even I had to admit the idea of giants in the sky was absurd. Maybe Jaber was just confused. Maybe he saw them climb a really high cliff or mountain, which sometimes *looks* like it's disappearing into the sky. That wasn't so hard to believe.

"It's true! It's true!" shouted Jaber above the laughter. "I saw them rip open the sky with a bolt of lightning, and their footsteps went *boom, boom, BOOM!*"

"He's describing the storm last night," said Horace. "Didn't I say it was a storm?"

"'Tweren't no storm!" shouted Jaber. "The giants,

they been stealing all over the country. I just came from a village that was ravaged by giants. They stole everything. The cows, the chickens, all the food from the fields— even the houses and the people in them! The whole ding-dong village, gone, like it was never there!"

"Maybe it *was* never there," said Mama.

"You know what I think?" Miss Lettie said. "I think it was you who took my cabbages!" She pointed a bony finger at Jaber.

"Me?" Jaber said.

"Yes, you! You probably carted my cabbages away and sold them in another village, and now you're feeding us all some crackpot story about giants falling from the sky! You ain't nothing but a swindler, is what you are!"

Jaber's face turned beet red. His eyes rolled up and down and side to side. "You think it was me? You think I'm stealin' from you? I ain't stealin'. Those giants will be back, and if they don't crush you beneath their feet, they'll snatch you up and grind your bones!" Jaber was in a frenzy. Spit flew out of his mouth and he waved his arms so wildly he lost his balance and fell to the ground. No one helped him up. They just walked away, hee-hawing about Jaber and his mad tales.

"He's a nutter," said Horace.

"Nuttier than my Nutty-Nutty Bread," said Baker Baker.

"He's nothing but a common crackpot cabbage thief!" said Miss Lettie.

"Come on, Jack," said Papa. "Back to work."

"I'm coming," I said, but as soon as Papa turned, I stepped toward Jaber. He was still sitting in the dirt, talking to himself.

"They'll take your cows, your pigs, your houses, and cabbages, and your chilluns. They'll take your legs, too. Eat them down to the bone, like chicken."

"Is that what happened to your leg?" I asked. "Did a giant eat it?"

Jaber looked up at me. I held out my hand. He regarded me, wondering if I was trying to trick him, but for all the tricks I'd played on people, I thought it'd be right low to trick a one-legged man on the ground. Jaber took my hand and I helped him up. He hopped a little until he caught his balance on his leg. "Thank you, boy," he said, brushing the dirt off his ragged clothing.

"What are they like?" I asked.

"Who?"

"The giants."

"Big," he said.

"And? What else?"

"Loud."

I folded my arms. "Have you *really* seen a giant? Or are you just pulling everybody's leg?" I bit my tongue. I probably shouldn't have used that expression. Jaber just stared at me, then he looked to the sky.

"Looks like dirt. Going to rain dirt soon."

"Dirt? Why would it rain dirt?"

Jaber looked at me now, his eyes all dark and mysterious. "There's another land up there above all that blue. And land's made of dirt. So when the giants open up their world to get to ours, what do you think is going to happen? Mark me, if it starts raining dirt, you run for your life."

Without another word, he picked up his cart and hobbled down the road, singing a song about some boy named Tommy.

> *Tommy boy, Tommy boy,*
> *Full of lies and mischief.*
> *Tommy boy, Tommy boy,*
> *Angerin' the mistress . . .*

The excitement was over, so I walked home, back to the fields and the boring work. Every now and then I looked up. The sky was clear blue, not a cloud—or a giant—in sight.

"Stop staring at the sky," Papa scolded.

But I couldn't help it. I looked once more, and something fell into my eyes.

Just a sprinkling of dirt.

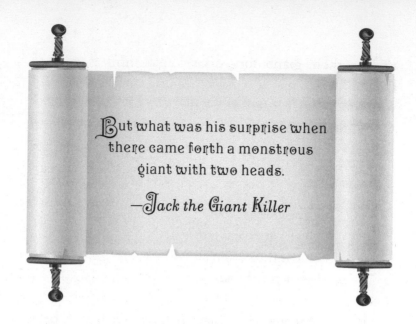

But what was his surprise when there came forth a monstrous giant with two heads.

—*Jack the Giant Killer*

CHAPTER TWO
Boom, Boom, BOOM!

"**A**re the giants going to come for us now?" Annabella asked that night at supper. "Are they going to take our food and our house and steal us away?"

Mama and Papa looked at each other across the table. I'd heard them fighting earlier. Papa had mentioned the giants and Mama could be heard shouting something that included the words *foolish*, *nonsense*, and *hogwash*.

Mama smiled weakly at Annabella. "No giants are coming, sweet. It was a storm that took Miss Lettie's cabbages. Unlucky, but unlikely to happen to us.

"It wasn't a storm," I said. "What about what Jaber

said? How the giants took houses and buildings and entire villages."

"You mustn't listen to Jaber," said Mama. "He's not right in the head."

"Why?" I asked. "Just because he has a wooden leg? Just because he likes to tell stories? That doesn't mean the giants aren't real. What about Grandpa Jack? What about all the giants he killed?"

Mama looked at Papa. He sighed. "Jack, we have no way of knowing if those stories are true, and the truth is, I've never seen a giant. No one has. Not anyone living, that is."

"But we've got to do something," I said. "If the giants are real, we could be next!"

"I'll hide," said Annabella with determination. "I'm good at hiding."

"There's no hiding from giants," I warned her. "They can smell you from a mile away."

"That's enough, Jack," said Mama.

"They'll hunt you down, snatch you right out of your bed."

Annabella squeaked and ducked under the table.

"Jack, I said stop!" said Mama.

"First they'll eat your flesh and then grind your bones to make bread. A *niiiice* golden loaf of Annabella Bone Bre—"

"Enough!" Papa pounded on the table. Everything went still. Papa was pale and trembling, his hands in tight fists. "That's enough talk."

"But if giants—"

"Eat your beans," Papa said between clenched teeth.

I may not be a good boy, but I'm not stupid. I took a bite of beans. I took a few more bites, slipping some beans into my pockets so I wouldn't have to eat them all.

Annabella came back from under the table. We ate in a cold silence for several minutes, until Papa broke it with the news that he'd be spending the night in the barn.

"Milky White's going to birth her calf tonight."

Mama nodded. "Good. At least we'll have milk through the winter."

"And the calf should bring a good price come spring," said Papa. "Might even give us a little extra."

"Sure would be nice to have extra," said Mama.

I tried to squish a bean between my fingers, but it slipped and hit Annabella on the forehead. She started screaming like it had been a boulder and not a bean.

"Jack!" shrieked Mama.

"It was an accident!"

"He threw it at my *head!*" cried Annabella.

"It didn't hurt, you big baby!"

"Jack, go to bed now." Papa stood and pointed at the ladder to my loft.

One thing I don't understand is why I get in the same amount of trouble for making mistakes as for being bad. I even get in trouble for things I can't control, like giants. Makes being bad all the more reasonable, if you ask me. I kicked my chair out from under me and yanked on

Annabella's braid. She howled, but at least now she had a reason.

"Henry, do something!" said Mama.

Papa tried to grab me, but I slipped by him and ran out the door.

"Such a naughty boy," I heard Mama say.

I ran past the barn and climbed the great oak tree at the edge of our fields. There was a pond below, and from up in the tree it looked like a giant footprint, with a rounded heel on one side and the narrow tip of a boot on the other. We called it Giant Foot Pond. Papa used to tell me it was made by the first giant who came to our land. It was said that he devoured a whole herd of cattle, so Grandpa Jack tricked the giant by luring him into a ditch and hit him on the head with a hammer. That story was one of my favorites, and I believed it was true. I believed all the stories.

I always thought Papa believed them, too.

Once, Papa had taken me to the seaside where there were cliffs a hundred feet high and filled with caves.

"A giant's lair if I ever saw one," Papa had said. The whole journey felt like we were on a quest for giants, just Papa and me. It made me feel special. Great, even.

So when he said the giants were just stories, it felt like he was ripping a big chunk out of me. I was Jack, named after my seven-greats-grandpa Jack, who had conquered nine giants. If giants weren't real, then what was so great about being Jack?

Papa went to the barn to take care of Milky White,

and Mama came to the door and called for me, but I ignored her. Finally she gave up and went inside. I pulled out my sling to do some target practice. I flung the beans from dinner high up into the sky, each one a little higher than the last. Once or twice I thought they'd gotten stuck up there in the clouds, but they all came down eventually. They landed in the dirt, where they'd probably grow into more beans that Mama would make me eat. I stopped throwing and just leaned against the trunk, swinging my legs until my eyes grew heavy.

Boom.

I woke with a start and nearly fell out of my tree. What just happened? I guess I fell asleep in the tree. Probably not the safest bed.

It was full dark now. A misty moon shone behind the clouds. There were no lights on in the house and only the glow of a single lantern in the barn.

MooooOOOOOoooo!

Milky White must be calving out now. That must have been what woke me.

Boom.

A vibration traveled up the tree and buzzed in my bones. I looked up. The clouds roiled and the sky rumbled liked a hungry stomach. There was a flash. Lightning. Thunder.

It started to rain, just a sprinkling at first, and then it got faster. Harder. Heavier. It stung my skin as it came down. I held out my hand and caught dark specks and clumps. It was dirt.

The dirt fell in spurts, like someone was throwing it down on us the way Mama threw grain to the chickens. Dirt pelted the barn and house. Inside, it probably sounded just like heavy rain, but I had dirt on my head and in my eyes.

Dirt shower.

The clouds were bulging and twitching like something was trying to get out. Or in.

Boom! CRACK!

The sky split open like a linen sack. Light poured through the hole, and something long and thin unraveled toward the ground. Something else followed. A foot. Then there were two feet, two legs, two arms, and a head. The dark shadow of a creature started to climb down the rope—out of the sky. The shadow got closer and closer, bigger and bigger, until it was skimming the treetops and then—

BOOM!

A giant landed right in the middle of our wheat.

He was twice as tall as the oak tree and wide as the barn. His arms and legs were like great tree trunks, his feet as big as wagons. Flung over his shoulder was an empty sack.

I clung to the branches of my tree with trembling limbs.

Crack!

With a flash of light, the sky split open again. More

dirt showered down, and a second giant emerged. He climbed down the rope and—

BOOM!

—landed next to the first giant. This one had more sacks and a bundle of crates slung over his shoulder.

The first giant looked around and sniffed. He bent down and scooped up a pile of wheat in one hand. He sniffed it and then stuffed it into his sack. He scooped the next pile and the next, until he had taken it all. A whole summer of work, gone in less than a minute. A whole winter of food.

The second giant did not seem as interested in his surroundings. He just stood there until—

MoooooOOOOOooooo!

Baaaaaaaaa!

Boom, boom, boom!

—he stomped over to the neighboring pasture, where there were cows and sheep in the fields.

He picked up a cow. The cow mooed and wriggled her legs like a bug on its back. The giant shoved her inside a crate. He then took the sheep by handfuls and the cows one by one, scooping them up like baby mice and runty kittens. Into crates they went, bleating and mooing.

Bok, bok, bok-berGEEK!

The hens were clucking wildly. The second giant stomped toward them and ripped the henhouse off the ground. He looked inside with one eye. He grunted and stuffed the whole thing into his sack.

The first giant was now ripping up the rest of the farm. He plucked trees from the ground just like carrots. He sniffed at them, picked at some of the branches, and then either stuffed them inside his sack or tossed them aside. I held my breath as he drew closer. Should I climb down and risk being crushed? Or stay in the tree and risk getting uprooted along with it?

The giant tore up another tree, not too far from me. He sniffed it and tossed it away, then turned down the road toward the village. I could just see the outline of him bending down to rip things out of the ground and stuff them in his sack as he went. A tornado with hands and feet. At least he was moving away from me.

Boom!

The tree shook as though a violent wind had rushed upon me, only there was no wind. The other giant! I hadn't been paying attention to him. His fist wrapped around the trunk, and his foot stomped down right alongside the Giant Foot Pond, almost the exact same size and shape.

Crack!

The giant yanked the tree out with one hand. I clung to the branches, whooshing up, up, up in the air. Soon I was level with the giant's face. Teeth the size of dinner plates sliced down just inches from my head. The giant crunched on the wood and leaves. He spat it out, then tossed the tree away. I sailed with it, clinging to the branches as the tree crashed down on our roof and ripped into the side of the house. I smacked my head on something and got scratched on all the branches. Some-one screamed. Inside the house.

Mama and Annabella. I pulled myself up from the branches, ignoring the throbbing pain in my head. Were they hurt? Had the tree crushed them?

The giant stomped toward the house. No doubt the cries had alerted him to a potential meal.

MooooOOOOOoooo!

The giant paused near the barn, searching for the cow he had missed. He got down on his hands and knees and crawled around, sniffing. My heart pounded. My hands grew clammy.

The giant tore off the barn roof. Planks cracked and flew in all directions.

MooooOOOOOooooo!

I needed to distract him. I had to get him away from Papa. I rummaged through my pockets and pulled out my sling and a green bean from dinner. It was all I had. I swung the bean around and around and let it fly. . . . The bean landed in the giant's ear. He didn't move. It wasn't big enough to bother him.

MooooOOOOOoooo!

The giant dug through the barn like he was search-ing for crawly critters under a log. A smile stretched over his face. He reached inside and pulled out the newborn calf. It mewled pitifully. But that was not all. Something else was clinging to the calf. Extra legs dangled from its middle. Papa was going up and up with the calf, too high to let go.

No. Not Papa.

I climbed down the tree as fast as I could. "Papa!" I shouted. "Papa!"

"Jack!" Papa searched for me, still clinging to the calf. He couldn't see me. "Take care of your mama and sister, Jack!" And with that, the giant stuffed Papa into his pocket.

"Papa! Papa! Hey, giant! Take me too! That's my papa! Take me too!"

Boom! Boom! Boom!

The giant couldn't hear me over the crash of his own footsteps. The other giant was coming back now, his sack bulging with the sharp corners of crates. They both returned to the ropes.

I searched for a stone—one big enough to hurt a giant—and whirled my sling, but the giants were too far away now. Too high. They got smaller and smaller until they disappeared in the clouds, with my papa in a giant pocket. There was a flash, a showering of dirt, and then . . .

BOOM!

Boom.

Boom.

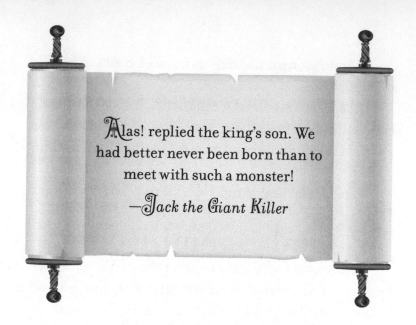

Alas! replied the king's son. We
had better never been born than to
meet with such a monster!

—*Jack the Giant Killer*

CHAPTER THREE

Sir Bluberys

The sky closed, and another dirt shower poured over my head.

"Papa!" I shouted. "PAPAAAAAA! Hey, giant! Come and get me! Don't you want me too? I'm Jack! You're supposed to take *me*."

I jumped up and up and up. I climbed to the loft of the roofless barn and jumped as high as I could, but it wasn't high enough.

Rope. If the giants could come down here with ropes, then maybe I could climb up to the sky on one.

I waded through the straw and rubble of the barn

until I found a rope. I also found a big hook in a jumble of Papa's tools and tied it to the end. I climbed back up to the loft and swung the rope around and around with the hook on the end and threw it as high as I could. It sailed up and up toward the dark sky. I thought it might catch onto the moon, but then it came down with a thud. I tried again. I swung it faster and threw it harder. I did it again and again until my arms were so weak I could hardly swing the rope.

I couldn't reach the top of the sky. I couldn't get to Papa.

"Help!" called a tiny, pitiful voice. Annabella! I had nearly forgotten about Mama and Annabella! They were still in the house, with a tree sticking through the side. I ran toward them. The tree had crushed one corner of the roof and torn through the wall next to the door. I crawled through a gap between the branches. Inside, Annabella was on the floor, sobbing next to Mama, who was trapped under a pile of wood and rubble.

"Jack," said Mama. "Oh, my boy! Thank goodness you're safe." She tried to lift herself up but fell back. "Where's your papa? Where's Henry? Can you get him for me?"

I shook my head and looked down at the floor. "He's gone."

Mama fell silent, and then her eyes got all shiny and her chin began to tremble.

"Papa's gone? Gone where?" said Annabella.

"The giants took him," I said. "And the newborn calf."

"Jack, please. Not now," Mama pleaded.

"But . . . didn't you see it? The giants threw that tree!" I pointed toward the hole in the house. "They came down from the sky and took all our animals and our food and . . . and . . . Papa!"

Annabella's hands flew to her mouth. "Are the giants going to eat him?"

"No! I'm going to find him first."

"I'll help. I can find him, too," said Annabella.

"You're not big enough," I said.

"I am so big enough!" she shouted.

"Enough, both of you," Mama groaned. "Please, no talk. I need your help. I need to get this wood off my leg." Mama ground her teeth and tried to sit up. Her face was white as wool.

I tried to lift the pile of wood off her, but my arms were limp and weak from all my throwing. "It's too heavy."

"One at a time, Jack," said Mama. "Start with the top and work your way down."

I lifted one piece and slid it off the top of the pile. I lifted another piece and another and another until I was sweating and my arms were shaking, but eventually I dug Mama out. Her leg was purple and swollen, and a big bleeding gash ran down her shin to her ankle. Annabella and I both cringed and sucked in our breath.

"Help me up, Jack."

I offered my arm, but when Mama tried to move her leg, she screamed.

She released my arm and took slow, steady breaths through her teeth. "I think it's broken," she said.

"Annabella, I need you to be a strong girl and help your mama."

Annabella came to the other side, and together we were able to lift Mama and help her to the bed. She whimpered as we propped her leg up on some pillows. Annabella inspected Mama's leg as though she were a doctor. "I don't think it's broken too badly, Mama. I'll boil some water so we can clean the cuts." Annabella quickly went to work. She built a fire, boiled water, and tended to Mama's leg, while I just stood there feeling numb and weak and hollow. All I could think of was Papa.

"We must search for your father," said Mama. "He could be nearby, injured. He could be stuck under a branch, or the wind might have carried him high up in a tree. Maybe he can't get down."

That much was true. It was pretty hard to get down from the sky.

"Jack," said Mama, "you must go to the village and ask for help. Gather a search party. Everyone and anyone willing to help."

Annabella and I looked at each other. She shook her head at me, and I knew she meant I shouldn't argue with Mama. I shouldn't tell her that Papa had been *taken* by giants, because she would not believe me. Mama thought the tales were all hogwash, and what was the use of telling her otherwise? She wouldn't know how to get to the giants any more than I did.

So I went to the village. The road had been trampled by giant footsteps, and I had to climb over uprooted trees and branches. When I got to the village, this is what I found:

Nothing and no one.

There were no horses or mules or chickens or goats. No cows or sheep. There was no mill. There was no cobbler's shop or smithy or bakery. All the shops and houses had been ripped up and taken away, leaving gaping holes in the ground.

"Hello . . . ?" I called out, but no one answered. Not the blacksmith or the cobbler or Baker Baker. Not the Widow Francis and her thirteen children or Horace and his pigs. I imagined he'd held on to Cindy the way Papa had held on to our calf, and the giants had just carried them up.

I sat down in the hole where the bakery should have been. The wind blew. It swirled the dust and lifted the faintest smell of fresh bread and sugar. What was I going to tell Mama now? Not only was there no one in the village to help, there was no village.

In the meantime, Papa could be in a cage or a dungeon now—just waiting for the giants to get hungry. . . .

Blurp-da-durr! Blah-durp-da-duuuurp!

A horn blew in the distance. It sounded official, like someone important was coming. I looked down the road and saw a waving flag, and a knight riding toward the village!

In the stories of my seven-greats-grandpa Jack, he befriends a brave knight, who helps him fight the giants. It seemed fitting that a knight in shining armor, riding a noble steed, should come now to assist me, except as the knight drew closer, I noticed that his armor was not exactly shining—it was dingy and rusty. And his noble steed was a swaybacked mule that kept bucking and veering off course.

"Whoa there! Ho, you lowly beast!" shouted the knight. "Heed my command!" The mule bellowed and bucked so hard, the knight nearly fell to the ground with a clatter. The knight quickly stood and bowed before me. His rusty armor creaked with every move.

"Lowly villagers!" He spoke as though an entire village was present to hear him. "I, Sir Bluberys the Chivalrous, have come to protect thee from giants who roam the land, attacking men, women, and children. Be warned, they will pillage your farms, steal your animals, and wreak terror and havoc, but never fear! I shall protect thee with my strength and valor!" He lifted his creaking arms as though he was expecting a great cheer.

"The giants already came," I said.

The knight looked down in surprise. "What's that you say? Speak up, peasant boy! My noble ears need a gallant voice!"

I nearly shouted at him. "The giants already came! They raided the village and took our food and animals, and they took my papa."

"Did they truly?" The knight blinked and looked around, taking in the evidence that giants had indeed already been to our village. He dropped his arms. "Drat! I thought we were fifty miles ahead of them at least."

"Have you fought any giants?" I asked. "Have you seen them?"

"Oh yes, hundreds!" said Sir Bluberys. "The last giant I met tried to bite my head off, but I chopped his off first." He drew a rusty sword that didn't look sharp enough to cut cheese. "The giants practically flee when they hear my name! That's probably why I missed them. They knew Sir Bluberys the Chivalrous was near and fled for their lives!"

"Where do they live?" I asked.

"Oh . . . here and there." Clearly he had no idea. "Is there any place to get some good grub around here? Stew? Pie? A little bread and butter perhaps for a chivalrous knight and his noble steed? I'm famished!" Sir Bluberys thumped his metal belly and looked around, as if he were expecting a feast to appear. What a blubberhead. I needed to get rid of this idiot fast.

"There's another village a short distance that way." I pointed down the road. "They probably have lots of food. Maybe you can catch up to the giants before they attack."

"Oh yes, of course!" Sir Bluberys tried to mount his mule, but it kept shifting and turning, so by the time he finally got on, he was backward. "Farewell, lowly peasants!" He waved as though bidding farewell to a large, cheering crowd and not just one disappointed boy. "I am Sir Bluberys the Chivalrous, sworn to defend and protect the meek and lowly. I will save ye from the giants!"

"Oh! And will you please look out for my papa?" I shouted after him. "His name is Henry!"

"Of course! Of course!" said Sir Bluberys. "I always rescue the fair maidens!"

The mule stumbled in one of the giant footprints, and Sir Bluberys pitched forward and grabbed onto its bottom. It bellowed again and then started trotting down the road with Sir Bluberys hanging backward and sideways.

I trudged home, worn and hopeless. In the daylight I could see our farm more clearly. It was a wreck, worse than Miss Lettie's cabbage field. I gazed at the ruined barn, wishing I had been inside last night. It always should have been me to face the giants, not Papa.

"It really does look like a storm hit," said a small voice behind me. I turned to see Annabella. She had a piece of bread in her hands and held it out to me. I took it, suddenly realizing how hungry I was.

"It was giants," I said. "I saw them."

"I believe you, Jack," she said, and that comforted me some, but not enough. What did it matter if my scrawny little sister believed me? What could she do?

Our fields were torn up and trampled. Our trees, our animals, our garden, all ripped up and taken. We had nothing. We'd been poorer than dirt before, so what were we now? Nothing. Nothing minus Papa.

MooooooOOOOO!

Annabella and I started.

MoooOOOOOO!

"That sounds like Milky White," she said. We raced to the barn. At first we didn't see any sign of the cow in the now-roofless barn. But she mewled and cried, and finally we found her buried under some hay and rubble. We pulled away the hay in tufts and lifted off the rubble, until at last Milky White was free. She heaved herself to a standing position.

MooOOOO!

"Oh, Jack, she's in pain," said Annabella as she rubbed at Milky White's neck.

"She just had her calf," I said, "and she probably needs to be milked." I found a dented bucket and milked the cow, but afterward she kept mooing and groaning like she was in horrible pain.

"I think she misses her baby," said Annabella. "Poor Milky White."

Of course. Her baby got taken right along with Papa. I didn't want to think what the giants had planned for them. If there was any truth in Grandpa Jack's tales, the prospects were not good.

"I'm sorry, Milky." I patted her on the neck. Even though she was just a cow, I could imagine how she must feel about losing her calf, not knowing where he was, or what was happening to him. . . . I imagined we felt about the same, Milky and I.

I would leave this instant to find Papa, if only I could find a way to the sky.

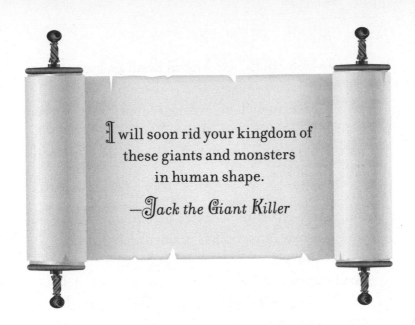

I will soon rid your kingdom of
these giants and monsters
in human shape.

—*Jack the Giant Killer*

CHAPTER FOUR
A Cow Worth Beans

I waited three days for the clouds to rain dirt, for the sky to split open, for the giants to reach down and take me with them, but the only thing that came out of the clouds was water, cold and wet. It turned the giant footprints into ponds and seeped through our roof. I plugged the holes with rags and straw while Annabella placed pots and buckets to catch the drips.

Mama stayed in bed with her broken leg and sore heart. It was clear Mama wouldn't or couldn't accept the truth about giants. Not even when I told her about the village. She just kept talking about storms and how we were lucky we didn't get hit too hard. At least we still had the cow.

"We'll have to sell her." said Mama. "Get a good price while she's worth something."

"But . . . she's all we have." I had seen Annabella scraping the bottom of the barrel that morning to make bread.

"She won't give milk forever," said Mama. "If we sell her now, we can buy enough grain to last through the winter."

"And then what?"

"We'll plant seed," said Mama. "We'll survive."

That was Mama, ever practical, even in dire distress. But I didn't want to survive. I wanted to *live*. I wanted Papa back.

"Go milk the cow, Jack," said Mama. "She won't be worth beans if she runs dry."

I milked Milky White and then took her out to graze in the muddy fields. It had finally stopped raining and the sun shone. I petted Milky's neck as she plodded along, tearing at bits of grass and scattered straw. She still seemed melancholy over her lost calf, but she wasn't crying anymore. Maybe she had given up hope like Mama.

I heard a distant melody. I turned toward the sound. A man was walking down the road, whistling, just like Papa did when he worked in the fields. Could it be . . . ?

I squinted and really looked. The man was walking funny. Limping. It wasn't Papa. Of all people, it was Jaber the tinker, hobbling down the road on his wooden leg, pulling his cart through the muddy ditches and around broken branches.

"Hello there!" he greeted me in a cheery voice. "Perfect morning, don't you think? Doesn't look like a dirt shower today, does it?" He smiled up at the blue sky.

"That's because we just had one," I said dully. "It rained dirt, like you said, and giants came in the night and took Papa. They took the village, too. All of it."

"Well, you're lucky they didn't take you," he said, "You've still got all your limbs, I see. Good. And a cow! Rare thing that the giants would leave a cow."

"They took her calf," I told him. "Papa was holding on to her. They took him up to the sky, and I'm going to go after him."

He cocked an eye. "How do you plan to do that?"

"I'll find a way. If the giants can come down, then there must be a way up."

"There must," Jaber agreed.

"Do you know a way?" Everything Jaber had told us about the giants had turned out to be true. But was that all he knew?

"I might," said Jaber.

"How? Tell me!"

Jaber gave me a hard look.

"Please," I said. "My papa . . ."

Jaber leaned against his cart and pulled up his wooden leg to rest on his good knee. He drummed his fingers on the wood and looked at the sky. "I knew a man once, had a son about your age. They were riding to market with a wagon full of turnips, just minding their own business, when all of a sudden—*Boom!*—a giant stomped down right in front of them. He stood fifty, maybe a hundred feet high. The giant picked up the wagon with one hand, horses and all."

"And the man and his son?"

"He took the son and left the man."

It sounded just like Papa, only the other way around.

"What happened then?"

"It rained dirt, of course."

"But what happened to the man and his son? Didn't his father go after him? Did he get to the giant world, too?"

"No. The boy was never heard from again."

"That's a terrible story," I said.

"Yes, it is."

We sat there and looked up at the sky. "Those giants, they've been coming down and taking everything from our world," said Jaber, "and no one has ever been able to stop 'em. I'm always asking myself, who's going to stop 'em? Who's going to go up there and show those giants they can't just take our crops and our people whenever they get the fancy?"

"I will," I said. "I was born to face giants. I'll chop off their heads!"

"I believe you, son, I do. And that's why I'm going to tell you a secret. I'm going to make you an offer I don't make to just anybody. . . ." Jaber dug inside one of his sacks. I held my breath, thinking maybe he held the secret to getting to the giant world. A magic rope, a flying carpet, a wand. "Mostly the giants just take and take, and never leave anything behind," said Jaber. "But once in a while they drop things. Things that are little to them but big to us."

Jaber held both his hands out to me like a bowl, and sitting inside were three . . . beans. Green beans just like the ones Mama grew in our garden, except they were as big as apples, but still . . .

"Beans?" I asked.

"*Giant* beans," he corrected.

"So? What good are those?"

"You're a smart boy! What do you get when you plant beans?"

I shrugged. "More beans?"

"Beanstalks!"

"So what? How's a *beanstalk* supposed to help me find Papa?" I was feeling a little annoyed now. Did he think I was stupid?

"Listen here," said Jaber. "I planted one of these once, just to see what would happen, and the beanstalk grew so tall, it went straight to the sky! Giant beanstalks can take you to the giant world!"

That got my attention.

"Where is it?" I asked. "This giant beanstalk you grew."

"Well, it's long since died and turned to dirt. They don't last forever, you know."

"You've been there, then? To the giants' world?"

His face fell and his eyes dimmed. "It's hard for someone like me to climb to the top of the sky." He tapped his wooden leg. "But that's why I only planted one, just to see what they would do. I saved the rest, waiting for the right person to take them. Someone with two good legs, and a reason!" He clutched my arm and drew close to my face. "A reason to go up there and face those giants and take back what they took from us! You, Jack. I've been waiting for *you*."

I'd been waiting, too, for my turn to face the giants, for a way to get to the giants, but . . .

Beans? I'd always hated them. I wasn't sorry that the giant had ripped them up from our garden. But now it looked as though these beans were my only hope of getting to Papa.

"How do you know that beanstalks reach all the way to the giant world, if you never climbed one?"

"Same way I know the giants are coming down. Dirt showers. You stand under that beanstalk every day while it's growing, and once you get that sprinkling of dirt, you know it's gone straight through the sky and struck land."

Well, what did I have to lose? "I'll take the beans." I reached for them, but Jaber yanked back his hand.

"Not so fast, young man. . . . These beans are valuable. I can't just *give* them away." He eyed Milky White. I knew what he was thinking.

"There's a full bucket of milk in the barn," I said. "I can give you that."

"A bucket of milk? Come, Jack. I'm a poor man with nothing to my name."

"I'll give you a bottle of milk every day."

"How will you do that when you're up in the sky?"

"When I get back, then."

Jaber clutched the beans to his chest. "What if you don't come back?"

He had a point. If I went after the giants, there was no guarantee that I'd return. And Mama would never agree to give Jaber milk every day. She wouldn't approve of the beans at all. Whatever I gave the tinker, I would have to give it now and be done.

"I'll take that cow for the beans," said Jaber. "You find your papa and your calf and maybe some riches besides. One hears tales of the giants' riches—diamonds and rubies the size of apples, sacks of silver and gold. . . . I think that's more than a fair trade for a cow."

It would be a foolish trade. Nuts. But Jaber had been right about everything else. And Papa . . . If there was even a sliver of a chance, I had to take it.

Slowly, I held out Milky White's rope. "You can take the cow," I said.

Jaber snatched it. "Done!" He dumped the three green beans into my hands. One tumbled to the ground, so I crouched to pick it up. When I stood, Jaber was already hobbling down the road, taking our last source of food with him.

Good-bye, Milky White. I hope you were worth the beans.

I tried to keep the news about the cow secret for as long as possible. I shuffled my feet all the way home. I didn't go inside. I went to the Giant Foot Pond, which had multiplied into several Giant Feet Ponds. The beans sat like heavy stones in my pockets. I took one out and turned it over in my hands. What if they didn't grow up to the sky like Jaber said they would? What if they didn't grow at all? But they had to. Jaber had been right about the giants when no one believed him. Why wouldn't he be right about the beans?

It was getting dark now. I was ready to plant the beans right away in one of the giant footprints, but then Annabella came running out, calling for me. I tried to hide, but she found me anyway. Sometimes I think her floppy braids are like bug antennae and they can sense whatever she's trying to find.

"Mama's asking for you. What's that?" She pointed to the bean in my hand.

"Nothing." I slid the bean into my pocket. "Just a stone."

As soon as I walked inside, Mama asked me to go milk Milky White. Since there was no Milky White to be milked, I had to spill the beans. I mean the beans about trading Milky White to Jaber. I was still trying to keep the giant beans secret.

"You did *what* with our cow?!"

"You said I should sell her," I reminded her.

Mama breathed deeply and twisted her apron in her hands. "Well then, it must have been a good offer for you to sell so quickly. What did that crackpot give you? Gold, I hope."

I glanced at Annabella, who was standing in the corner quietly, listening. "Not quite gold, no." I fingered the beans in my pocket, which was a stupid thing to do because Mama's eyes went right to them. She knew my pockets were always full of mischief.

"Turn out your pockets, Jack. Now." Mother spoke soft and low through clenched teeth, like a growling animal about to attack. Even though Mama had an injured leg, I was certain that rage would give her whatever strength she needed to rip the hair out of my head. Slowly, I pulled out the giant beans and held them in my cupped hands.

"What. On earth. Are those?"

"Beans," I said. "Giant beans."

"Beans," said Mama. Her face drained of whatever color she had left, and then I spilled my explanation.

"I know you won't believe me, but you have to listen. These are giant beans. See how big they are? Papa was taken by giants. The entire village was taken! Tell her, Annabella!"

Annabella squeaked from the corner like a shy little mouse. "It has to be giants, Mama. Where could everything have gone?"

"Did you *see* the giants?" Mama asked.

Annabella glanced at me and then looked at the floor. "No. I didn't see them."

"*I* saw the giants!" I said. "I saw them take Papa up to the sky! And these beans will grow us a ladder that leads to Papa. Jaber told me so."

"Jaber told you so." Mama stared at the beans for a while, cold and blank. She had to believe me. But without warning she seized the beans from my hands and thrust them out her shattered window, into the dark night.

"No!" I shouted.

"Jack! Stop it! Stop your foolishness! Your papa was lost in the storm, and you won't find him with beans." Mama was crying now, and so was Annabella, but I was too mad to cry.

"I saw them!" I shouted. "I saw them take Papa."

I tore through the hole in the house and ran to the place where Mama had thrown the beans. I searched all around, tore up the garden like a mole until I found them all. Then I dug down deep into the earth with my bare hands, turning the soil, pulling up weeds to prepare a space for my beans. A strange calm came over me as I placed the beans in the earth and covered them with dirt. Safe in the ground. I drew water from the well and poured it over the spot where the beans were buried.

When I was done, I stayed in the garden, seething about Mama. How could she give up on Papa so easily? Why couldn't she just believe me?

When I came inside, Annabella was asleep, curled up like a kitten next to Mama. Mama was just sitting in her bed, drumming her fingers on something in her lap. It was Papa's old book of giant tales. Papa never needed to read them, since he knew all the stories by heart. I did too, but the book was still a treasure passed down through the generations.

Mama handed the book to me. "He would want you to have it," she said, and looked away, tears brimming in her eyes. The worn leather and cracked binding was familiar in my hands. It should have been a comfort, but I knew what Mama was really saying. She didn't think Papa was coming back. She was giving up.

I went to bed with the book pressed to my chest, trying to crush the swelling pain underneath. I tried to comfort myself with the stories, imagining Papa's voice in the words.

There once was a worthy farmer who had only one son, named Jack. . . .

I started to cry. I cried myself to sleep wishing that when I woke up, Papa would be here.

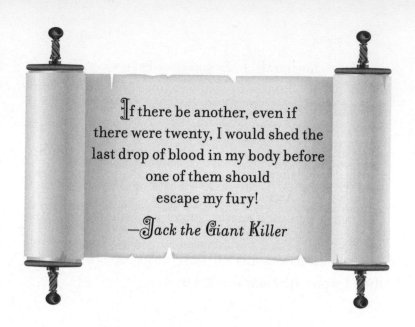

If there be another, even if
there were twenty, I would shed the
last drop of blood in my body before
one of them should
escape my fury!

—*Jack the Giant Killer*

CHAPTER FIVE

Up the Green, into the Blue

Snap!
Crack!
Thwack!

My eyes flew open. It was morning, but my room was full of moving shadows. Something big and dark was lurking outside my window. Was it the giants? Had they come back to snatch the rest of us?

Slowly, I crept out of bed and poked my head out the window. Something green unfurled and nearly smacked my face. I didn't know what it was, but it didn't look like a giant, unless giants were green.

Thwack!
Snap!
Crack!

"Aaaack!" I screamed as a long green sort of finger shot through the window and poked my face. I slapped at it and scrambled away from the window. I grabbed Papa's book of giant tales and raised it above my head to smash whatever green monster had just reached inside my bedroom. I lowered the book and stared as the green finger split and swelled and something unfurled and flopped on the floor. It was just a leaf, but a big one. Too big to be normal.

I remembered what was below my window. The garden. I remembered what I had planted there just yesterday. The giant beans!

I climbed down my ladder, raced out the door and around back.

Snakes and toads! The beans! They were swelling and growing right before my eyes. They were as tall as the house already. The beanstalks snapped and groaned as they tore at the thatch and wrapped around the stone chimney as though circling a bean pole.

"Jack?" Mama called. "What is that racket? Who's here?"

Annabella raced outside, her braids flopping wildly. When she saw the beanstalks, she crashed right into me. We both stood there craning our necks. The three stalks were twisting around each other, making one giant beanstalk. It was taller than the tallest trees now.

"Jack! Annabella! What is going on?" Mama came

out of the house, awkwardly hopping along behind a chair so she wouldn't put any weight on her broken foot. She didn't have to go far.

"Oh my . . ." She stared openmouthed at the beanstalk, still twisting and stretching toward the sky.

"See? I wasn't lying. Those were giant beans, and this beanstalk will lead us to the giants! To Papa!"

Mama didn't say anything. She just gaped upward. Then, for the first time since the giants had come, she took a look around the farm. Her jaw dropped as she saw the empty fields, the torn-up barn, the uprooted trees. The heaps of dirt and the holes from the giant footsteps, just like in Miss Lettie's cabbage field. Mama looked back to the giant beanstalk and then lastly to the sky. I knew she wouldn't admit it—Mama was far too practical—but I could see she was considering the possibility of giants. The seed had been planted and the idea was growing in her.

"You'd best give it plenty of water," said Mama. "Beans need lots of water to grow. I suspect *this* will need a great deal more." And that was all she said. She took the chair and hopped back into the house.

Annabella and I looked at each other, and then we raced to the well and drew water for the beanstalk. We poured bucket after bucket until the garden was properly drenched.

"How fast do you think it will grow?" Annabella asked. "When will we be able to reach the sky?"

I laughed. "You're not going up there."

Annabella gaped. "What do you mean? You said the beanstalk would take us to Papa."

"It will take *me* to Papa. You're too small."

Annabella's confused look crumpled into a scowl. "No I'm not! I can climb just as well as you can!" She stomped her foot in the muddy garden, spraying mud all over her skirt.

"But who will take care of Mama? She still needs help with her hurt leg."

"She's getting stronger, though." Annabella was determined. "Maybe by the time the beanstalk reaches the sky, she'll be better, and I can come."

"If you're sure . . ." I gave an exaggerated sigh. "It will be dangerous, though. The giants could stomp you flat! They could cook you in a stew, bake you into a pie, or peel the skin right off your bones like a chicken. You want that to happen?"

"I'm not afraid," said Annabella, but her eyes were wide. Her resolve was weakening. Just to be thorough, I gathered a bucket of snakes and toads and dumped the whole thing directly around the base of the beanstalk. The next morning when we came to water the beanstalk, a toad hopped right on Annabella's foot, and then a snake slithered over the other one. She dropped the bucket of water and ran away screaming.

No problem a bucket of snakes and toads can't fix.

I watered the beanstalk every morning, and it grew uncommonly fast. Sometimes I could see it growing before my very eyes, slowly swelling and creeping skyward. It was like the beanstalk was seized by some magic, like it knew it did not belong in this world and so it stretched and grew toward its own land. By the end of the first day, I could barely see the top of the beanstalk, and by the second, the tips of the beanstalk seemed to graze the clouds and the base was as thick and large as a tree trunk.

On the third day, bean pods swelled, and after a week, they were as tall as me, some even taller. I cut a bunch down and built a fort out of the beans at the base. I'd live in it until the beanstalk reached the sky! I showed my bean fort to Mama and then wished I hadn't.

"Oh, Jack! We're saved!" She clapped her hands together at the sight of the beans. "You wonderful boy—you made a good trade after all!"

"I did?" I wasn't sure what she meant, but I guessed she liked my fort.

"Of course! These beans will feed us all winter!"

I felt my face go as green as the beans. *Eat* them? Snakes and toads, I hadn't thought for a moment that we would actually *eat* the beans. Gross.

Mama made me go up the beanstalk and harvest all the beans that were fully grown. Before the day was done, our cellar was piled to the ceiling with nothing but giant green beans, and Mama started cooking again. She boiled the beans, pickled them, dried them, mashed them into soups and cakes. She even made a bean porridge for breakfast. Blech! I thought dirt and worms would taste better. I was almost ready to try it.

"Why couldn't it have been a giant apple tree, or a blackberry bush?" I said, rolling a giant boiled bean around on my plate.

"Too thorny," said Mama. "Imagine a thousand daggers coming at you every time you tried to pick a berry." She ate a spoonful of bean porridge and grinned like a little girl. It was the first time I'd seen her smile since Papa had gone. Of course she was happy, now that we had enough food for the winter, but I got the feeling she was also enjoying my misery—and especially the fact that I had no one to blame but myself.

I slept inside my bean fort that night, and it reminded me of the times Papa and I had camped out under the stars, beside the great oak tree. Papa would tell the tale of the giant who found Grandpa Jack asleep beneath a tree and carried him off to his castle to eat him.

"What if a giant comes and finds me here?" I would ask.

"Then I'd protect you," said Papa.

"What if they take me away?"

"Then I'd come and find you," said Papa.

But it all felt different when the giants took Papa. That had never been in the stories. The giant always took Jack, never someone he really loved and cared about. Never the one person he needed more than anything in the world.

I woke in the middle of the night to rain. It trickled through the cracks of my bean fort and sprinkled on my face. I rolled over, and it got in my ear. I sat up and held out my hand. The rain didn't trickle off in little streams—it sat on my hand in solid clumps. I smiled. Dirt.

It was time to climb.

Heart racing, I grabbed Papa's axe and tied it around my waist with some rope. I had my sling and a pocketful of stones. I had the beanstalk that led to the giant world, to Papa. I waited for nothing else. I did not say good-bye to Mama and Annabella. I left no message. They would figure out soon enough where I had gone.

I started to climb, quickly at first, and when the sun began to peek up from the horizon, it was like I was racing it into the sky. Who could climb the sky faster, Jack or the sun? Who could climb higher?

Every now and then I looked down to see my world getting smaller and smaller, until our farm was nothing more than a little square, our house just a dot.

I climbed for what felt like hours, and then I heard a rumbling. *Oh no, the giants have seen the beanstalk!* I froze, wondering if I should climb down or speed up and try to get to the top. The rumbling came again, louder this time, and very near. It was my stomach! Ha! I was starving. No wonder I could barely climb. I should have brought food with me, but in my excitement and rush I hadn't thought of it. I supposed it didn't matter all that much, since I was climbing the same food we had at home.

I wedged myself in a crevice next to a giant bean. Then I took my axe and split open the pod. I nibbled on a bean just until I was no longer starving, and then I tossed the rest and watched it fall down and disappear. I couldn't see our house and the far-off village didn't seem like my home anymore. Just Below.

Feeling stronger, I started to climb again, higher and higher, until I met the sun, and then the sun started going down. I had climbed nearly all day. It was a long way to the sky.

Eventually the clouds hovered above my head. They looked as warm and soft as thistledown, so I plunged into the fluffy white and gasped. The clouds were cold and wet! It was like a milky ocean. I could still breathe, but I couldn't see—not even my hand in front of my face— and I completely lost my sense of direction. Which way was up? Which way down? I clung to the beanstalk, shivering as the cold wetness seeped down into my bones. Finally, I tipped my head back and spat. When the spit came back down in my face, I knew which way was up again. I climbed a little faster.

At last I pushed through the top of the clouds and came to the Blue, which wasn't just blue, but a barrier of sorts. The top of the sky, the end of my world, the beginning of another.

The Blue was a soft, shimmery curtain. I reached a finger out and poked it. It jiggled like jelly but resumed its glossy smoothness. The beanstalk seemed to be growing upside down out of the Blue. I took out my axe and stabbed at it. It split open and dirt sprinkled down on my face. Beyond the Blue was a ceiling of dirt, stretching as far as the eye could see.

The beanstalk bent and twisted between the dirt ceiling and the Blue until it found an opening that allowed it to grow upward. A hole so wide it could fit a giant. This must be the hole the giants had come down through. It looked endless, with no light above, and my muscles ached with the thought of more climbing.

"Don't give up now, Jack," I said to myself. "You haven't even gotten to the giants yet. Take courage!"

I climbed through the hole and up the beanstalk. The spot of Blue below me began to darken until I could no longer see it. It must be night, but then at last a pinprick of light appeared above me. The top!

I ignored the scream of my arms and legs and climbed faster. The opening at the top was small, just big enough for the beanstalk to push through, but far too small for a giant. It must have been covered up somehow.

At last I emerged from the hole. I pushed through some leaves and landed facedown in the dirt, heaving and coughing—and laughing.

Ha, ha! I made it! I was in a land beyond the sky. Giants, beware!

Haste, valiant stranger,
haste away,
Lest you become the
giant's prey.

—*Jack the Giant Killer*

CHAPTER SIX

A Giant World

The first thing I saw in the giant world was the sky. It was just like the one in my world—big and blue, streaked with clouds—only the sun was in the wrong place. It was sunset down Below, but clearly it was a fresh dawn here. I guessed my day was this world's night, and my night was this world's day. Otherwise, everything seemed quite normal. Clouds, dirt, trees, rocks . . .

Whoosh!

Dragons!

A dragon screeched and swooped down at me, talons outstretched.

I stumbled back into the beanstalk hole and wedged myself between the twisting vines. The dragon tore at the stalk and leaves with its dagger talons and curved beak. It flapped its wings, and a giant feather fell down through the hole. That's when I realized that it wasn't a dragon. It was a giant bird. An eagle or a hawk. The bird screeched and shook at the vines. I curled into a ball and clutched at my ears. I'd been in the giant world for only a minute and I was about to be torn apart by a giant bird. It wasn't fair! The tales of Grandpa Jack never said anything about giant birds.

The bird screeched again, released the beanstalk, and flew back into the sky. It circled high above, waiting for me to emerge. After a few minutes it gave up and soared out of sight in search of some other edible creature. I stayed in the tangle of vines a while longer.

I crept out of the hole slowly, looking side to side, up and down for any sign of predators. Now I knew how a mouse must feel. My heart beat as fast as a mouse's, too. Perhaps mouse hearts beat so fast because they're always frightened of owls or cats.

I scurried to a tree and crouched behind it. The tree trunk bent and swayed. Weird. These trees didn't have rough bark but were waxy and ribbed, like celery. The tops didn't have leaves but were round and white and fluffy like . . . dandelions. They were giant dandelions.

Of course. This wasn't just a world where giants lived. It was a giant world. I guess I should have figured that out by the giant beanstalk. *Everything* was giant! The hawks and the grass and trees and—whoa!—the bugs.

A wood louse the size of a squirrel lay dead beneath one of the dandelions. It was rolled on its back with its many legs all shriveled and contorted. Even dead it was terrifying. I imagined the delightful scream from Annabella if she were to find *that* in her bed!

Some distance away I saw a real giant tree, so I scurried over to get a better view of things. I couldn't reach the branches, of course, but the giant bark made perfect hand- and footholds for climbing, like a series of paths on a wall. The tree was sticky with sap, which got all over my hands and made my nose and eyes itch with the spicy smell. A beetle the size of my head crawled out from under the bark. I held still as it scuttled over my hand, tickled my arm with its wriggly antennae, and disappeared around the other side of the tree.

Once I was high enough, I twisted around to see.

A whole city spread out before me. Giant houses and shops lined the streets. Big plumes of smoke rose from chimneys as tall and wide as my house. There were wagons the size of whales, and giant horses pulling them. And there were giants, not just one or two, but dozens and dozens, all milling about like ordinary people, except . . . giant.

"Ho, ho, villainous giants! None shall escape the wrath of mighty Jack!" I tried to speak the way Grandpa Jack did in the tales. Gallant and brave.

Directly across the road there was a bakery with a giant loaf of bread and pie painted on the sign, and it reminded me of Baker Baker and his bakery that had been taken. I wondered where it could be now. What did giants need with a tiny bakery when they had a giant one of their own?

A giant emerged from the bakery, dressed in fine robes and a plumed, poufy hat. He was stuffing his face with a pie. Dark juice slid down the sides of his mouth. My stomach twisted, wondering what exactly was in that pie. Blackberries? Blueberries? Or people-berries?

A giant peddler pushed a cart through the streets, calling out his sales for the day in a deep, booming voice that vibrated in my chest. "We got roots! Mushrooms! Crickets! Only ten gold pieces for a dozen!"

Ten gold pieces for crickets? I could catch a hundred in ten minutes for free. But maybe crickets were rare in the giant world and full of luck or something, because the peddler was thronged with giants, and they all opened their purses full of gold and poured it into the peddler's hands. One giant man took a cricket right away and popped it into his mouth! He crunched the cricket between his giant teeth. His face twisted up and he didn't seem to think it tasted all that good, but he ate two more on the spot and patted his belly when he finished. "That's better," he said.

Giants eating crickets . . . at least it wasn't people-berries.

Speaking of people, I didn't see anyone my size. But there were so many giants! Way more than nine. There were big man giants with horses and wagons, woman giants with baskets and carts, and child giants. I'd never considered that there were woman and child giants before. All the giants in Grandpa Jack's tales had been brutish men. Ogres. But man or woman, ogre or not, one of these giants had taken Papa.

"Which of you brutes took my father? I'll chop the villain's head off!"

No one seemed to hear.

Many of the giants were moving uphill, away from the shops. I watched them go up and up and up some more, and—aha!—at the top of the hill there was a giant castle. So enormous I couldn't see the ends of it. Great towers rose into the sky, glistening in the morning sun like gold. In fact, it looked like they really were gold. Every part of the castle glowed with golden light, and the windows sparkled like great shining lakes. Papa had to be there. In the tales, the giants always kept their human captives in castle towers or dungeons.

I would probably have to face many giants. Maybe even more than Grandpa Jack. But that didn't matter. I was born for this! I could conquer them all with my axe and my wit and bravery.

I raised my axe with a flourish. "Beware, wretched ogres! Ye shall fall by the mighty hand of Jack!"

With a sudden crack, the bark I was holding on to broke off the tree, and I tumbled to the ground.

One step closer to my destination.

I didn't think it wise to reveal myself to the giants when there were so many at once. So I tried to stay hidden behind rocks or grass as I followed the road toward the castle. I soon realized that the giant world was incredibly barren. There were only a few patches of grass in the dusty ground and very little of it green. Whatever giant shrubs or flowers I came upon were either shriveled or full of holes and wilting as though ill. I noticed, too, that the trees had few leaves, and their branches seemed to sag. It looked like the land was in a drought, except I saw plenty of streams and puddles, and the warm air told me it wasn't winter. I guessed the giant world was just brown.

I climbed and climbed and climbed, and yet I seemed to make very little progress up the mountain. The castle was so high and far away. There had to be an easier way to get there.

I watched the giants wend their way upward on carts and horses and by foot. I couldn't see much more than boots and skirts and wheels. The child giants were easier to see, since they were closer to the ground. They had big hungry eyes and great sharp teeth that gnashed open and shut with a fearsome appetite.

A giant little boy spotted me. "Ooh! Pixie! Pixie!" He charged after me with fat hands outstretched. The boy's mother grabbed his arm and yanked him away. "No, Gunther! Don't touch the pixies. They'll bite you!" Gunther stuck out his lip in a pout, but his mother carried him off. I let out my breath. Safe. Whatever pixies were, I was glad that giants didn't like them and I looked like one. There must be creatures in this world that we didn't have Below.

Just then a strange creature waddled right by me. He

was much smaller than the giants, maybe the size of a cat to them, but much bigger than me. He was twice the height of Papa and several times as wide, with stout legs, a round, chubby face, and a fat, bulbous nose like a squash.

"Message for Ferdinand! Message for Ferdinand!" the creature chanted in a raspy voice. Whatever he was, he could talk and he didn't look vicious or threatening. Maybe I could ask him for help.

"Excuse me, sir!" I called, but the creature didn't stop. He kept running and calling, "Message for Ferdinand! Message for Ferdinand!" I supposed the message was really urgent, but a few minutes later another of the creatures waddled by. This one looked to be a girl, her hair in pigtails. "Message for Bertha! Message for Bertha!" she chanted.

"Excuse me!" I called. "I need some help, please! Please could you help?" Now that I'd noticed the creatures, they were everywhere, but it seemed like they couldn't hear me. Another one passed, this time bearing a message for Gus, and then another for Isabelle. All their messages seemed to be terribly important, but even the ones who were not chanting about messages wouldn't stop when I called for help. Unless . . .

"Hey!" I called. "I've got a message! Message!" Sure enough, one of the creatures waddled straight to me. This one had a little button nose and a wide mouth, like a toad. He wore tattered rags and no shoes. He looked down at me and blinked. "Message?" he said.

"I'm looking for my papa. He's small, like me. Can you help me find him?"

The creature just stared at me, then repeated my words exactly in a croaky voice. "I'm looking for my papa. He's small like me. Can you help me find him?"

"Ummm . . . he was taken. By . . . a giant?"

"He was taken by a giant?" he asked.

"Yes. Do you have any idea where he could be?"

"Yes. Do you have any idea where he could be?"

"Stop repeating what I say and just answer me!"

"Stop repeating what I say and just answer me!"

"Hey, pea brain, do you know anything?"

"Hey, pea brain, do you know anything?"

I growled and kicked at the dwarf-giant—whatever this creature was—not thinking about how he was still three times my size and could probably crush me, but he didn't do anything. He just stared blankly, as if our entire exchange had been forgotten. "Message?"

I sighed. "My papa's name is Henry and—" Before I could say any more, the dwarf-giant waddled off calling, "Message for Henry! Message for Henry!"

"Wait!" I shouted, but the creature waddled on without a backward glance. "Message for Henry! Message for Henry!"

So the pudgy giant-dwarf creatures wouldn't be any help. No matter. I didn't *need* help. Grandpa Jack faced a giant with three heads all on his own.

Turning my attention back to the castle, I leapt high and grabbed onto a giant woman's skirts and hid myself between the folds. As the giantess walked I swung wildly back and forth, like I was being thrashed about in a gale. It was rather fun, and I was moving at a very fast pace, upward and onward, until someone bumped into the woman. I lost my grip and went tumbling down the hill, *thumpity, bumpity,* until I came to a stop in the middle of the road. A hoof stomped down on one side of me and a wheel rolled by the other. A long tail brushed over my head, and without a second thought, I grasped at the coarse threads.

Before coming to the giant world, I would have thought riding on a horsetail would be no more threatening than hanging from a tree, but a tree only bends with the wind, while a tail has a mind of its own. It flicked me side to side and up and down. It was like hanging on to the end of a whip and you never knew which direction it would go. I got dizzy, giant flies buzzed in my face, and it smelled pretty awful, which shouldn't be surprising considering where a tail is placed.

Once inside the castle gates, the horse halted but the tail did not. The horse must have felt me because I got whipped around so violently, it was impossible to hold on. I went flying. I tumbled to the ground and bounced and rolled until I came to a stop directly beneath the stone steps of the castle.

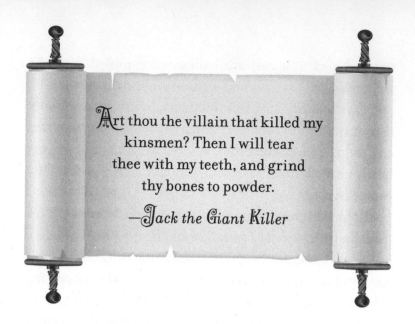

Art thou the villain that killed my
kinsmen? Then I will tear
thee with my teeth, and grind
thy bones to powder.

—*Jack the Giant Killer*

CHAPTER SEVEN

Cat and Mouse and Giant

The walls of the giant castle rose above me like endless mountains and cliffs. To my left was a set of stairs leading to some doors, but each step was twice my height, and frankly I'd had enough of climbing for one day. Besides, it was better to enter with stealth and strategy, and take the giants who held Papa by surprise.

I slid through a crack in the stone and entered a tunnel, probably for mice and rats. The air was stale and moldy. Only a few shafts of light pried through other holes in the stone. Above me there were great wooden beams covered in dust and cobwebs and rather elaborate spiderwebs. . . .

"AaaaAyACK!" I leaped back as a giant spider dropped down from one of the beams right above me. Its body was the size of a pumpkin, with eight hairy legs, two sharp pincers, and four shiny black eyes all fixed on me. I held my axe, ready to swing, but the spider didn't attack me. It merely looked at me as though curious and then scuttled back up its silk thread.

A mouse as big as a sheep scurried by, twitching his whiskers and sniffing at the ground for food. He crawled up one of the beams and then disappeared through another hole. If a mouse could go through the hole safely, then so could I. I climbed up the beam, pulling myself up on giant nails and digging my feet into the knots in the wood. The spider continued its spinning, but I felt its eyes on me. Well, I suppose when you have eight limbs, it's hilarious to watch little humans climb.

As I climbed, I got whiffs of the most heavenly smells. Roasted meat and onions, fresh bread, and baked cheese. My stomach growled. The thought of eating something besides beans was almost too much for me. I climbed faster.

Finally I reached the hole the mouse had gone into. It was a tunnel, just big enough to crawl through on my hands and knees. The mouse was crouched behind a sack, nibbling on some grain that was spilling out of a rip at the bottom. He watched me closely with his beady eyes. I must have made him nervous, because he quickly finished his meal and scurried off. I scooped up a handful of grain. It was wheat. Just regular wheat, not giant.

I climbed on top of the sack of grain to get a better view of things. This was undoubtedly a kitchen. There were more giant sacks of grain and baskets of fruits and vegetables. A giant table rose up above me twice as high as a house. The walls were lined with shelves and pots and pans, rolling pins and dishes and giant wooden spoons. Across the room was a giant fireplace with a black kettle, and two stone ovens, each with a fire blazing inside. The smells of bread and meat and cheese were so strong I could almost taste them now, but there was no sign of giants. Perhaps I could grab some food without anyone noticing.

I hopped down from the sack. The floors were made of great slats of wood that I'm sure were flat and smooth to the giants, but to me they had cracks and ridges that were easy to trip over, not to mention giant nails and splinters of wood poking out like daggers and swords. I wasn't afraid, but I pulled out my axe, just to be prepared.

Some hot liquid splashed down at my feet. I jumped back and looked up. Hanging from the sky-high ceiling was an enormous iron chandelier with a dozen blazing candles. I added dripping hot wax to the list of things to watch out for.

Suddenly a bell rang. There was a rumble and the ground trembled like the earth before a stampede.

"The king demands his supper!" boomed a voice.

Through an open doorway to my left came a rush of

giants. They stomped and boomed into the kitchen, and I was right in their path.

"I need the soup!" someone shouted.

"Hand me the pie!"

"Careful now, it's hot!"

"Oomf! Watch yourself, clumsy!"

"You watch *yourself*! I've got the king's pie."

I ran back toward the mousehole, but my path was blocked by something large and furry. My heart gave a sickening jump. It was a giant cat, its fluffy tail swishing back and forth, patiently waiting for a mouse—or some tasty morsel—to come out of the hole.

I slowly backed away but then tripped over one of the slats of wood and fell with a *thud!* The cat meowed and turned around. It was orange with a squashed face and yellow eyes that narrowed when they saw me. Before I could blink, the cat pounced. Giant claws like curved daggers slashed down at me. I ran for my life.

ReeeeaaAAARRRrr!

I hurtled over a giant nail and then dodged a giant foot. I ran around chair and table legs and giant feet and skirts, all with the cat snarling and clawing at my heels.

Where to hide? I couldn't run fast enough, and there were no holes in the middle of the floor. I wedged myself between the jugs and jars, but the cat pushed them aside and tipped them over, swiping me with its giant claws.

"Out of the way, stupid cat!" One of the giants shoved the cat aside, which gave me enough time to scramble on top of one of the sacks and jump in.

Ale. Yech! Better than claws, but it was sticky and

smelled rancid. Through the hole at the top I could see the cat attacking the jug. It clawed and swiped at the opening. The jar rocked back and forth, threatening to topple over.

"Rufus!" said a voice. "What in the world are you doing, you silly cat!"

The cat growled and hissed.

"Did you find a mouse? Did you?" The jug was suddenly picked up, causing me to tumble back into sloshing ale. A giant eye came over the opening, and then the jar was tipped. Liquid sloshed over me and I went down, down, down in a whirlpool of ale. I tumbled out of the opening into a bowl. I coughed and coughed and flopped onto my back, unable to move.

"Good kitty, Rufus! You caught us a big, fat— Oh my! What have we here?" The cat snarled and jumped at me again, but the giant scooped me up in the palm of her hand so fast, my stomach dropped and flipped. And then we were face-to-face. Big blue eyes twinkled and an enormous mouth stretched wide to show rows of teeth the size of axeheads. My axe! I was in the hands of a giant and I had an axe! But there was no time for it.

"Oh, what fortune!" said the giant woman. "I just *love* little boys!"

And she dropped me into her apron pocket.

Men's hearts,
eaten with pepper and vinegar,
were his nicest food.

—Jack the Giant Killer

CHAPTER EIGHT

Mum Martha and Tom Thumb

The giant went about her business, shouting orders and bumping into things, therefore bumping me into things. I was smacked and slammed and tossed to and fro so viciously, I couldn't help but think of all the spiders and grasshoppers I'd put into Annabella's pocket. Poor grasshoppers! I promised that if I ever got out, I'd never put another living creature into anyone's pocket again.

"I need a serving spoon!" shouted a giant.

"I need a knife!" shouted another.

"Out of my way!"

I smelled food. Delicious food. Bread. Bacon. Turkey.

Leg of lamb cooked in sage and onions. Or maybe it was leg of *man*. Boy stew. Human hearts. My own hunger shrank and curdled in my stomach. What was this giant going to do with me?

I tried to make an escape hole with my axe, but I nearly chopped off my own arms, so I gave up and tried to stay still.

After what felt like hours of being jostled around, the noise quieted and the giant plucked me between two fingers and pulled me out. It was evening. The windows were dim and the kitchen was lit by a single candle on a table as big as a wheat field. Menacing shadows stretched along the walls and ceiling. Dark shapes lurked in the corners.

The giant brought me to her face, cupped in the center of her palm. All the giants Grandpa Jack faced were brutish men with disfigured faces and breath like rotten meat. This giantess was not disfigured. She had round rosy cheeks and twinkly eyes. She smelled like freshbaked bread and melted cheese. My stomach grumbled loudly and the giantess chuckled.

"I'm hungry, too," she said. "It's been a busy day in the kitchen, and goodness knows I am always the last to eat, but I am so glad I found you! Such a sweet thing."

Sweet. Sweet things were good for eating. Snakes and toads, wake up, Jack! Just because she's a woman giant doesn't mean she won't eat you.

I slid the axe from my waist and raised it above my head. "Thou barbarous and villainous giant! I am Jack, the great-great-great—"

"Oh dear, that does look sharp." The giantess plucked the axe right out of my hands as easily as pulling a pin out of a cushion. "Don't want to chop any fingers or toes, now do we? I prefer to keep you in one piece."

She dropped the axe into her apron pocket.

That did not go the way I'd pictured.

"Oh my, you *are* dirty. Let's wash for supper." The giantess plopped me into a washbasin and poured water over my head. She held me between her thumb and forefinger and rubbed me against a bar of soap. Up and down and all around so the soap lathered and bits of foam got into my mouth. I coughed and spat, and then the giantess dunked me back in the water and swished me around like a dirty rag in the wash bucket.

Swish, swish, swash.

"All clean!" She shook me a few times, wrapped me tight inside a handkerchief, and set me beside a stub of candle. The flame was like a blazing fire in front of me, and it was nice and warm.

"Now, my name is Martha," said the giantess. "You can call me Mum Martha."

Mum?

"What's your name, little one?"

I looked at her, confused. Did giants enjoy knowing the names of their meals? Roast Jack. Jack Stew. Jack Pudding and Pie. Delicious.

"Oh, poor thing," said Martha. "Perhaps you have no name. Some do come that way. But don't worry. We'll find you the perfect name! You could be Hans or Fritz or Gus, or . . ."

The giantess continued to rattle off names, but a movement at the corner of my eye caught my attention. A sugar bowl as big as a chicken coop sat on a shelf just above me. It wobbled from side to side and finally tipped over. The lid popped off and a boy tumbled out. A boy who was my size, and looked about my age.

"Well, if it isn't Tom Thumb!" said the giantess with delight. She held out her hand, and the boy climbed into her palm without hesitation. "I'm sorry, I forgot I put you in the sugar bowl for dinner, but now that you're here, I have a surprise for you." Martha set the boy down next to me. "A new brother! Oh dear, I never did choose a name for him, did I? He doesn't seem to have one. What do you think his name should be, Tom?"

Tom shrugged. "How about Tim?"

Martha clapped her hands. "Oh perfect! Tim and Tom Thumb! We're going to be such a happy little family! My own baby boy is all grown up and gone off in the world, and you little ones just fill the cracks in my heart!" A giant tear trickled down her cheek and made a puddle at our feet. She scooped us both up and pressed us against her chest so I could barely breathe. I suddenly wished for my own mother, even if she met me with a good tongue-lashing.

Finally Martha let us down, and I fell to my knees, gasping for air.

"We must celebrate," said Martha. "With cheese! Cheese and children! My two favorite things!"

Martha went to a cupboard and took out a large

wooden block with a slab of cheese as big as a cow and a giant knife.

I struggled to get out of the handkerchief and tipped over. Tom helped me up and unraveled me.

"Thanks," I said, but before I could say anything more, Martha placed the cheese right between us. She cut off a chunk and popped it into her mouth. The smell was sharp and acrid.

"Mmm. Mm. Mm! I just love cheese."

Tom poked his head over the top of the cheese and climbed down the other side. He ripped off a chunk for me.

"Here, Tim, have some cheese." The smell was overwhelming, but I was dizzy with hunger, so I dug in. It tasted better than it smelled, and I instantly felt better.

"My name is actually Jack," I said.

"Well why didn't you say so? My name is *actually* Tom. Martha calls me Tom Thumb since I'm about as big as her thumb."

"I thought she was going to eat me."

Tom laughed. "Not Martha. We're her pets, like a toad you keep in your pocket."

Tom's clothes were rather odd. He wore a giant acorn shell on his head like a helmet, a vest and pants made of leaves and thistledown, and fur boots. He had bright-blue eyes, and a sprinkle of freckles over round cheeks and a button nose.

"How long have you been here? Did Martha kidnap you?"

"Of course not. She paid another giant an entire round of cheese for me, which is a lot for Martha. She loves cheese. She prefers it over any other food."

"Do the other giants prefer to eat children?"

"I don't think so, but giants are the least of your worries when it comes to getting eaten. Once I got eaten by a giant cow!"

"How could you be alive if you were eaten by a cow?" I asked.

"I got swallowed whole. I went straight down the throat like a big mud slide, traveled through all four stomachs, and came out the other end."

"You mean you came out in the cow's . . . ?"

"*Exactly!*" said Tom, grinning with pride. "It was amazing!"

I pictured this event in my mind and slowed down on the cheese. It too came out of a cow.

Now that I had some food in my stomach, and I knew I wasn't going to be eaten, exhaustion settled in. My limbs were sore and heavy, and the warmth of the candle made my eyelids droop.

I shook myself awake. I couldn't sleep now! Perhaps I was not in danger, but Papa might be.

"Tom, have you seen other people like us? People who have been taken by giants?"

"Oh sure. There are lots of elves in the castle."

"Elves?"

"Yeah, elves like us."

"I'm not an elf. I'm a human boy."

"Not in this world. Do you think the giants call

each other giants? Here in The Kingdom, they're regular sized and we're little, so we're called elves. You'll get used to it."

I felt a little dizzy. "Okay. Can you tell me where I might find more of these . . . elves? I'm looking for my papa."

Tom froze. He lowered his cheese and looked at me as though I'd just told him it was poisoned. "Your papa?"

I nodded. "Giants took him. They took all our crops and animals, and they snatched my papa right out of the barn with our newborn calf."

Tom's eyes lost focus. He looked as though he had gone somewhere very far away.

"His name is Henry," I said. "He looks like me, only taller. Have you seen him?"

Tom snapped to attention. "Nope, haven't seen anyone's papa lately." He took a huge bite out of his cheese.

"Do you have any idea where he could have been taken?"

"No idea."

"Would Martha know?" She was steadfastly feasting upon cheese with her eyes closed. The giant slab was now half gone.

"She hardly ever leaves the kitchen," said Tom. "I see a lot more than she does. I've been all over the place. Want to duel?" Tom picked up two giant toothpicks off the cheese board and held one out to me. Normally I would have jumped at the chance, but seeing the giant toothpick gave me horrible visions of things that might have happened to Papa.

"Not now. I'm on a quest." I walked along the edge of the table. Looking for a way down.

Tom tossed the toothpicks aside. "A quest! I love a quest! I'll join you. What is our quest? Treasure? Trolls?"

"No. I'm on a quest to find my papa, of course."

Tom's smiled faded. "Oh. Well that's not as fun as treasure or trolls. You know, there's lots of treasure in the castle. The giant king is *extremely* rich. He has mountains of gold—giant-sized mountains. And he makes it with *magic*. Mum Martha's seen it before. Haven't you, Martha?"

I got a tingling feeling at the back of my neck. A giant king. Gold. Magic. It was like Grandpa Jack's tales.

Martha opened her eyes as though she'd been woken from a dream. "What? Oh, yes. The king has plenty of gold, but I daresay it would be better if he could grow some magic potatoes. Such a famine we're in, we can't grow a bean these days! Our cows don't give milk, the hens don't lay eggs, and if we didn't have you little elves, we'd all be starved!"

Martha's words took me by surprise. "So that was why those giants took all our food? Because you're in a famine?" Of course, I had noticed how brown and droopy all the plants were, but I hadn't made the connection to famine.

"It's a *curse*," said Tom. "An evil magician put a spell on the land."

"Tom, stop telling tales," Martha chided. "I know it's horribly beastly of us, but what can we do? We would have starved by now without you dear little elves." Her eyes started to brim with tears.

"Don't cry, Martha," said Tom, patting her big hand. "We know it's not your fault and you're very kind to us."

"But why do you take people, too?" I asked. "Why not just the food?"

"Giants couldn't very well handle our food on their own, could they?" said Tom defensively. "Can you imagine Martha trying to milk one of our cows with her giant hands? She'd crush it! I had to milk seventeen cows for that one slab of cheese, you know."

"Such a good, sweet boy, my Tom Thumb." Martha patted him on the head so his knees buckled beneath him. "Now, that's enough chatter for one night. It's off to the sugar bowl with you boys."

Martha scooped us up and dropped us in.

The sugar bowl was very comfortably lined with feathers and thistledown and other soft things. "Good night, sweet boys! Sleep tight, don't let the cats bite!" Martha placed the lid over the top, and all became pitch-black.

"Isn't Martha great?" said Tom.

"Sure," I said. "Great."

"Just wait until tomorrow," said Tom. "After we milk the cows, we can duel and joust and play tug-of-war. We can eat whatever we want, and I can even take you to the armory, where there are helmets that make terrific forts and swords you can slide down and axes and spears you can climb like trees."

"Okay," I said, wondering if I would ever get my own

axe back out of Martha's pocket. At least I still had my sling, though I didn't see how that would do me any good against the giants.

I was so confused. Martha was not at all like the giants in Grandpa Jack's tales, and apparently they had stolen from our world only because they were having a famine. That didn't make it all right, but it was less monstrous than I'd assumed. Still, it didn't make my quest any easier. Where was Papa? What giant was I supposed to conquer here? Clearly not Martha.

Yawning, I nestled into the soft down. It had been a long, long day. Two days in one, really, and I was all out of ideas. I'd figure it out in the morning.

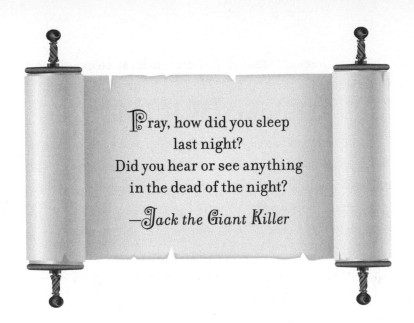

Pray, how did you sleep
last night?
Did you hear or see anything
in the dead of the night?

—Jack the Giant Killer

CHAPTER NINE
Spoon Shot and Pudding Pond

I dreamed of Papa. He was standing in the middle of the wheat field before harvest, brushing his hands over the feathery tops, just like he always did.

"Isn't she beautiful, Jack? Just like gold."

As Papa brushed his hands over the wheat, a breeze rushed through and the wheat glimmered golden in the sun. Not just golden, but gold. The wheat had turned into *real* gold.

I bounded through the fields. We were rich! I'd never be hungry again!

The ground started to tremble. I stopped and looked up.

Boom, Boom, BOOM!

The sky tore open and a giant hand reached down. It ripped up the gold wheat in handfuls. It tore up the entire field, and then the giant snatched Papa.

"Papa!" I shouted.

"Jack! Take care of your mama and sister, Jack!"

"Papa!"

I woke up, but the earth was still shaking and I couldn't see a thing. I slammed into a wall and then something that felt like a foot hit me in the gut. I went rolling all over again, until I slammed into another wall.

"Mama!" I shouted. "The giants are coming!"

"Don't worry," grumbled Tom sleepily. "It's just Mum Martha."

I suddenly remembered. I was in a sugar bowl, in a giant kitchen, in a giant castle, in a giant world, where the giants really *had* taken Papa.

"Wake up! Wake up!" came a warbly voice. "It's a beautiful day for milking! A lovely day for making cheese!"

Martha popped the top of the sugar bowl off, and I was blinded by light. She tipped the bowl, and Tom and I rolled out into her hand.

"Good morning, children! Did you sleep well? Are you hungry? Eat up! Eat up! We must get some meat on those skinny little bones, and then it's off to the milking pen!" Martha set us down on the table and gave us hot porridge with cream. Tom ate his porridge out of a thimble, and I slurped mine out of an empty acorn.

It was early morning, just the first rays of sun trickling through the windows, but bright enough that I could see the whole giant kitchen now. It was an enormous, noisy, bustling place. There were giant maids stirring pots of porridge, kneading dough, washing dishes, scrubbing the floor, and stoking fires. In the giant fireplace was a big black kettle, and in the blazing ovens on either side were loaves of bread, or hills of bread, more like.

Four giant tables stretched across the kitchen in two rows. Two of the tables were being used for preparation. Another table was covered with food. Not giant food. Food from my world, and more than I had ever seen all at once. There were great mounds of cabbages, hills of apples and pears, giant buckets of peas, carrots, beets, and radishes. Cascades of wheat and barley filled one whole end of the table, all neatly bundled and stacked. And on the fourth table—

MooooOOOOOOOoooo.

Baaaaaaaaa!

Bok, bok!

—there were all manner of farm animals. Cows and sheep and pigs and chickens.

Above this table hung three shelves. They seemed to hold giant birdhouses, except the birdhouses were real houses from Below—log cabins, brick houses, and whitewashed cottages with thatched roofs and smoking chimneys.

And people. There were people my size on the shelves!

A woman swept the dirt out of her door and off the shelf. Another hung laundry to dry on a huge dish rack, and below her a man was bathing in a giant tankard, all of them going about their business as if it were a normal day in a normal world.

I couldn't believe I hadn't noticed any of this yesterday. But one does not expect to find cows in a kitchen or an entire village sitting on a shelf.

"Good morning, my elves!" Martha sang cheerfully. "It's a lovely day, isn't it? And so much work to do. Dear me, I could never do it all without you sweet elves. We need to chop carrots and peel potatoes, gather eggs, pluck chickens, and milk cows! Of course, there will be plenty for all of you, so let us work hard, my elves. Many hands make light work!" Martha held out both her hands. Several people readily climbed onto her palm as though stepping into a carriage. "Hello, Sally, Mary, Thelma, Francis, George, Harold, and . . . oh I forgot your name!"

"Maude," said a woman.

"A wise and sensible name. Thank you, Maude."

Martha delivered two handfuls of people to the animal table and a few more loads to the food table, calling each of them by name. I strained to hear her say "Henry." Papa could be on one of those shelves. He could be in Martha's hands right now.

"Amazing, isn't it?" said Tom, slurping the dregs of porridge out of his thimble. "We can climb potato mountains and cheese walls and jump on the bread . . . it'll be loads of fun!"

"Tom, why didn't you tell me all these people were here?"

"I did! I told you I saw lots of elves every day."

"But . . . I told you that my papa was taken with all our wheat and our calf. Wouldn't they have been brought here? I can see a calf over there right now!" I said, pointing to the table full of animals. I needed to find a way over there, but suddenly Martha was in front of us.

"There you are!" she said. "It's time for the milking." She scooped me in one hand and Tom in the other.

I wriggled and protested. "But I needed to—"

"Now, Tim, you mustn't allow your brother to do all the work. We reap what we sow—except in The Kingdom, where nothing seems to grow anymore . . . Dear me, I do wish I could at least grow a tomato. I sowed some seeds in the spring, and I gave them plenty of sun and water, but they didn't even sprout!"

Martha carried us to a barn with peeling red paint. It sat on the end of the table full of animals. At least she was taking me where I needed to go. She unlatched the doors with her giant fingers, and a whole herd of cows streamed out, mooing.

"Now be good boys and milk the cows," said Martha. "And, Tom, dear, do try not to squirt the milk at Harold or the chickens. You know how that upsets him, and it spooks the hens, and we need every tiny egg if we are to feed the king, not to mention every drop of milk. Goodness, it seems he never stops eating. If he could eat only gold, then I'd never have to cook again!" Martha left us to see to the king's breakfast.

"Come on," said Tom. "Let's do the milking and then we can duel!"

"But my papa . . ." I reminded him, looking down the row of barns.

Tom sighed. "Go ahead and look, but you still have to help with the milking. Martha gets terribly upset if it isn't done, and I don't like her to cry. There's a real risk of drowning."

"I'll be back!" I promised. Maybe with Papa, even!

I ran down the center of the table, which was like a road through a strange village. Sheep and pigs were penned up in fences made of giant clothespins and yarn. Chickens nested in coops made of giant lanterns, tea-cups, and an upside-down hat stuffed with straw. The table was lined with a fence made of forks stuck in the wood for posts and wire stretched between them. A man was spreading the hay using a giant fork as a pitchfork.

"Excuse me, sir," I said. "I'm looking for my papa. His name is Henry and he was taken by giants with our newborn calf. Have you seen him?"

"No," said the man, and he continued spreading the hay, not at all concerned with my troubles.

I moved on. I came to a barn made out of books. There were three books for walls, and a fourth split open across the top to make an A-shaped roof. There was even a man reading the open book on the ceiling as he milked a cow. The words were large and looped. It reminded me of Papa's book full of giant tales.

"Excuse me, sir," I said to the man. He looked down from his book on the ceiling but continued to milk the cow. "I'm looking for my papa. His name is Henry, and giants took him with our newborn calf. Have you seen him?"

"There's a newcomer in the bread-bin barn," said the man. "Came here a week or two ago. Don't quite recall if it was a calf or a pig he had." A pinprick of hope flared in my chest.

I raced down the table until I found the bread-bin. There was a man inside, but it wasn't Papa. He was much too big, and he was holding a pig in his arms, feeding it an apple by hand. The man looked up.

"Halloo! Come to throw a pail of slops on me, eh, Jack?"

I squinted. "Horace?" He had grown a beard, but I recognized him and his pig, Cindy. I smiled. It wasn't Papa, but seeing someone from home was like finding a clue or a sign on the trail, telling you you're on the right track.

"Is my papa here?" I asked.

"Haven't seen him, but I don't see much beyond this bread bin. Just pigs. I tend most of the pigs here on this table, feed them their slops and such, until they all become giant bacon."

I grimaced.

"I know," said Horace. "But at least they didn't turn *us* into bacon. And they let me keep my Cindy."

"Do you remember anything about the night the giants took you? Do you remember anything about my papa?"

Horace scratched his head. "No. Not much. It was

dark and loud and stuffy. Couldn't hardly breathe. One of the giants kept picking up my pigs and saying he wanted to keep some for pets, but the other giant wouldn't let him. I just held tight to my Cindy until it all passed."

The pig snorted in his arms, reminding Horace that he was supposed to feed her. He gave the pig the rest of the apple, and then he held a fresh one out to me.

"You want an apple?" I took it, though I wasn't hungry. "You need a place to sleep? You can stay in my bread bin. It's not much, but we got all we need."

"Thank you, but I'm not staying. I'm going to go look for my papa."

"You be careful, now. They say some of those giants can be real ogres."

"I will. Thanks for the apple."

I left Horace and walked slowly back to the barn where Tom was milking a cow.

"Come on," said Tom. "I've already milked four."

I took a bucket and picked a cow to milk.

Across from where we sat, Martha and the rest of the kitchen servants were busy preparing the royal breakfast trays. They set out bowls of porridge and tea and toast, but one tray stood out among the rest. Firstly, the tray and all the dishes were made of pure gold, right down to the sugar spoon, and secondly, it had about a hundred poached eggs, fifty slabs of bacon, and a mountain of fruit. Finally, Martha unlocked a cupboard and brought out a glass bowl filled with gold flakes. She sprinkled the gold all over the food, like one might dust sugar over a cake.

"Is that the giant king's breakfast?" I asked.

Tom nodded. "Can you imagine being so rich you can *eat* gold?"

I couldn't.

"And guess what his name is?" said Tom. "King *Barf!*" He burst out laughing.

Martha cleared her throat, suddenly towering over us. "His *Royal Majesty's* name is King Bartholomew Archibald Reginald Fife, Tom dear, and you had better watch your tongue. The king is not merciful to those who cross him, no matter how small. Why, just last week a chambermaid told me she saw the king throw an elf straight into the fire!"

I gulped. I had a terrible vision of Papa being thrown into flames. "Does the king keep elves, then?" I asked.

"Why, I suppose so, yes, though for what purpose I'm sure I don't know. His Majesty gave me all my elf helpers—all except you and Tim—but all elves are given by His Majesty's command."

Ding! A bell rang.

"Oh my! And now the king demands his breakfast!" Martha sprinkled the king's breakfast with one more spoonful of gold before it was whisked away.

Could King Barf have Papa? Either way, Martha said he was the one in charge of where they all went. That meant he had to have seen Papa at some time and sent him somewhere. It clearly wasn't the kitchen.

"Heads up!" said Tom. He squirted some milk right in my eye. "Bull's-eye!"

Milk was dripping down my face, but I went right back to work, pretending I didn't care. Then, when he wasn't expecting it, I squirted Tom in the ear, and suddenly we were in a milking duel and not so much milk got into the buckets.

Abandoning his cow altogether, Tom picked up a giant fork. "Let's joust like knights!" he said, raising the fork like a lance.

I scoured the barn until I found a fork leaning against a bale of hay. I struggled to lift it. It was *heavy!*

"Charge!" Tom cried, and raced toward me.

"I will vanquish thee, villain!" I lumbered forward in an awkward trot. Our forks clanged together as we passed. Tom knocked me over and nearly stabbed me in the gut. I tumbled to the ground.

"Are you okay?" asked Tom.

I grinned. "Let's do it again!"

We clashed the forks again and again, until my mind wandered to the times when Papa and I used to play swords. He'd play the villain or the giant, and I'd be the hero. We had these amazing death scenes where I'd stab him and he'd grunt and choke and fall down on the ground and twitch and lie still. I'd wait for a few moments, and then I'd creep up on him and whisper, "Papa?" but he'd stay silent, and then I'd poke him a little. He wouldn't move. Finally I would bend down and check for his breathing or a heartbeat, and that was when he'd growl and grab me and throw me up in the air.

Then he'd tickle me until I laughed so hard, my stomach hurt. Thinking of this made my chest hurt.

I put down my fork-lance. The sunlight had moved above the windows now, which meant it was probably close to midday. I looked around at the lunch preparations. A giant maid was shaking salt and pepper into a pot of bubbling soup. Another was placing bread and cheese on a tray, and Martha had just taken a pudding out of the oven and set it on the table to cool.

I needed to find Papa, and finding the king was my best chance. I'd meet him face-to-face—or face-to-foot. I'd demand he give me Papa. Or else!

"Tom, is there a way to get to the other table? The one where Martha is?"

"Sure, we just need a spoon."

"A spoon?"

"You'd be surprised how much you can do with a giant spoon." Tom disappeared and then came back a minute later, dragging a soup spoon. He set it down and rubbed his hands together. "Stand on the end there."

"How is a spoon supposed to get me across the table? Does it fly?"

Tom smiled. "Something like that. Get on!"

I tentatively stepped onto the end of the spoon's handle, not sure what to expect.

"Terrific. Now wait a minute." Tom climbed up some bales of hay and onto the roof of the barn. He shouted down at me. "Bend your knees! One! Two—"

I suddenly realized what he was doing. "Tom, I don't—" But it was too late.

"Three!" Tom jumped off the barn and landed on the other end of the spoon. I catapulted into the air.

"Snakes and tooooooooads!" I soared over the table, arms and legs flailing, and landed on top of a mountain of potatoes. I tumbled down in a potato avalanche.

Tom swung across the kitchen to join me on a rope tied to one of the chandeliers. "That was amazing! You should have seen how high you flew."

"Why didn't you just tell me about the rope?" I grumbled.

"Where's the fun in that?" Tom seemed perplexed. "No elf has ever traveled by catapult before! You should feel honored."

I cracked a smile. I had to admit it was fun. I also had to admit that I liked Tom quite a bit. Maybe he didn't understand what it was like to lose your papa, but he was exactly the friend I'd always wished for back home, someone who liked big adventure and a little mischief.

Tom found another spoon and was dragging it into place beneath a giant block of cheese.

"Come on! It's my turn! You can jump from the cheese."

"Okay." I had time to send Tom up into the air once. If I shot him somewhere across the room, he wouldn't be able to stop me from sneaking off on the king's lunch tray. I climbed the cheese, which made a great squelching sound every time I stuck my hands in or pulled them out. When I reached the top, I was covered in sticky, stinky cheese. I hoped Martha wouldn't find me, or she'd give me another bath.

Tom was on the end of the spoon, knees bent and ready.

"Count to three!" shouted Tom, grinning like he was about to get his greatest wish.

"One, two, three!" I jumped and landed on the end of the spoon. Tom went flying.

"Wheeeeeee!" he shouted with glee.

And I, being gooey and slick with cheese, slipped off the spoon and stumbled to the edge of the table. I flailed my arms and nearly fell, but luckily caught myself on Tom's rope. Safe.

Ding! The bell rang.

"Lunch!" Martha sang.

The kitchen broke into chaos. A maid swept right in my path and caught her arm on the rope, so I swung wildly across the table. I jumped on a loaf of bread and bounced a few times on the spongy surface before I flew off and—*splat!*—landed in something warm and wet and squishy. I licked the crumbs around my mouth. Whatever I had landed in, it was tasty.

"Don't forget the king's pudding!" Martha picked up the dish.

The king's pudding . . .

"Wait!" I shouted. "Martha! I'm here! It's me Jack—I mean Tim! I'm in the pudding!" I yelled and waved my arms, but she could neither hear nor see me—the kitchen was too loud. She quickly passed the dish off to a servant, and I was whisked away.

I tried to get out of the pudding, but it was like swimming through thick, gooey mud—impossible.

The servant walked briskly down dimly lit corridors, turned a corner, and entered an enormous dining hall with sky-high arched ceilings, giant-sized paintings of lords and ladies, and an endless table covered with golden plates and goblets, steaming food, and lighted candles as tall as trees.

The servant set the pudding down right in front of a giant. His face was pudgy and pink, with dark beady eyes and a sneering mouth. His upturned nose gave him the distinct look of a pig. He was dressed entirely in gold—gold robes, gold chains, gold rings, and two gold crowns upon his head, one stacked on top of the other.

There was no mistaking it. This was the giant king. King Barf. And I was in his lunch.

Will no other diet serve
you but poor Jack?

—*Jack the Giant Killer*

CHAPTER TEN

Fee, Fie, Fo, Fum!

The king lifted a golden spoon and crashed it into the pudding, narrowly missing me. A moment later the spoon plunged down right next to my ear. King Barf ate with speed and greed, scooping up more as soon as he had shoveled the last glob into his mouth. I dodged one bite and then another, and as the pudding dish cleared, I made my way toward the edge.

Just when I thought I was out of danger, the spoon scooped beneath my feet and scraped me against the edge of the dish. Suddenly I was barreling toward the king's mouth—a huge cave lined with yellowish boulders. I was going to be eaten by a giant.

The spoon tipped. I slid down onto a squishy, slimy tongue.

The mouth-cave closed, and everything went black.

King Barf's tongue squished me to the roof of his mouth. Luckily, the king chewed with his mouth open, so every bite I got just enough light to dodge his teeth. Unluckily, his mouth didn't open wide enough for me to escape without being sliced in half on the way out.

I slid to the back of the throat and kicked out my legs. The tongue swelled up in defense and squished me hard, but I yanked and twisted and punched. The king gagged and coughed once, twice, and with a great gust of foul breath shot me out of his mouth.

I soared past the pudding and right over a candle-stick, narrowly missing the flame, and landed—*plop!*—in a hot green pond. Some of the liquid splashed into my mouth. Blech! Green bean soup! I swam to the shore of the tureen, seeking shelter in the crevice where the ladle rested. I'd nearly been *eaten!* But it looked like I'd escaped, miraculously, with no giant teeth marks.

The king coughed and hacked some more. "This pudding is full of gristle," he spat in a cold, nasal voice. "Servant! Take this disgusting mush away!" A servant picked up the dish and walked quickly out of the room, but before he disappeared, I saw him dig his hands into the pudding and stuff some into his mouth. No food goes to waste in a famine.

The king took another dish and went on with

shoveling food into his mouth. Crumbs and juice dribbled down to the table.

Cluck, cluck.

Snakes and toads, there was a giant *chicken* on the table! A live hen, pecking at King Barf's scraps. She was attached to the king's wrist by a gold chain, and the king stroked her feathers while he ate.

Across from the king sat a giant woman—the queen, I believed. She had fair skin, bright-blue eyes, golden hair, and ruby-red lips. She was very beautiful, except every now and then her tongue flicked out like a frog's.

In her lap the queen held a giant baby. The prince, I guessed, not more than a year old with chubby cheeks, two shiny sharp teeth, and a fountain of drool dripping down onto the queen's plate.

"Fee! Fee! Fo!" the giant baby said as he pounded on the table.

The king glowered at the baby as though he smelled something foul. "Must you bring that troll to supper, woman?"

"My name is not '*woman*,'" she said defiantly. "It's *Queen* Opal, and this is not a troll. He's your son and heir and has more right to be at the table than that *animal*."

The king petted the hen. "My Treasure shall stay with me always and everywhere I go, isn't that so, Magician?"

The king addressed another giant who sat between the king and queen. He had carroty orange hair that stuck up in all directions, and eyes that looked permanently mystified. "Oh, yes, Your Goldness," said the magician. "Nothing is so important as your Treasure."

"Yes, you are my only delight, my Treasure," the king cooed, and then he shouted, "Lay!"

Suddenly the hen went rigid. She trembled a little, gave a loud squawk, and laid an egg. The king seized the egg and held it up to the candlelight. It was not an ordinary egg—neither brown nor white, not even blue or speckled. It was gold. That hen just laid a golden egg.

The magician clapped his hands fast three times. "Oh very good, Your Goldness! It is such clever magic, is it not?"

"Thank you, Magician," said the king. "It is clever magic, though it would be even cleverer if you could make *more*. Ever since the queen stopped spinning golden straw, my gold supply is running dangerously low."

The queen's eyes grew wide with fear. She flicked out her tongue.

The magician sat up straight in his chair, like a soldier at attention. "I'm trying ever so hard, Your Goldness. Yesterday I *nearly* succeeded in turning a scullery maid's hair to gold. I was certain I had it right. I'll never understand why it caught fire. . . ."

The king waved his hand dismissively. "It's of little consequence to me if you set someone's hair on fire. I only wish you could make another golden hen. Or a golden goose or *something*. I do fear Treasure is wearing out, just like the queen, and then what will I do?"

The magician sighed mournfully. "Indeed, I did try to make a golden goose, but the first froze into a statue, and the second laid eggs of *coal*, not gold, so I gave that one to the blacksmith for his fires, only I don't think he appreciated it, because he chopped its head off right away and cooked it for supper."

The king clutched his hen close to his chest. "Don't let that brute near my Treasure!"

Bok, bok! said the hen.

"Fee, fee!" laughed the baby, and pounded on the table while globs of drool ran down his chin.

"Oh, take that slimy thing away," barked the king. He turned to the queen. "And what is that horrid dress you're wearing? Haven't you any golden gown?"

Queen Opal shuddered. "I . . . I don't like to wear gold. It irritates my skin."

"How can you not like gold?" said the king. "I can't stand to wear anything *but* gold. It's the coziest thing in the world, isn't it, Treasure? Lay!"

The hen seized up, trembled, and expelled another golden egg.

"That hen would serve better for a supper," said the queen. "Your subjects have hardly any food at all, so I hear."

"What are you talking about?" said the king. "We have plenty of food. It comes in by the wagonload nearly every day!"

"From the elf lands Below!" shouted the queen. "And how long can it possibly last? It's all so tiny. How many elf villages are there?"

"How should I know?" said the king. "Ask your brothers. They're the ones who go down to that filthy place."

"Frederick and Bruno?"

My ears perked up at this. Frederick and Bruno. They must be the brutes who had taken Papa.

"Yes," said the king. "They've finally proven useful to me, unlike you and your treacherous father. You're lucky you didn't suffer his fate after I found out you could no longer spin straw into gold."

The queen flicked out her tongue. "You can't exile me! Not when I have Archie!" She clutched her baby to her chest.

"Well, be thankful your brothers are working to pay off the debt. They're in the armory now, I believe, preparing for another raid."

"But the elf food is so *tiny*," said the queen, picking up a potato between her fingers. "How long can it possibly feed us?"

"What does it matter? When we run out, we get more! There's always more."

"But . . . what about the elves? Isn't that stealing?" asked the queen. "Aren't you afraid they'll get angry?"

Yes, it was stealing. And yes, I was angry!

"What can they possibly do? They're no bigger than my finger."

"Sometimes small things have a way of surprising you," said the queen.

"Fie! Fum!" sang the baby.

The king stabbed his fork into a hunk of meat and stuffed it into his mouth. He spoke while he chewed. "That village was under my kingdom and therefore under my rule. All the food, all the animals, all the land, even the elves—they're all mine, even if they *are* pitifully small."

"Well, it doesn't seem fair," said the queen. "How would you like it if a giant came down from the sky and stole all your gold?"

The king choked and coughed. "Don't be ridiculous! I'm too powerful to be defeated. I'd chop off their head!"

"If you're so powerful, why can't you grow food? Or *make* it with magic? Can't you have your magician make more food?"

The magician perked up. "Yes, yes! Of course I could! I'll turn this fork into a carrot!"

"Not my gold!" cried the king. "Pick something else— that thing there!" He pointed to the baby prince, who was gnawing on a piece of bread.

"Oh, goody, goody!" said the magician, reaching for the baby.

The queen slapped him away. "Not my Archie, you monster! Turn your*self* into food!"

The magician screwed up his face. "I suppose I could. I never thought of that. You're very clever, Your Majesty. Yes, I think it could work." He held his hand very close to his face. He went cross-eyed as he mumbled some words very quickly under his breath.

His fingers began to stretch and grow.

They got longer and more pointed. They turned a little green, then white and orange, until finally all five fingers on his left hand were long, pointy carrots. The greens sprouted over his knuckles and bunched at his wrist like a frilly cuff.

"Finger food!" said the magician. He bit the end off his pinky finger. "How convenient. No need to worry, Your Majesty. If we run out of food, we can simply eat ourselves!"

The queen stared at him in horror. The king laughed and stuffed some bread into his mouth.

"Fee, fee, foe!" The baby was up on the table now. He dug his hands into a bowl of potatoes and stuffed them into his mouth, smearing potato all over his face and belly. "Fum!" he said, smiling and clapping his hands so the potatoes sprayed everywhere. Then he looked right at me.

Snakes and toads, I'd been spotted.

"Fee, fee, fum!" The baby crawled so fast, I hardly had time to think. I slipped back into the soup. Maybe if he didn't see me, he would go away.

"No, Archie!" the queen shouted just as the baby pounded his fists on the edge of the tureen. I went gushing out of the bowl on a wave of gooey green beans. I splattered onto the baby's belly and slid down into the doughy folds of his legs.

"Fie, fo!" The baby poked and prodded and tried to pick me up, but we were both too slimy and slippery with soup, and luckily his chubby hands could not grasp me.

"Get that slimy creature off the table!" shouted the king.

The queen picked up the baby as I crawled onto a butter dish. She held the prince out at arm's length. He was covered with soup, and he wriggled in the queen's arms and splattered green slime on her face and blue gown.

"How disgusting!" said the king. "He looks like a prince of frogs!"

"Ooh! Ooh! I can turn him into a frog!" said the magician, clapping his hands so excitedly one of his carrot fingers snapped right off. "Oh, let me! Let me! Please, please, please!"

"Don't you touch him!" said the queen. "Haven't you done enough harm?"

"But I think he'd be charming as a frog, don't you, Your Goldness?"

"Could you make him lay golden frog eggs?" asked the king.

"You're horrid!" shouted the queen. "Don't you think of anything besides gold?"

"What else is there to think of?"

"Food," said the queen. "And family."

"Pfft! We have plenty of food. And of course I've thought about family. As I said, your brothers are preparing for another raid on the elves. Tomorrow they'll feed The Kingdom." The king petted the hen and she clucked. "And I shall have my gold, too. Now lay!"

The hen obeyed.

"Lay! Lay! Lay!"

The hen shuddered violently but released three more eggs.

"See?" he challenged the queen. "Gold is my destiny." And with that, he marched out of the room, cradling the hen in his arms. The magician followed like a faithful pup, trotting at his heels.

"A curse, more like," grumbled the queen. "All gold comes with a curse."

"Fee, fie, fo, fum!" said the baby. He put a slimy hand on the queen's face, splotching her with green.

"As for you, Prince Frog, time for a swim, and may you prove to be a better king than your father." The queen carried the giant baby away, leaving me alone on the butter. Now that lunch was over, I needed to go to the armory to find the giants who had taken Papa.

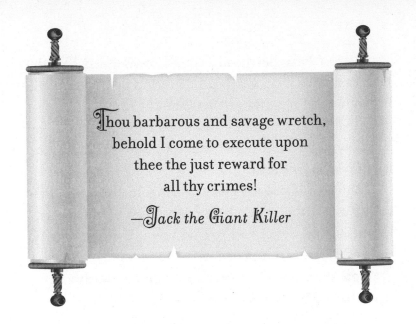

Thou barbarous and savage wretch,
behold I come to execute upon
thee the just reward for
all thy crimes!

—*Jack the Giant Killer*

CHAPTER ELEVEN

Bruno, the Cowardly Giant

"I th-thought you had b-been eaten!" Martha cried when she found me in the butter.

"I was," I said. "But I'm all right. The king spat me out."

Martha burst into tears and made puddles at my feet.

"Did he bite you at all?" Tom asked. "Did you see down his throat? How high in the air did you fly?"

"Higher than when I flew off the spoon," I said, smiling, for while it had been terrifying at the time, telling the tale made it seem like it had been a great adventure.

"Amazing!" said Tom. "I wish it had been me!"

Martha blew her nose so loud, it sounded like the blast of a horn. "Hush, Tom. There will be no more falling into puddings and getting eaten by kings or cows or anyone else. Tim is very lucky to be alive, and if he had been caught by the king . . . well, let's just say His Majesty is not one to be merciful."

I shivered. I hoped Papa had not gone to the king. At least I was fairly certain he'd been taken by the queen's brothers. And now I had to find them, but first Martha insisted I wash for supper.

I growled as she plopped me into the washbasin. I never had to bathe two days in a row at home!

"You're so filthy, a servant might mistake you for a potato, and then you really *will* get eaten," she clucked at me.

After I was washed and dry, Martha pulled out some bread and cheese. I was famished, even though I had just come from a giant feast. Tom and I gobbled up great big chunks of it.

"Want to catapult off the spoons again?" said Tom.

"Not now," I said.

"How about a duel?"

"Maybe later." I glanced at Martha. I would need someone's help in finding the queen's brothers, but I was afraid if Martha knew my plans, she would lock me in the sugar bowl.

"Tom," I whispered. "I know who came down and took my papa. It was the queen's brothers, Frederick and Bruno."

"That's great," he said in a bored tone.

"I need to find them." I urged.

"Oh, sure," said Tom. I wasn't sure he was listening.

"The king said they were in the armory, preparing for another raid."

"The armory?" Tom was interested now.

I nodded. I was beginning to realize that the only way to get Tom to help me was to make it seem like an adventure. "Maybe, if you want to come with me, we could have a battle."

Tom dropped his bread. "Yes! With giant swords and axes and spike balls. I haven't slid down a sword in ages. And I have the best way to get there! All we need is a little bit of cheese."

"Cheese?" I asked.

"You'll see," said Tom, already stuffing chunks of cheese in both his pockets. "Quick, before Martha puts us in the sugar bowl!"

Tom slid down from the table on a length of Martha's yarn. I followed, being careful to make sure Rufus wasn't in sight, and then we hopped over the cracks and crevices and giant nails and crawled through a hole in the corner of the kitchen. We were greeted by cobwebs and some ants.

Ants had always been something I could squash beneath my feet without a second thought, but giant ants . . . they had misshapen square heads and sharp pincers, but much like the spider, they paid me no mind at all. They were intent on their work, picking up crumbs and marching toward their hole like dutiful soldiers.

"Now pull out just a small handful of cheese," said Tom. I did, and we both held the cheese out.

"What are we waiting for?" I asked.

"A ride," said Tom. I looked at him like he was crazy, but Tom stood still and patiently held out his handful of cheese.

Soon, squeaks could be heard getting louder and louder, and then a few mice came scurrying down the wooden beams toward us.

A brown mouse approached Tom, twitched its whiskers, and squeaked as though greeting him. "This one's mine! You take the next!" Tom hopped onto the mouse's back and lobbed the cheese so the mouse scurried after it.

Brilliant! They were like horse-mice! A mouse came to me and sniffed at my pockets. Its long whiskers tickled my arms as I pulled out a chunk of cheese and dropped it to the ground. The mouse snatched it up. Hesitantly I grabbed onto the mouse's fur and swung myself over its back. The mouse squeaked in protest, but then I flung the cheese forward and off we went. Riding a mouse reminded me of when I was little and Papa used to let me ride the sheep, a sort of lumpy trot with lots of side-to-side movement. The mouse scurried to the cheese and gnawed away at it. After it finished, I took another chunk out of my pocket and threw that one even farther so I could catch up to Tom and his mount.

"Isn't this incredible?" Tom shouted back at me.

"Incredible!" I shouted back, because it was.

"Turn here!" said Tom, and we threw our chunks of

cheese to the left and scurried down that way until we came to a dead end.

"Now what?" I asked.

"We have to go up," said Tom. *Up* was about a hundred feet to the next rafter, with lots of spiderwebs and giant nails poking out of the beams. "Aim the cheese for the rafters. The first one up will lure the second mouse to follow." Tom threw his cheese, but it didn't catch on the upper beam, and when it came down, the mouse devoured it. Tom tried again with the same result.

"Let me try." I took out my sling, put a chunk of cheese in the middle, and flung it up so it landed perfectly on an upper beam.

"Terrific!" said Tom.

My mouse scurried up the wall and Tom's followed. Once we got to the top of that rafter, we turned down a short passage and dismounted.

"Just through here," said Tom, and we crawled on our hands and knees through a small crevice. When we came out on the other side, we were between two metal pillars. I looked up. We were underneath a giant suit of armor.

"Isn't it amazing?" said Tom.

The armory was like a metal forest. A very sharp one. There were giant swords as tall as towers stacked in neat rows, spears fanned in a circle on the wall, spiked metal balls and chains the size of boulders, crossbows and quivers of arrows, suits of armor like mountainous cliffs, and axes with shining blades crossed all along the walls. It was amazing, but I didn't see or hear anyone.

"Come on! Let's duel!" said Tom, and he pulled out two needles from the back of his shirt and handed one to me. Before I could even protest, he attacked, stabbing the needle at my chest, so I jumped back behind the foot of armor.

"*En garde!*" said Tom, and he waved his needle-sword around. It was either fight or be stabbed, so I made a cut at Tom, and we clashed our needle-swords back and forth in a fierce duel.

"Ha! I'll slice you in half!" said Tom.

"Nay, thou pompous wretch! I, Jack the Great, shall chop off thy head and slice thee to bits!"

We sparred back and forth, and I was having such a great time I almost forgot what I was doing until a horse whinnied.

I stopped and looked around. "Are there horses in the armory?"

Tom shrugged. "Probably just outside." He tried to engage me again, but then came the sound of clashing swords not our own, and most definitely within the armory. I ran from leg to leg of the suits of armor until I reached a corner.

I peered around to see a giant boy, perhaps a little older than me, sitting cross-legged on the floor, a sword by his side. He was playing with what looked to be a toy knight and horse, except they were not toys at all. The horse, which was actually a mule, bellowed and brayed, and the knight's rusty armor creaked and clattered as he swiped his sword through the air at the giant boy.

"Thou pompous wretch! I, Sir Bluberys the Chivalrous, shall chop off thy head and slice thee to bits!"

That blubberhead stole my line!

Sir Bluberys charged at the giant, but just as he reached his foot, the mule bucked wildly. Sir Bluberys fell to the ground with a terrific clatter and crunch of armor.

"Are you hurt?" The giant boy scooped up the knight and, in doing so, stabbed his thumb on Sir Bluberys's lance. "Ouch!"

"Hurt?!" said Sir Bluberys. "A noble knight is never injured. Repeat, young squire!"

"A noble knight is never injured," said the giant boy, his chin quivering.

"Louder, lad! With conviction!"

"A noble knight is never injured!" And then a drop of blood appeared on the boy's thumb and his eyes brimmed with tears. He sniffled.

"Soldiers don't cry! Get ahold of yourself." Sir Bluberys tried to slap the giant, but I doubt he felt more than a tingle.

"I'm s-sorry," sobbed the giant boy. "It's just . . . it reminds me of the pixies, you know, when they attacked me. What if it happens again? What if they eat me alive?"

"Nonsense! Don't be ridiculous!" said Sir Bluberys. "Look how large you are. A strapping lad like you has nothing to fear. How could anything so small ever hurt a big brute like you?"

"Pixies can. They attacked me and bit me everywhere with their poisonous fangs, and it hurt like a thousand needles sticking in me." The giant boy's sniffling turned to sobs. He stuck his bleeding thumb into his mouth.

"Is that true?" I whispered to Tom, who had just peeked his head out from the other side of the leg of armor.

"Yes, pixies are the worst. They're no bigger than us, but they're awful. If they bite you, you'll explode."

"Explode? How?"

"You don't want to know."

I pictured myself exploding. "I hope I never meet a pixie."

"If you do, just throw dirt at it," said Tom. "Pixies hate dirt."

"Right," I said. "Pixies. Explode. Dirt."

"Fear not, lad!" said Sir Bluberys. "We can battle again tomorrow, and with some help from me, soon you'll be a brave and strong warrior. In the meantime, do you have any grub? Pie? A turkey leg, perhaps?"

"Yes. Thank you, Sir Bluberys. I don't know what I'd do without you. You're the only elf I've never been afraid of."

"Nonsense, Bruno, lad!" said the knight.

Bruno! The queen's brother!

"That's him," I whispered to Tom. "That's the giant who took my papa."

"Well then, what are you waiting for?" whispered Tom. "Charge the villain! Chop off his fingers one by one!"

Yes, that was the thing to do. Charge. Chop. Conquer the giant. I gripped the needle so hard, my hands shook. I'd jump on his head and poke his eyeballs!

Bruno lifted Sir Bluberys and his mule and placed them gently on a table, where an elf's feast was laid out: roast turkey, bread, potatoes, cheese, and even some straw for the mule. Sir Bluberys tore off a turkey leg and ate greedily, and Bruno watched him with his chin cupped in his hands, smiling as though watching a puppet show.

Footsteps echoed from the doorway across the room. "Bruno!" shouted a voice.

"It's Frederick!" Bruno panicked. His eyes darted around the room, then narrowed on the suit of armor where Tom and I were hiding. I shrunk back behind the foot. Bruno grabbed the helmet off of the top and placed it over Sir Bluberys and his mule. "Don't make a sound!"

Another giant entered the armory—Frederick. He looked much like Bruno, except he was taller, with such a hulking build, it made his arms stick out from his sides. He had bushy eyebrows and lips that curled up in a snarl. He was the kind of ogre Grandpa Jack would have chopped to bits.

"What are you doing in here?" said Frederick. "Playing dolls?"

Bruno looked from side to side. He leaned against the table, blocking his brother's view of the helmet. "No. I was j-just—"

"Hey, guess what," Frederick interrupted. "I brought you a present." His hands were cupped around something.

Bruno flinched a little. "W-what is it?"

"A pixie!" Frederick flicked out his hands, which

turned out to be empty, but Bruno screamed and jumped back. He bumped into the table and made the helmet shift.

"Frederick! Don't do that!"

Frederick cackled. "You're such a sissy, Bruno!"

I hated to admit it, but I'd played that exact trick on Annabella before. Did I look as mean and awful as Frederick when I did it?

Bruno didn't run away, crying like Annabella. He growled and rushed at his brother and crashed into him, knocking him into our suit of armor. Tom and I jumped back against the wall as the armor toppled over and made such a terrific crash, I had to cover my ears. The boys pushed and shoved, knocking over giant swords and shields and armor. It sounded like all the metal pots and pans in the world were crashing together at once. They wrestled each other to the floor, rolling and grunting and punching. The whole room seemed to shake and tilt as they fought. Tom and I cowered behind the fallen armor until Frederick had Bruno pinned.

"Get off me!" Bruno struggled to get free. They stood and backed away from each other, breathing hard and sweating.

Tom watched the giant brawl with rapt attention. "That was amazing!" he whispered. "I've never seen a giant fight before."

Frederick dusted himself off. "Get your things ready. You know the king's orders."

"I don't want to," said Bruno. "I don't like going down there."

"Why not? Are you afraid the elves will bite you?" Frederick gave Bruno a poke.

"Stop! I just don't like it, is all. It's . . . it's mean. It isn't fair to the elves."

"Fair? Who said anything about fair? If things were supposed to be fair, then we wouldn't be so much bigger and stronger, would we?" Frederick walked toward Bruno, and Bruno continued to back up toward the table. "If things were supposed to be fair, then I wouldn't be able to lick you in a fight. If things were supposed to be fair, then we wouldn't have a king to tell us what to do. Are you going to disobey the king?" Frederick was inches from Bruno's face now.

"N-no. It's just—"

Sir Bluberys's mule bellowed a long and low neigh that echoed inside the helmet.

"What was that?" Frederick asked.

"Nothing," said Bruno, shifting again to block Frederick's view of the table, but the mule bellowed again.

"What's under that helmet?" Frederick lunged for the table, but Bruno blocked him, shifting this way and that, until finally Frederick grabbed Bruno and shoved him aside. He picked up the helmet.

"Well, what do we have here?"

Sir Bluberys was now mounted on the mule with his sword drawn and raised. "Stand back, villainous giant! I shall vanquish thee!" He waved his sword in random twists and flourishes. I rolled my eyes. I'd better stop saying things like "vanquish" and "villainous" if I sounded like this blubberhead.

Frederick laughed and pinched the mule around its midsection. "You really were playing dolls!"

"Put him down, Frederick! He's mine!" Bruno rushed forward, but Frederick simply lifted Sir Bluberys higher.

"Yours? You know very well that all elves are property of the king. Is this the elf that should have gone to the cobbler with the last batch? You told me he got away, you little liar."

"Give him back, Frederick!" Bruno leaped into the air but fell short. "The cobbler has enough elves already. Last time we gave him thirteen children and a calf, remember? He didn't need Sir Bluberys or his mule!"

Thirteen children. A calf. Was it possible? Could he be speaking of the Widow Francis's children and Milky White's calf? If it was the same, then Papa had to have gone there, too. . . .

"You can't keep elves without the king's permission. You broke the law."

"Just give him back!" Bruno tried to grab for Sir Bluberys, but Frederick jumped to the side and switched the mule and Sir Bluberys to his other hand.

"I'll give him back . . . after we take another village. Otherwise, I'll tell the king you stole him."

Bruno froze with his hands still in the air. His face turned a pale shade of gray. "You wouldn't," he whispered.

Frederick sneered. "Try me."

Bruno dropped his hands in defeat.

"What would the king do?" I asked Tom.

"Beats me," said Tom. "I've never heard of anyone who stole from the king and lived to tell the tale."

I shivered, thinking of all the awful things King Barf might do to a thief. Sharp blades came to mind. Shackles. Fires. Whatever it was, the threat was enough to frighten Bruno into doing what Frederick wanted.

"I'll go," said Bruno. "Now give him back." He reached for Sir Bluberys, but Frederick pulled away. "You can have him *after* we get the village."

"No! That's not fair!" Bruno lunged at his brother, but Frederick dodged him easily.

"Keep trying, little brother. One day you'll be able to best me. Or not."

Frederick leered at Bruno and then walked out the door with Sir Bluberys, who was still waving his sword and shouting, "I'll slice thee to bits! I'll chop off thy nose! I'll . . ." His cries faded as Frederick walked away.

Bruno stood in the midst of the armory, helpless against his brute of a brother. Huge tears trickled down his cheeks. I almost felt sorry for him. Almost, except for the fact that he had taken Papa, and apparently gave him to a cobbler.

Bruno wiped his tears and slumped out of the room.

"C'mon!" shouted Tom as soon as the footsteps had faded. He jumped onto a spear leaning against the table and climbed up to where Sir Bluberys had been and where his feast still remained. I climbed up after him. Tom ripped off the other turkey leg and tore into it. I picked at some of the bread, but I wasn't very hungry.

"So . . . the cobbler," I said.

Tom slurped some drink from a nutshell and wiped his mouth on his sleeve. "What about him?"

"That giant Frederick said Sir Bluberys should have gone to a cobbler with other elves and a calf. . . . Do you think my papa could have gone there?"

"Maybe. Maybe not." Tom dug into a pie like he didn't care. Well, why should he? It wasn't his papa. But it was almost like he didn't want me to find him.

"Tom, did you have a family Below? A mother, a father?"

Tom shrugged. "Maybe. I don't remember."

"How long have you been here? When did the giants take you?"

"I guess about a year ago. Maybe longer. I can't remember, really."

"How do you not remember your family after just a year?"

"Because I don't," snapped Tom.

I fell silent. Maybe his parents weren't very nice people, or maybe he had been an orphan back home. I guessed I would prefer Martha in the giant world to either of those, and I wouldn't care whether or not someone else found his own papa.

"Listen, Jack," said Tom in a very serious tone, "I didn't want to say this at first, but chances are you're not going to find your papa. It's a giant world out there, and if you go wandering around confronting all these giants, you're going to get hurt. You don't want that to happen, do you?"

"No, but—"

"Then take my advice. Don't worry about your papa. He's a grown-up, right? Grown-ups can take care of themselves. He should be the one to find *you*."

"But . . . I *came* here to find my papa. If I don't find him, he might be lost forever." The very thought of this made my throat tighten up so I could hardly breathe.

Tom looked away from me. "It's dark now. Martha will be worried."

We went back to the kitchens by mouse and cheese, but it wasn't such fun this time. My chest was still tight from what Tom had said about not finding Papa.

When we returned, Martha tucked us into the sugar bowl, but I slept fitfully. I kept thinking about the cobbler, shoes, Papa. It all just churned in my brain, and I woke with an idea. It was so brilliant, yet so simple, I almost laughed out loud.

I knew just how I was going to get to the cobbler.

Now I will show you a fine trick.
—Jack the Giant Killer

CHAPTER TWELVE
Cobbler, Cobbler, Mend the Shoe

When Martha took us out of the sugar bowl the next morning, I was ready to put my plan in place, except of course there was the milking to be done. And then there was Tom. I decided not to share my plan with him. I still felt a prickly annoyance at the things he'd said in the armory, and it was clear he had no interest in helping me find Papa. That was fine. I would find him on my own, but getting Tom to leave me alone was a separate task. He kept squirting me with milk. He tried to get me to joust, race, and play tug-of-war or spoon catapult.

"How about hide-and-seek?" I suggested. "You can hide first."

"Great!" said Tom. "You'll never find me in a hundred years!"

"Great," I echoed, and Tom ran off while I started counting. I stopped at ten. Yes, I was ditching Tom. Yes, it was a little mean, but what could I do?

I ran to the other end of the table, where Martha sat squinting at a pile of tiny carrots as she attempted to chop off the green tops. A bunch of elves were making much faster work of their own pile.

"You would think we could grow some carrots, but no, we must rely on slivers. Ouch! I cut my finger again!" Martha wrapped her finger in her apron, which created a little cloth bridge between the table and her pocket.

I easily crawled inside and found my axe nestled in the corner. Ha! I slipped the axe into the rope around my waist and slid down the rest of Martha's skirts to her giant shoe. I took out my axe and very carefully and slowly worked the blade into the threads of Martha's shoe, sawing and cutting as much as I could between the leather and the wooden sole. It was hard work getting through the stitching, like cutting through thick cords, and Martha shifted her feet every now and then. Sometimes she tapped her toe, and I just had to sit there and bounce until she stopped, but eventually I got through several stitches, and when I finished, there was a fine gap in the toe. Big enough that she would need someone to fix it. A cobbler.

I tucked the axe back at my waist and climbed up

Martha's skirts and apron. Martha was still talking and chopping carrots, and no one seemed to have noticed my disappearance at all, not even Tom. He was still hiding. I smiled, pleased that my years of troublemaking had been put to good use. Wouldn't Mama be proud?

After Martha had finished with the carrot tops, she stood up and dusted her hands. "All right, my little elves. It is time to prepare the stew. Let us— Oh!" Martha tripped and fell forward. She knocked over the giant bowl of little carrots and caught herself on the edge of the table. A dozen elves ran to the spilled carrots and started scooping them back inside.

"Oh deary me, what a nuisance! I seem to have worked a hole into my shoe!" She slipped off the shoe and set it on the table, displaying the gaping hole at the toe. "This will never do."

While the other elves busied themselves picking up carrots, I slipped inside the shoe.

"I need a gnome. Where's a gnome?" Martha asked. Peering through the toe hole I saw her go to the window over the sink and sing, "Messaaaaage!" A moment later she yanked up one of those stupid pudgy creatures that kept copying me. He wriggled his feet in the air. So those were gnomes.

"A message for Siegfried the cobbler," said Martha.

> Dearest Siegfried,
>   As you can see, I have worn a large hole in my shoe, and I simply cannot prepare the king's supper under such conditions. Please stitch it up as best you

can, and I shall give you a pie or a slab of cheese in return, whichever you prefer. I prefer the cheese, but perhaps you would favor the pie since I gave you cheese in return for making boots for my dear little boy Tom Thumb. He is doing well, such a sweet thing, and I have a new little son, too. Tim Thumb! He was nearly eaten by my cat, poor dear, and then the king nearly swallowed him whole when he fell into the pudding. But he is safe and sound with me. Where is he now? Oh well, probably hiding in a teacup somewhere. Those boys are full of such mischief. I thank you for mending my poor shoe. It is also in service to His Royal Majesty, King Bartholomew Archibald Reginald Fife.

Yours Truly,
Martha, the Royal Cook

"Now repeat that, please," said Martha, and the gnome repeated the message, except he jumbled a few phrases. Instead of "Please stitch it up," he said, "Please hiccup," and "He was nearly eaten by my cat" became "He was nearly beaten by a rat."

"Close enough," said Martha. "Take the shoe and be off with you."

Martha handed the shoe to the gnome, and then to my surprise she picked him up by the hair and flung him out the window. I expected us to crash and roll in the dirt, and myself to fly out of the shoe, but the gnome landed on his feet, lithe as a cat, and started running. "Message for Siegfried the cobbler!" he chanted as he ran down the path and out the palace gates. Down the hill we went. In less than ten minutes, without so much as a flea getting in my way, we arrived at the cobbler's door. My plan had worked beautifully!

"Message for Siegfried! Message for Siegfried!" The gnome shouted louder and louder until at last the door opened. I peered through the hole of the shoe as a wizened old man stepped out. He had enormous bat-like ears, and a face so wrinkly it looked like tree bark. He wore spectacles and a long leather apron full of giant hammers and scissors and chisels and other tools.

"I am Siegfried the cobbler," the old man wheezed.

The gnome rattled off his message, and the cobbler seemed to fall asleep while he listened. His eyes drooped and his head nodded. When the gnome had finished, the cobbler jolted awake with a snort. "Wha? Who? Oh yes. Very good. I will take the shoe. And message for Martha. Her shoe will be fixed by tomorrow morning. I'll take a pie. And some ale if she can spare it. The end," said the cobbler.

The gnome toddled out the door chanting, "Message for Martha! Message for Martha!"

The cobbler looked closely at the ripped seam in the shoe. He sniffed at the gap, and his giant nostrils almost suctioned me up. I crouched low against the side.

"Let's see," mumbled the cobbler. "There's a hole . . . it needs five, three, six, or ten stitches and a good hammering on the heel and a polish. Easy as pie, and a pie for payment!"

The cobbler tossed the shoe onto his worktable, and

I tumbled out of the hole when it crashed to the surface. Standing up, I found myself in a garden of shoes. Giant boots like tree trunks, long shoes with curled tips that looked like boats, and lovely slippers embroidered with silk and gold threads and shiny beads.

Two men emerged from among the shoes carrying rags blackened with leather polish. It was smeared on their noses and cheeks, so they looked like chimney sweeps.

"We've got 'er, Mr. Siegfried." They marched over to Martha's shoe, heaved it up on their shoulders like a log. They carried it over to a tall stand with a giant shoe mold on the top. I had seen one in the cobbler's shop back home, but of course this was quite a bit larger, a giant foot sticking upside down in the air.

More elves joined in the task, emerging from shoes like termites coming out of the woodwork. Two elves climbed up to the top of the shoe mold and dropped down ropes. Below them, two more elves affixed the ropes to Martha's shoe.

"Heave 'er up!" they called, and the elves on the top pulled and tugged on the shoe until it slid upside down over the mold. The top elves then unwound a giant rope ladder with pins and needles for the rungs, and half a dozen elves climbed up to the shoe. A few of them pounded the old leather, and began to stitch with a giant needle and thread. It looked like they were raising a barn.

"Oh, very good," said the cobber. "You are such fine little cobblers. Here, let me get that stitch. I can do it." The cobbler pulled the needle away from the elves.

He squinted his crinkly eyes and took aim with shaky hands. He jabbed the needle toward the shoe and nearly stabbed a tall, skinny elf with curly black hair, who tumbled off the tip of the shoe and had to be pulled up by the others. Meanwhile, the cobbler had slid the needle right through the gap in the shoe and pulled it back out without making a stitch at all.

"There," said the cobber, smiling. "I make a fine stitch, don't you think? It's these steady hands." He held his hands to his face. They quivered like a leaf in the wind. "Strong, steady hands. Now it's time to hammer the sole."

The cobbler raised a hammer the size of an oak tree above his head. The elves scattered in all directions, except for one, a short and portly elf with a long red beard who called out to the cobbler.

"Pardon me, Mr. Siegfried, but yer lookin' a bit tired. Maybe ye should take a wee nap."

"No, no. I've so much work to do." The cobbler yawned. The hammer teetered dangerously.

"Why don't ye give that hammer ta old Duncan," said the red-bearded elf. "I can pound the shoe fur ye, good as new, and you can take a wee rest in yer chair by the fire."

"I suppose I could rest for just a minute." The cobbler dropped the hammer into Duncan's arms. The elf buckled under the weight of it until several more came to his rescue.

"Pound it hard," said the cobbler, tottering over to his chair by the fire. "And don't forget to trim the strings. You don't want people tripping about on their shoestrings. That's a mark of a poor craftsman."

"Nay, sir! Aye, sir!" said Duncan.

The old cobbler sat, almost squashing a cow-sized puppy that had been sleeping in his chair. The furry white dog yapped and wriggled out from under him, and in less than ten seconds the cobbler was asleep and snoring. The dog trotted over to watch the elves at work, wagging his tail excitedly.

"Poor old chap," said Duncan, nodding toward the cobbler. "He canna stay awake fur more than a minute."

"And he canna hold a needle steady to save his life," said the tall skinny elf whom the cobbler had nearly stabbed. "He almost ended mine!" He was nearly twice the height of Duncan, yet clearly Duncan was in charge.

"Ah, quit your blubberin', Bruce," said Duncan. "We got a job ta do."

"I don't see why," said Bruce. "I didna ask to come here. I ne'er wanted ta make giant shoes."

"Oh, fine, then," said Duncan, glaring up at Bruce. "Go on and go out there, then, why don't ye. If yer not crushed in a moment, maybe you can go work in a stable and change giant *horse*shoes."

Bruce cowered and pulled at his curly hair. He clearly saw giant horseshoes as a real and terrifying possibility. "I suppose things could be worse."

"Tha's right, they could! Now get this hammer to the heel and pound the nails! An' you get back ta the stitchin'."

Papa was not on top of the shoe, but there were elves

all over the table, cutting leather with giant scissors, polishing boots, and sewing beads on slippers. I weaved in and out of all the shoes, searching. Still no Papa.

I looked inside some of the shoes and found piles of cotton fluff and blankets, crudely made candlesticks set in giant buttons, and a few small piles of potatoes and cabbages. It looked as though these elves worked on shoes during the day and slept in them at night. They didn't have shelves full of cows and chickens, or giant slabs of cheese, as we did in the kitchen, so they stashed what food they could find. I'm sure one of Martha's pies was a very good trade for a mended shoe. Better than gold, maybe.

A woman stood by a large witchy-looking shoe with a brass buckle. She held infants on both hips and looked quite frazzled. "Now, children," said the woman. "Stay out of my way. Go play, and mind the needles and scissors and the ledge. If you're good, there'll be a nice supper tonight." Children in raggedy clothes crawled out of the shoe and scampered in all directions. I recognized them! It was Widow Francis and her thirteen children. And there was a calf! One of the younger children was riding it like a pony. It was Milky White's calf, I was sure of it.

"Stay close to the shoe!" said Widow Francis. "Don't fall!" The children laughed and went about playing Hunt the Slipper, singing the song:

> Cobbler, Cobbler, mend my shoe.
> Stitch it up and make it new.

One, two, three, four
Stitches will do!

"Widow Francis!" I called. The old woman turned to me. She looked confused for a moment, and then she frowned and I knew she recognized me. When I was younger, I used to play with her triplet sons, Larry and Barry and Jerry, but she said they weren't allowed to talk to me after I accidentally set fire to the blacksmith shop.

"Oh," she said. "Look what the cat dragged in."

"Actually it was a gnome who dragged me in. The cat tried to eat me."

Widow Francis just blinked. I shifted and looked around. "I'm looking for my papa. Have you seen him?"

"Yes, of course I have."

My heart soared. I knew it! I knew he would be here! "Where is he?!" I shouted.

"Well, I'm sure I don't know," said Widow Francis.

"But you just said—"

"He *was* here, but not anymore."

My heart crashed. "What do you mean? What happened to him?"

Widow Francis caught sight of one of her babies knocking over a big glass jar.

"Ned! Don't eat the polish! I'm sorry, dear. What?"

"My father, Henry. What happened to him?"

"Well, he was here, just as I said. And then one of those babbly fellows came and talked to him, said the most peculiar things, but it seemed to make sense to your father, because as soon as he heard it, he flew the coop, or the shoe, I should say. John, will you please put down the scissors? I've told you a hundred times, you cannot cut Jane's braids! You'll cut her head off one of these days!"

"When was that?" I asked.

"When what?"

"When did my papa fly the shoe?"

"Oh, it must have been an hour or two ago—"

"An hour!" I shouted. "You mean he was just here an *hour* ago?"

"The babbly creature said he had a message for Henry, and then he rambled some strange things about where his papa was and some other things I won't mention."

One of the triplets shouted from the top of a boot. Larry, or Barry, or Jerry—I couldn't tell which. "He called your father a *pea brain*!"

Widow Francis frowned. "Yes, well, at that point your father was convinced the message had come from you."

The gnome! That must have been the gnome I met when I first arrived and tried to ask for help. When I said Papa's name, the gnome must have searched high and low until he found the right Henry and then repeated our whole conversation. Papa was alive! But he was still missing.

"He said he was going to go search for you," said Widow Francis. "I told him it was a fool's errand, but he didn't listen, and this morning he slipped away in an outgoing shoe, and now he's gone."

"He gave us George before he left!" said the little girl riding the calf.

"Don't let George chew on the shoelaces!" said Widow Francis.

"Do you have any idea where he could have gone?" I asked. "Did you see which way the shoe went?"

"Mind the fire!" Widow Francis shouted. Two of the children had climbed atop one of the candles and dipped their feet in the melted wax, making themselves little waxen shoes molded perfectly to their bare feet.

"Well, by the looks of the shoe he escaped in, I imagine he's now at the giant castle, up on the hill. I can't imagine where else that shoe could have gone."

"Why do you say that?"

"Because, child, the shoe was made of gold. Who but royalty would wear a gold shoe?"

A gold shoe. That could only belong to one person.

King Barf.

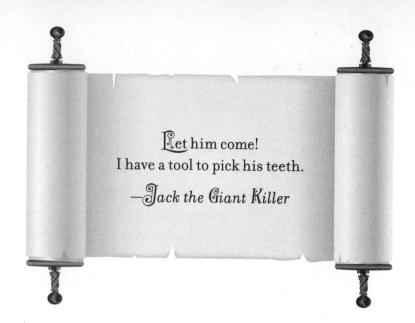

Let him come!
I have a tool to pick his teeth.

—*Jack the Giant Killer*

CHAPTER THIRTEEN
Flying the Shoe

I slumped down against a boot and groaned. Up the hill, down the hill, now up the hill again! Papa and I had probably passed right by each other. This was starting to feel like an enormous game of cat and mouse. I needed to get back to the castle and fast, but how?

Widow Francis was pulling two of her babies away from the edge of the table. She plopped them each inside a child's clog, where they immediately began their escape attempts.

"Widow Francis, ma'am, is there any other way to get out of this place? Besides the shoes?"

"You mean leave the cobbler? You can't do that."

"Why not?"

"Because, it's too dan— Oh good grief, not the hammer. They'll crush everyone's bones! Put that down!" Widow Francis dashed after Barry and Jerry, who had managed to lift one of the cobbler's giant hammers. They dropped it so the wooden end landed on Larry's shoeless toe. He started to wail and scream, but the other two ignored him and ran off to join the game of Hunt the Slipper.

Cobbler, Cobbler, mend my shoe!
Fix it up and make it new!

I looked up at Martha's shoe. The elves were still stitching the gap, and every now and then the dog would yip and jump up at them. The cobbler had told Martha it would not be finished until tomorrow morning, and I wasn't patient enough to wait that long. If I could get past the dog, I could ride a wagon or boot straight to the castle this very day.

First I had to get off the table.

I ran to a giant spool of twine and unwound it several lengths. I dangled it over the edge of the table, as far as possible from where the dog sat. Easy. I'd be out of here in no time. But just as I began to climb, an elf caught me. It was the one named Bruce, whom the cobbler had nearly stabbed with a needle. He was dragging a giant pair of scissors toward Martha's shoe. "What do ye think yer doin'?" he shouted angrily. "Get back from there!"

Fleeing instincts took hold. I grasped the rope and looked behind me. It was a long way down. I was better at going up than down, but in this case it didn't matter. The elf pulled open the giant scissors and—*snip!*—cut the twine. My rope slid to the floor, and Bruce caught me by the back of my pants and lifted me off the ground.

"Duncan! We got ourselves a runner!"

"Put me down!" I flailed and kicked. Bruce released me, and I fell flat on my stomach. I scrambled to my feet. Bruce stood in front of me, holding up the giant scissors and glaring like he'd snip off one of my limbs if I made a move.

"Where's the runner? Show me the rascal!" Duncan shouted as he came barreling toward us with a giant needle in hand.

Bruce grabbed me by the arm again as though he'd caught a prize lizard. "I caught the lad trying to escape down some rope. I cut it just in time."

"And a good thing, too," said Duncan. "What were ye thinkin', lad? Ye canna go down there! Did ye not see the great beast of dog? He'll rip you to pieces, that one."

"I was being careful," I said, which was true but sounded ridiculous spoken aloud.

"Oh, ye was being careful, was ye? Well, say ye get past the wee beastie, what then? There's all kinds of monsters outside. Ye'll get yerself stomped on or snatched."

"Or eaten!" added Bruce. "There's some giants who'll eat us, ye know."

The other elves all trembled.

"So ye see, lad, ye canna ever leave this table. It's

safest here, and if ye do the work, Mr. Siegfried will take good care o' ye."

"But you don't understand. I'm looking for my papa. I came here to find him, and he left to find me. He left in a golden shoe."

"That was your papa? The rascal! If I'da known what he was doin', why, I woulda . . . well . . . no matter. No takin' chances now." Duncan grabbed me by the neck of my shirt and dragged me toward the giant shoe mold.

"Let me go! I have to go find my papa!"

"It's fer yer own good," said Duncan.

I twisted and pulled away, but Duncan was very strong, despite being so short and portly, and he pulled me along like a floppy fish on the end of a hook. "Lower the ladder!" he shouted, and the pin ladder unfurled a moment later. "Up ye go." Duncan gave me a prod.

"You can't make me stay here," I argued.

"Oh, yes I can, and ye'll thank me for it one day. A young lad like you has got no chance runnin' about in this giant world. Ye'll be crushed or eaten in a second."

Bruce nodded. "We elves have to stick together!"

Others mumbled their agreement. It was clear that Duncan had a tight hold on everyone here. They believed that leaving the cobbler would risk their very lives. I didn't blame them. But did they really want to stay here and make giant shoes forever?

"What if I told you I knew a way to get home?" I asked in desperation. "Back to our world Below."

A hush fell over the crowd of elves. The only sound that could be heard was the thumping of the dog's tail.

Even the children stopped their games to listen. Home is something that pulls at you no matter how much fun you're having.

"Back to our world, ye say?" said Bruce. "How?"

"A beanstalk. A giant beanstalk. It grows in the soil Below and reaches from our world up to this one. That's how I got here. I climbed it just like a ladder."

Someone stifled a cough, then they all started laughing. "A beanstalk! You can't *climb* a beanstalk!" Bruce doubled over and slapped his knee.

"That's quite a tale, lad," said Duncan, his red beard twitching with a smile.

"It's true," I insisted.

"The boy has always had a fondness for telling tales," said Widow Francis.

"It's not a tale!" I said. "I planted the beanstalk myself."

There were a few more chuckles, and then the other elves went back to their polishing and stitching and cutting. Now I knew how Jaber felt when he warned our village about the giants.

"Okay, bean boy. Up ye go." Duncan gave me a nudge, and I was forced to go up the pin ladder. Duncan followed close behind. Once at the top, he rolled up the ladder and stood over it like a guard dog. "Let's get back to work! I'm hungry for me pie."

Trapped. On the very shoe that brought me here, and by elves, no less. I didn't expect to be imprisoned by my own kind.

Now that the stitching was done, Duncan gave me the job of holding the nails they were pounding into the heel of the shoe, which was probably the worst job ever, if you ask me.

WHAM!

The hammer shot down and missed the nail. The whole shoe tipped and shook.

"Hold her steady, lad!" said Bruce, as though missing the nail had been my fault. Three elves lifted the hammer and hurled it down again. I shut my eyes as the hammer drove the nail into the shoe, narrowly avoiding my fingers. Duncan strutted back and forth, shouting orders. Anytime he caught me looking at the ladder, he'd place his foot on top of it and smirk at me.

Maybe the cobbler could help, but he'd been asleep for over an hour. So much for a wee nap. The longer I was here, the more anxious I got. Where was Papa now? He could be in big trouble for all I knew.

WHAM!

I peered down at the table, where Widow Francis's children were frolicking about. The triplets were giving each other rides in a blue slipper with a curled tip. Two pushed while one sat inside. They pushed the slipper to the table's edge, where it rocked precariously.

"Larry! Barry!" shouted Widow Francis. "Stop that at once!"

The boys abandoned the slipper, leaving it teetering on the edge.

"Hold the nail, lad!" Bruce chided me.

I adjusted my grip.

WHAM!

The hammer whistled right by my ear. The slipper was filled with blankets and fluff. If I jumped down and wedged myself in the toe, I could tip it over the edge and they would cushion my fall. It'd be like jumping from the barn into a pile of hay. Tom would have loved the idea.

WHAM!

This time the hammer grazed my arm. If I didn't get out of here soon, I might not stay in one piece.

The elves raised the hammer.

"Set the next nail, lad!" shouted Bruce.

I looked at the shoemaker's elves, struggling to hold the hammer up. Duncan was watching me closely, his foot propped on the ladder.

He stretched and yawned, and in an instant I dropped all the nails in my hands and jumped off the shoe-mold tower into the slipper below.

"Boy overshoe!" shouted Bruce. I crawled into the toe of the slipper and heaved.

Duncan was coming down the ladder now, and others were behind him.

I gave another push, and the slipper rocked and tipped, but stayed put.

"Get him!"

"Stop that elf boy!"

I thrust all my weight forward and that did the trick.

Down the slipper went and landed with a bounce and flip. My brains were scrambled, but at least I didn't break any bones.

I crawled to the opening and heard a low growl.

Snakes and toads, I forgot about the dog!

"Watch out, lad!" shouted Bruce. But it was too late. The dog sank its teeth into the slipper and started to thrash it around. With nothing to hold on to, I went flying out of the slipper. I tumbled and rolled, bumping and crashing against the hard floor, until I came to a stop. The room was spinning and tilting. I scraped myself off the ground just in time to see a giant white fur ball running toward me. Mouth open. Tongue flopping.

"Run, lad! Grab the rope!" The elves shook the rope dangling off the table's edge.

I ran past the rope and straight under the table. No way I was going back. The door was only twenty steps away, and there was a gap under it big enough for me to slide through.

I ran as fast as I could, with the dog nipping at my heels, until I thought my heart would burst. Just a few more leaps and then . . . I tripped—over my own awkward feet, of all things. I crashed to the floor and skidded to a halt.

The dog was upon me now. I could feel his warm breath on my face. The smell of slobber and fur. This was it. The great and terrible end of Jack. I pulled my axe out from the back of my pants, ready to swipe at the monster.

The dog leaned down . . .

. . . and he licked me with his giant pink tongue. In a wave of slobber, he pushed me right through the crack under the door to freedom.

I must say, I've always preferred dogs to cats.

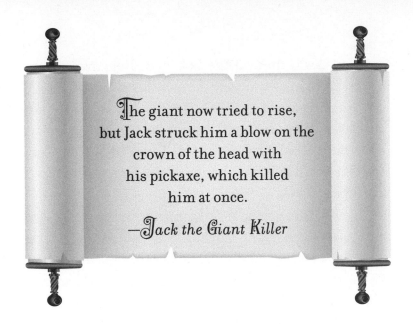

The giant now tried to rise,
but Jack struck him a blow on the
crown of the head with
his pickaxe, which killed
him at once.

—*Jack the Giant Killer*

CHAPTER FOURTEEN

Pest

Free of the cobbler—or more accurately, the cobbler's elves—I began searching for a ride back to the castle. I was ready to hop onto a wheel when I caught sight of the beanstalk across the street, just peeking above the boulder that covered the hole.

The tip of it shimmied a little, like something was crawling around in the leaves. There were probably all sorts of creatures devouring the beans and leaves now, seeing as it was one of the few green things in this land. A smile grew on my face as I imagined a giant slug or beetle crawling down through the hole and dropping into our world. Wouldn't Mama and Annabella be surprised!

But slugs could also be a danger. What if they nibbled away at the stalk until it shriveled up and died? Jaber had said it wouldn't last forever. I had to be sure Papa and I had a way home. I crossed the street for a closer inspection.

It was still green, mostly, minus a few holes and brown spots. A giant ladybug crawled up one of the leaves in search of aphids. A snail with a shell big enough for me to wear as a helmet was sliming along a bean pod. The stalk shimmied a little more, as though something was shaking it. Maybe a mouse or a bird—or a pixie. Remembering what Tom had said, I scooped up a handful of dirt. I walked around the stalk very slowly, checking under each leaf.

Something wiggled and squeaked beneath the upper leaves of the stalk.

"Ha!" I shouted, thrusting aside the leaf that covered the hole and throwing the dirt down at the creature.

The creature screamed and raised her arms for protection. I dropped the rest of the dirt, and my jaw dropped with it.

The creature was not a pixie or a mouse. It was my little sister.

Once, when I was nine and Annabella was five, I wanted to go on a quest in the forest. I made careful preparations. I had my stick sword and my sling and pockets full of rocks and acorns. I filled a cloth with bread and cheese and boiled eggs, and I announced that I was off to find the giants.

Then Annabella decided she was coming, too.

"You're too small," I told her.

"I am not!" she cried, wailing and stomping her feet so much that Mama finally said I couldn't go anywhere unless I took Annabella with me. I was so mad at her, I hid in the trees every now and then and snarled and growled when she came near. It frightened her, but she didn't turn back. She stayed with me the whole day, searching all the best caves and trees before I could get to them, and asking endless questions about the giants. "Could that be one of their footprints? Do you think they ripped up that tree? How come we haven't seen one yet? Maybe they're like bats and only come out at night."

The whole quest was ruined, so I decided to get back at her. That night I released a nest of newly hatched spiders in her bed. I told her they must have nested in her hair while we searched for giants and now they were hatching. Maybe it was nasty of me, but Annabella never interrupted one of my quests again.

Until now.

"What are you doing here?" I spoke sharply, as though the words might cut her down to size.

Annabella flinched. "I came here to help you find Papa." She smiled hesitantly.

"Does Mama know you're here?"

Her smile disappeared. "Well, she does now, I

suppose. She told me to go see if I could harvest some more beans, but we'd harvested the ones closest to the bottom, and then I wanted to see how high I could go, so I just kept climbing and climbing, and then I made it here!"

I folded my arms. "You have to go home, Annabella. Mama must be worried sick."

Now it was Annabella's turn to fold her arms. "Mama's already worried sick—over *you*."

"She is?"

Annabella twisted her apron in her hands, the way Mama always did when she was in distress. "Oh, Jack! My naughty boy! I shall never see him again! Oh!" She placed her hand on her heart.

Annabella did quite a fine impersonation of Mama. I laughed in spite of myself, but I stifled it quickly. "So what do you think Mama will do when she sees *you* gone? What were you thinking?"

Annabella turned pink in the face. I thought it was because she felt shame, but I was wrong. "What were *you* thinking?! You came up here and you didn't even tell us where you were going or what you were doing! For a whole day she was so upset she wouldn't eat unless I spooned the food into her mouth."

I didn't know Mama cared enough about me to not eat. I was always a burden. Jack, her naughty boy, the great pest. It made me feel sort of happy that Mama was sad when I left, but if she was that sad over me, she'd be all the more distressed over Annabella, her one good child.

"You have to go home, Bells," I said.

"Says who?"

"Says me. Mama needs you, and you're not big enough to stay here."

"You're not big enough either. *You* go home to Mama. I'll find Papa by myself." She stomped her foot on the ground as though she meant to plant herself here and spread roots.

I sighed. Jack the Giant Killer never ran around with a pesky little sister. *He* had knights and kings and noblemen. Although it would be funny to hear her scream the first time she saw a giant spider. . . . She'd be running home in no time. And if that didn't work, then there was always Rufus.

I'm sorry, Mama. Annabella was eaten by a cat. But don't feel too bad. You always thought she was so tenderhearted, I'm sure she made a nice meal. Aren't you proud?

"Fine, you can stay."

Annabella beamed.

"But if you get eaten by a giant snake, it isn't my fault!"

"Giant snakes?" Her smile faltered.

"Why of course." I grinned. "You didn't think it was just the humans that were giant, did you?"

"Well, I . . . I . . . no. Of course not. I knew there would be giant snakes here."

"Oh yesss," I hissed. "Giant snakes and bats and cats and rats. I even heard of a boy who was eaten by a cow."

"A cow?"

"Yep, swallowed whole." I left out the part where he survived and escaped.

Annabella's chin quivered a little. But she didn't cry. She lifted her chin and forced a shrug. "I've always been very good around animals."

"Well, we'll see how you fare at the size of a mouse. Come on. We need to get to the castle before dark, when the owls and bats come out to hunt little girls. . . ."

I left Annabella and started walking up the hill. I paused and turned around, expecting to see her hightailing it down the beanstalk, but to my surprise she walked right past me, trudging up the hill with her braids bouncing. I trotted after her and then pulled ahead, so she'd know who the leader was.

"Do you know where Papa is?" Annabella asked after we'd walked a few minutes in silence.

"He's at the giant castle."

"How do you know? Is he being held captive like Grandpa Jack?"

"Maybe."

"Is the giant going to eat him?"

"No. The giants don't really eat us." I paused. "I don't think they do anyway. Not the ones I've met."

"You've met giants? And they didn't eat you?"

"They don't take us for eating. They take our food and our animals, since there's a famine going on here."

"Oh. That makes sense, I suppose." Annabella looked all around at the brown and shriveled plants. "Then why did they take Papa?"

"They take people to do their work for them. They call us elves."

"Elves . . . how strange. But I guess the giants don't think of themselves as giants, do they?"

It unnerved me how quickly she was catching on to everything, as though she found it all quite logical. "No. They think of themselves as people, just like we do."

"But not very nice people, if they took away Papa."

"Yeah, some of them."

"We'll beat the giants, Jack," said Annabella. "We'll get Papa back and beat the giants just like Grandpa Jack."

I kept walking. Annabella didn't really know what it was like to face a giant. Even if they were kind giants, like Martha, they could still pick you up between their fingers and do whatever they pleased with you.

We trudged on through dust and dead grass. The castle looked so far away, it would take forever to get there on foot, but I had very little confidence that Annabella would be able to ride a cart or skirt or shoe. She'd fly off in an instant, so we stayed off the road and walked. Hours later we weren't even halfway up the hill.

Gribit!

"What was that?" Annabella grasped my arm.

Something large and green hopped into our path. It had bulging eyes and a mouth that stretched clear across its face.

It was a giant toad.

Brrrgibit!

The toad hopped toward us, and Annabella squeaked with fright and stumbled back.

"What's the matter?" I said. "I thought you liked animals."

Annabella swallowed. "I do. . . . It's just—"

Rigibit! croaked the toad.

"Hello," said Annabella.

The toad flicked out its enormous tongue and hopped a little closer. Its bulging eyes were fixed on Annabella. She glanced uneasily at me.

"Go on," I goaded. "Make friends with it."

"My name is Annabella," she said, desperately trying to keep her voice steady. "What's yours?"

Gribit!

"Oh!" Annabella smiled. "She says her name is Gusta."

Gusta? So it was a girl toad, apparently. I rolled my eyes. "Great, now give Gusta a kiss and say good-bye."

"Oh, I don't think—"

Brrgibit! The toad flicked out her tongue, wrapped it around Annabella's waist, and plucked her off the ground like a flower out of a garden.

"Jack!" cried Annabella. The toad started to hop away.

"Hey!" I shouted. I loaded my sling and flung a stone as hard as I could but missed as the toad leaped away, in the opposite direction from the castle, with Annabella wrapped up in her tongue.

I guess that's what happens when you kiss a toad.

Is goggle eyes were like
flames of fire, his countenance
grim and ugly, and his cheeks like a
couple of large flitches of bacon.

—*Jack the Giant Killer*

CHAPTER FIFTEEN

The Swampy Stream

Snakes and toads. Snakes and TOADS! My sister had just been taken by a giant toad! This is the kind of thing that I would have dreamed about back in my own world, and the very thought of it would have made me laugh. But dreams are not quite the same when they become reality. I'd never imagined how long a giant toad's tongue could be. It was as long as Annabella herself, and those bulging eyes . . . so goggling and hungry.

I ran after the toad, leaping over pebbles and dodging blades of grass. I had always been good at catching toads, but a giant toad is something else altogether. It was like trying to catch a trotting deer or a wild boar. No matter how hard I ran, the toad got farther and farther away, and Annabella's screams grew fainter, until the toad hopped over a rise of land and disappeared from sight.

I ran harder, ignoring the stitch in my side and the scream in my legs. The brown grass whipped and tripped me by the ankles, like it was trying to hinder me on purpose.

I crested the hill and the earth fell away. At the bottom of a steep slope was a swampy river snaking through a wooded area—probably nothing more than a trickling stream or puddle to the giants, but a huge swamp to me. I had to find Annabella before it was too late. Was it already too late? An image flashed through my mind of the toad with just a skinny little leg hanging out the side of her mouth.

I pushed the thought aside and ran down the hill. I tripped on stones and branches and dead leaves. I rolled and bumbled down the slope until at last I reached the bottom, where the land leveled out and the swamp began.

The water was covered with a greenish-brown film. Brown grass and reeds stuck up along the bank. A fallen tree stretched across the water, its roots corroded and rotten. Giant snails clung to the slimy tree roots, and wood lice crawled all over the place. A giant worm as big as a snake slurped down into the mud.

The air smelled moldy and putrid, like rotting fish guts. Every time I took a step, my foot made a suctiony *pop!* And the air was filled with the sinister sounds of a hundred hungry insects.

Brrrreeeeeeeeeeeeeeeeeeeeeeee

Pckpckpckpckpckpckpckpck

VzzzzZZZzzzzVzzz

Giant mosquitoes swooped low over the water. Their noses were like great black swords, thirsty for blood. The mosquitoes were too big to sneak up on me like they did back home, but not so big that I couldn't fight them off.

Great. The one thing I could fight in this world was a mosquito.

I made my way along the water's edge, and within a minute I was soaked up to my shins. The swamp was so loud I couldn't pick apart the separate noises. Could that sound be Annabella? Or that one?

Pckpckpckpckpckpckpckpck

Kk-kk-Kk-kk-Kk-kk-Kk-kk

ststststststststsssssssssssssss

"Bells!" I shouted. "Annabella! Annabellaaaaaa!"

I tripped over a log and fell facefirst in the mud. Then the log started to slither.

Hsssssssssssssssss

Snakes and toads. Toads and SNAKES! A giant snake reared its head. It was brown with black markings, the perfect disguise for a predator in a rotting swamp. It flicked out its forked tongue and tickled beneath my chin. I was frozen. It unhinged its jaws wide enough to fit over my head and shoulders.

Move, Jack!

The serpent's jaws snapped shut, and I dove out of the way at the last second, hiding behind a rock. The snake slithered slowly around, through the dried reeds and grass.

Think, Jack! Your axe!

I pulled my axe out from my waist. The snake lunged again, but I swiped the blade in the air, so it reared back. I continued to wave my axe around, backing away from the snake, but then I stepped in a sinkhole and lost my balance. The axe slipped out of my hands and wedged itself in the swampy ground. I tried to reach for it, but I was stuck in the mud, and the snake was slithering toward me again.

The snake hissed and circled me. I looked all around for something, anything I could use for a weapon. There was a pebble just a few feet from where I was stuck. If I could just reach it . . . I snatched up the rock, and at the same time the snake coiled up and cinched my legs and waist. It raised its head above me and flicked out its tongue. It looked like it was smiling, triumphant.

Whoosh! I flung the rock at the snake's head. My aim was not sure, but the rock smacked the tender underside of its neck with enough force to make it hiss and release me. I reached down and grabbed for another stone and loaded my sling. This time I hit it square on the jaw. The snake's head flipped back. It flopped to the ground and slithered away, disappearing in the grass.

I retrieved my axe from the mud and held it at the ready, just in case, but the snake did not return.

I kept walking. The late afternoon sun beat down

on the swamp and created a sweltering fog. I wiped the sweat from my face, but moments later I was just as wet and sticky as if I'd gone swimming. It was like my body was telling me to give up now. Should I give up? I could at least rest. I sat down in the mud and rested my head against a reed. A fly buzzed toward me.

VzzzzZZZzzzzVzzz

I swatted and the fly zoomed into a spiderweb in the bush above me. Immediately the giant spider went to work stringing up the fly and wrapping it like a mummy. No famine for spiders.

Pckpckpckpckpckpckpckpck

Uhrrrr-urh-urhurh-urh-urh-urhurh

Gribitrigibit

I sat up straight.

Rigibigit . . . Gribit

That had to be a toad, but was it *the* toad? This swamp was probably full of them.

Gribigibit

I walked toward the sound. Soon I heard a soft whimpering.

I pulled apart some reeds, and not twenty feet away, there was Annabella sitting like a lonely flower in the center of a lily pad. Her knees were tucked up to her chest, and she was trembling with fright. The toad watched her closely with goggly eyes, but seemed uninterested in eating her.

I let out a rush of air. I really didn't want to break the news to Mama that Annabella had been eaten by a toad, no matter how funny the prospect had once seemed.

"Bells!" I whispered as loud as I could, hoping to get Annabella's attention but not the toad's. "Bells!"

Annabella looked up. Her eyes were red and puffy, but when she saw me, her whole face lit up with relief.

"Jack! Oh, Jack, you found me!" She jumped up, forgetting that she was on a lily pad and not solid ground. The pad swayed and moved beneath her. She teetered, flailing her arms, until she toppled off and—*kerplink!*—fell into the water.

"Bells!" I shouted this time.

Brrrrigigit!

The toad hopped in after her and a moment later popped back up with Annabella wrapped in her tongue. The toad deposited her on the lily pad in a soppy, coughing puddle. Annabella brushed the soggy leaves and weeds off her face, but they stuck to her hair and clothes, and she shivered as a strong breeze swept through.

Rigibit? The toad flicked out her tongue and licked Annabella on the cheek. Annabella flinched, and for a moment I thought she would burst into tears, but instead she gave a shaky laugh. "That tickles." The toad did it again and Bells giggled some more.

Rigibit

"I thought she wanted to eat me," said Annabella, "but it seems like she'd rather keep me as a pet."

"Bells," I said, "see if you can get away. Can you paddle your arms in the water and make the lily pad move?"

Annabella scrunched her nose at the mucky water, even though she was already drenched in it, but she dug her arms in and tried her best to paddle toward the bank. Slowly, the pad started to move.

Brrigit . . . Rrrgibit!

Before she'd gotten halfway to shore, the toad lashed out her tongue and pulled her back to the center of the lily pad. Annabella screamed and wriggled free. She faced the toad with hands on hips. "Stop grabbing me with your tongue!" she scolded. "It's horribly rude, you know!"

Gribit! The toad shrank back with shame.

"Oh, I'm sorry," said Annabella in a more soothing tone. "You're just lonely, aren't you? Haven't you any other toads for friends?"

Rigibit, the toad croaked mournfully.

"You poor, sad creature, all alone. No one should be alone." Annabella talked with the toad like she would anyone, listening carefully to each croak.

She turned to me. "Jack, I have a feeling it's going to be difficult to escape. She thinks I'm her new friend. She wants me to live here."

"Well, she can't watch you forever, can she? We'll just have to wait."

But the toad stared at Annabella with such intense, bulging eyes, it was difficult to believe she'd ever let her guard down.

Grrrrribit! Birgibigit!

"Yes, you have a lovely home," said Annabella. "But I can't live here. I would starve here in a day, you know. Oh, look! How beautiful!"

A giant butterfly with bright-blue wings fluttered low

over Annabella's head. I'd never taken much of an interest in butterflies. In our world they weren't ugly or scary enough to use as pranks, but that wasn't so here. This giant butterfly was probably the ugliest creature I'd ever seen. The wings were fine, but the body was like a giant furry grasshopper, and it had huge, bulging eyes and wriggling antennae. Annabella didn't seem to mind, though. She spoke to the butterfly like it was her long-lost friend.

"Hello, Mr. Butterfly!" Annabella reached out her hand as if she were petting a puppy, but just then the toad hopped up and caught the butterfly with one neat flick of her tongue. The toad held out her catch to Annabella, like a bird might offer worms to its babies.

Annabella's face twisted in horror. "I didn't mean I wanted to *eat* the butterfly! How awful!"

The toad sat there for a moment, then stuffed the butterfly into her own mouth, pushing it down with her huge tongue. With a good crunch, she swallowed it in two gulps, except for one antenna that stuck to her lip, still wriggling.

Rigibit

"Blech!" Annabella was looking green.

The toad turned her attention to a dragonfly hovering nearby, but before she could get it, a whale-sized fish burst from the water and swallowed the dragonfly whole. The fish splashed down on its side, and huge waves rocked the lily pad. Annabella had to lie flat and hold on to the sides as the water came crashing down.

Gribit! Rigibit! The toad croaked angrily at the fish.

She hopped to another lily pad and then another, as if to chase down the fish and make it share the dragonfly.

Annabella teetered on the very edge of the lily pad. She was preparing to jump, but I knew for a fact she was not a strong swimmer.

"You can do it, Bells. Just jump as far as you can, and I'll help you." I waded toward her.

Gribit! Rrrigibit! The toad was still distracted, but it wouldn't be for long.

"Bells, jump! Now!"

She plunged into the water and came up gasping for air. Her eyes were closed and she splashed her arms about. I waded farther and was able to reach a piece of her skirt. I pulled her after me. "Stand up, Bells!"

Annabella stopped thrashing. She put her feet down and stood.

Gribit! Brigigibit! The toad had given up her chase and was swimming toward us now. We sloshed through the mucky water to the bank. I wanted to take off running, but Annabella stopped me.

"We're not big enough to outrun her. We have to hide!" She piled dead grass and leaves on top of herself until she was totally covered.

Rigibit! The toad was getting closer.

"Jack, hide!" Annabella commanded.

I burrowed into the leaves beside her, just in time to see the toad break through the reeds. We waited, holding our breath, as the toad hopped all around. She croaked mournfully, calling out to Annabella. Finally her croaks faded in the distance.

"Wait just a while longer," Annabella whispered.

When we were sure the coast was clear, we sat up and looked at each other. "Grandpa Jack didn't prepare us for that one, did he?" asked Annabella.

"I don't think he prepared us for a lot of things," I replied. "Come on. We'd better get as far as we can before your toad friend comes back."

As we walked away from the stream, the land got more solid and started to slope upward. The castle looked miles and miles away—at least a full day's walk. It was evening now, and the sky was cloudy and gray. Soon it would be full dark, and the bats and owls and other night creatures would be searching for their supper.

I kept my sling and axe at the ready. Annabella picked up a few stones for herself, but with the night coming on, we wouldn't be able to spot a predator so easily.

A wind swept through, and Annabella shivered uncontrollably in her wet clothes. I took off my jacket, which was only partially dry but still better than nothing, and draped it around her shoulders. She clutched it to her. "Th-thank you," she stammered through blue lips.

We walked on, slipping and tripping as we made our way up the hill. I no longer knew which way the road was. I just kept going toward the castle, using the glowing tower windows like guiding stars.

Suddenly Annabella screamed. I whipped around

expecting some frightful beast, but there was none. Annabella just stood in shock, dripping wet again, as though someone had emptied a bucket of water on her head. Another bucketful splashed at my feet and then to my side and all around. It was giant rain. Each raindrop was like a jug of water. Within thirty seconds the ground beneath us was a muddy river, and we began to slide back down the hill.

"Jack! I can't hold on!"

I grabbed Annabella's arm and pulled her up, digging into the mud. Lightning flashed in the sky and lit the hillside in a cold white light.

"Let's head for that fallen tree," I said. "We can find cover beneath the branches. Can you make it?"

Annabella nodded, and we slogged through the mud as well as we could. When we reached the tree, Annabella slumped beneath a branch. I tried to find any kind of opening, but the tree did not appear to be hollow.

"Jack! I found something!" Annabella cried.

I turned back toward Annabella. Amid the leafless branches she had found a nest woven tightly with grass and twigs so it formed a round little shelter. "It's empty," she said.

"Are you sure?" I said. "What if it belongs to a rat or a giant bird?"

"It must have been abandoned when the tree fell. The animal probably found a better shelter."

The rain fell harder, and Annabella shivered. She needed to dry off soon or she was going to catch cold. I stepped inside the nest, holding my axe over my shoulder.

Everything was still and quiet and—miraculously—dry and warm. It was lined with leaves and feathers and fluff. An old bird's nest, I guessed.

I shouted for Annabella to come inside. She smiled at the little fort and curled up in a pile of fluff. I stood by the hole awhile to make sure no one was coming. Finally satisfied that we would be left alone, I dropped my axe and sank down into the nest, ready for a long sleep after a long day.

"Jack?" whispered Annabella.

"What?"

"I'm sorry I got kidnapped by a toad."

"It's not your fault," I said. "And it was kind of fun to watch you get all wrapped up in that giant tongue."

Annabella giggled. "I really thought I was going to get eaten."

"What did the tongue feel like? Slimy?"

"Mostly sticky, and when she licked me, it tickled. I didn't mind so much."

"Does this mean you won't scream anymore when I put a toad in your bed?"

"That was *you*?!"

I looked at her incredulously. "Did you really think they just hopped through the window and found their way beneath your covers?"

"And the grasshoppers in my apron, and the spiders?" She seemed fairly shocked.

"Yep."

"I knew it! One of these days your tricks are going to come back to bite you!"

I smiled.

We listened to the rain pelt the top of the nest. Soon it lightened and then stopped altogether. Through the small opening in the nest we could see a sliver of misty moon.

"Do you think that's the same moon we see in our world?" Annabella asked.

"It looks the same to me," I said.

"I hope Papa can see it," said Annabella. "He always loved the moon."

"He loved the land," I said.

"He loved us, and Mama, too."

Yes, Papa loved us. You could see it in the way he lifted Annabella and swung her around, the way he kissed Mama and pulled her tight to his chest, and the way he clapped his hand on my shoulder and told me I was great, just like Grandpa Jack.

I wanted to show him that I loved him just as much. More than fame or fortune or giant adventures. I wanted him back more than I wanted to be great.

"He still loves us, Bells," I said. "We're going to find him."

Annabella didn't say anything. She was asleep, and in a moment I was, too.

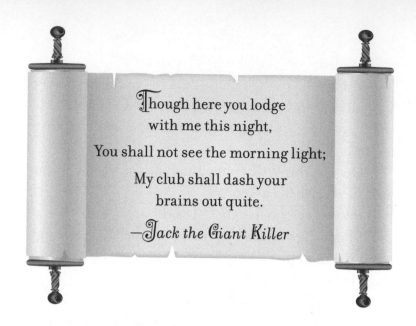

Though here you lodge
with me this night,
You shall not see the morning light;
My club shall dash your
brains out quite.

—*Jack the Giant Killer*

CHAPTER SIXTEEN

Squeak and Bite

I was woken by a squeaky voice and a sharp tug at my hair.

"Leave me alone, Bells," I mumbled. "It's too early." I dug myself deeper into the fluff and squeezed my eyes shut, but she kept pestering me. She pulled my hair and poked me in the face and chattered like she was a squirrel or something. I couldn't understand a word she was saying. I slapped at her. She squealed and fluttered away.

Fluttered? How would Annabella flutter?

My eyes flew open. I saw a flash of color and lots of shimmer and sparkle, like sunshine or . . . gold.

The whole nest gleamed and glistened as the sunlight streamed in through the opening. It was not made of grass or sticks at all, but neatly woven strands of gold.

It was also swarming with creatures—some kind of hornet or hummingbird. I couldn't see because there were so many and they were moving so fast, but whatever they were, this was clearly their nest and they were not happy to find it occupied. They pulled my hair, tugged at my clothing, and scratched my arms and legs with sharp nails. They squeaked and chirped a sort of gibberish that sounded halfway between a bird and a squirrel.

I pulled out my axe and swung haphazardly. The creatures shrieked and dispersed, flying to the far corners of the nest. I lowered my axe and stared.

They were neither birds nor insects, but *people* my size, with hair in all colors of the rainbow—and wings! Sparkling translucent dragonfly wings, shiny green leaf wings, blue butterfly wings, and pink flower-petal wings.

These must be pixies.

Great.

This was probably the absolutely worst place we could have chosen to sleep—a pixie nest. According to Tom, pixie bites could make you explode, but maybe if we backed out slowly, with no sudden movements, they'd let us be.

"Annabella," I whispered. "Bells. Wake up."

Annabella groaned and turned over. The pixies turned their attention to her, and one went over to investigate. He had dragonfly wings and hair as green as spring grass. And he was wearing grass, too, and leaves and tree bark all stitched haphazardly together with gold threads. He cocked his head and looked at Annabella like a curious bird.

I tightened my grip on the axe, but my hands were sweaty and slipped along the handle.

Annabella yawned and stretched. Her eyes fluttered open. She stared at the pixie for a moment, and then she gasped and sprang up. The pixie flew back a little. Annabella looked all around the nest, her eyes wide with awe.

"Jack," whispered Annabella, "We must be in a fairy palace!"

"Pixies," I said. "The giants call them pixies."

"Pixies . . . ," muttered Annabella, taking it all in. "Aren't they beautiful?"

The green pixie squeaked gibberish and moved closer to Annabella. I raised my axe, ready to strike.

"No, Jack! Stop!" The pixies were hissing at me now, baring sharp teeth, glossy with venom.

"Bells, we need to get out of here, now."

But their anger at me was once again overcome by their interest in Annabella. Something about her seemed to fascinate them.

The green pixie approached her.

"*Eeks Saakt ist ooch kist*," screeched the green pixie.

Annabella bowed her head. "It's an honor to meet you. I'm Annabella, and this is my brother, Jack."

"Wait, you understand them?"

Annabella looked at me in surprise. "You don't?"

"Of course not! They're talking nonsense."

"It's not nonsense. He says his name is Saakt. He's the pixie prince, or something like that."

The pixie gestured at me and squealed more nonsense. *"Hech tistken urch wak gotter ost vutten skkkeeet!"*

"He also says you're trespassing on pixie territory, and you now owe them a debt."

"A debt?"

"Uchsa Rast gold stiks twodx uuuurttttsss!"

"They prefer to be paid in gold. If you don't pay, there will be a punishment—I think he said the Bite of Eternal . . . Itching? Twitching? Or maybe he said your legs would fall off? I didn't quite catch it all."

I rubbed at my leg. "What about you?"

She smirked. "He likes me. I'm a guest of honor, he says."

"But I'm your brother! Can't you tell them to like me, too?"

"That's not how it works."

"What do you mean? You've spent two minutes with pixies and now you know all about them? I've heard about these beasts! They're vicious, even to giants."

"Don't be ridiculous! They're not vicious. They're highly sensitive creatures. Look how sweet they are." Two more pixies had now descended from the ceiling, each chirping at Annabella. They were bigger and wilder than the others, with bent, scarred moth wings that looked like they'd been thrashed by a cat's claws or something.

"This one's name is Eetsl, and this one is Kazzi. They're Saakt's guardians, I think."

I snorted. "You think?"

One of the pixies picked up Annabella's tangled hair and inspected it closely. *"Etek ist gold!"*

More pixies flocked to Annabella, picking up strands of hair and pulling them in all directions. Annabella giggled. "They think my hair looks like gold."

"So they like gold, huh?"

"They *love* it. I think it gives them some kind of power, I'm not sure what. Maybe to fly? Hey, maybe they could help us find Papa! Wouldn't that be wonderful? If we had flying friends, then we could find him much faster."

"No, Bells," I said. "I don't think that's such a good idea." I didn't really want help from creatures who had threatened to make my legs fall off.

"Don't be silly!" She turned to the green-dragonfly pixie. "Saakt, can you help us? We're trying to find our papa in the giant's castle."

At this several pixies bounced and squeaked.

"Gold! Gold! GOLD! Gold! Goooooold!"

"They're chanting gold over and over," Annabella translated.

"Yes, I understood that much! Gold is all they care about, and the castle is full of it. Come on, Bells—we're wasting time."

"No, wait. I think there's more."

The green pixie was gesturing wildly and squeaking so loud and fast, it made my ears itch.

"What is he saying?"

"I'm not sure, but he's very excited. He keeps saying something about gold and he'll fly us. Or at least me."

"What? No, Bells. We can't trust them."

"But, Jack—"

"No, no, no! NO! I already rescued you from a toad, and we can't afford to waste any more time." I grabbed Annabella's hand and yanked her toward the opening of the nest. The green pixie chattered an angry command, and his guardians blocked my path. They spread their jagged wings and snarled, revealing razor-sharp teeth.

"He thinks you're trying to steal me," said Annabella.

"She's *my* sister," I said, "and we have to go find our papa."

The guardians, Schnitzel and Catsy, or whatever, stood their ground, screeching like bats.

"Jack, you're making them angry. . . . You don't want to do that."

"Well, they're making *me* angry!" I turned to the pixie prince. "I'm sorry we slept in your nest. If you must know, it was *her* idea, but now we'd like to be going. I'm sorry I have no gold to pay you. It looks like you have quite enough here. Good day."

With that, I jumped forward, swinging my axe like a madman, and the pixies shot into the air.

"Jack! What are you doing?"

"Getting out of this crazy place."

"Jack, if you just—"

"Bells, let's go now!"

I grabbed Annabella and shoved her toward the

opening. She screamed as she tumbled out of the nest. A few of the pixies flew after her, but the rest swarmed around me. I swung my axe to keep them at bay. The green pixie snapped and snarled, his black eyes glaring with malevolence.

I managed to clear a path and jump out of the nest, but the pixies quickly regrouped. They hovered above, pelting me with rocks. I needed dirt. Tom said that was the only real defense against pixies. I clawed at the muddy ground and threw clumps of dirt at them. They shrieked and flew away, but in a moment they circled around and launched a dive-bomb attack. "Bells! Throw dirt at them!" I shouted.

"Why?"

"Just do it!"

I threw another handful, but one of the pixies managed to dodge it and shoved me onto my back so all the air got knocked out of me. He yanked my hair and scratched my face, and finally I felt a sharp sting on my leg.

Here it was. My demise was near, and it would come not at the hand of a giant but a pixie—one with pink hair and yellow butterfly wings.

Dirt and pebbles showered down, and the pixies screamed and scattered. More dirt fell on me. I dared to peek between my arms and saw Annabella shaking a mud-caked tree branch with all her might. The pixies flew away in a swarm until they were nothing more than a moving shadow in the blue sky. I sat up. Annabella wiped her muddy hands on her apron. Then she turned on me.

"Why did you have to do that?" she snapped.

"You're *welcome*. They were going to bite you!"

"No, they were not! They were only curious. And I could have gotten them to help us, but you had to play the hero and attack them, and now they're gone."

I felt my face go hot. "Well, if you hadn't climbed up the beanstalk in the first place, I never would have come here, and I probably could have found Papa by now."

Annabella's eyes widened. She covered her mouth as though she were about to cry or be sick.

"Bells, I'm sorry, I just . . ." I didn't mean to make her feel *that* bad.

But Annabella shook her head and pointed. "Oh, Jack, your leg . . ." She grimaced and shut her eyes.

I looked down and yelped. My left leg had ballooned to twice the size of my right. It was more like a log than a leg. The pixie bite. In the mad rush and my anger at Annabella, I had forgotten all about it, but now that I noticed it, my brain registered a sharp pain shooting from my hip down to my toe. My foot was swelling fast, too, stretching the leather of my shoe. I scrambled to pull it off and watched my foot become as round as a ball with five fat knobs at the end.

My chest got tight. My breathing got short. Was my leg about to fall off? Was I going to explode?

Annabella looked around, and then she ran behind me, out of sight.

"Where are you going? Don't leave me!" But a few seconds later she was back, her hands full of dark, slimy mud. It smelled like rotten potatoes.

"Where's the bite, Jack?"

My leg had swollen to such proportions that my pants were splitting open, so I split them the rest of the way, revealing the bite just above my knee. It was just a graze really, but the whole area was red and angry. Annabella slapped a handful of mud on the wound. It stung at first, but then the slimy coolness seeped into the cut and took the edge off the pain. Annabella ripped a strip of fabric off my torn pants and tied it around my leg to keep the mud in place.

"It will take hours for the swelling to go down," she said. "But we can't stay here. The pixies might come back and finish you off. They're not forgiving creatures." She said it as though she dealt with pixies every day. "Can you move at all?"

I tried to lift myself off the ground, but I could hardly feel my leg anymore. What if I had to get a wooden stump like Jaber the tinker? "I can't bend my leg," I said.

"You've got to," said Annabella. She came behind me and put her arms underneath mine. "I'll push you up, and then you swing your right arm around my neck."

"Bells, you're not strong enough," I said. "I'm too big."

"Hogwash," said Annabella, sounding very much like Mama. "You may be tall, but you're just as skinny as I am. Now, on three. One, two, three." Annabella heaved and pulled. I tried to push myself up but fell back almost immediately and took Annabella with me.

"I told you I can't bend my leg."

"Not your left, but you can still bend your right, silly. Why are you keeping it straight?"

"Oh." I forgot my right leg still worked. I bent my knee, and Annabella positioned herself behind me once more. "Let's try it again. On three, push on your good leg and hold on to me. One, two, three." She heaved and pulled, and I pushed up on my right leg and cried out at the pain shooting down my left, but I stayed standing and swung my arm over Annabella's shoulder. She teetered under my weight but steadied herself, and I was able to hobble along, dragging my log-leg behind me. Every step was a stab of pain. I started to sweat and breathe hard even though we were moving about as slow as a snail—slower than giant snails.

"I can't make it much farther," I said.

"Let's just make it to that bush over there. There are leaves to give us cover. We should be safe."

The bush she was speaking of was more like a copse of trees, and it was miles away. I felt dizzy just looking at it, but we continued to hobble onward and upward, one excruciating step at a time. Annabella started to sink beneath my weight, but she kept going and pulled me along like she'd been hauling bales of hay her whole life.

The pain in my left leg doubled, and my right side burned with the strain of trying to carry all that weight. "Bells, I can't go any farther."

"We're almost there." Annabella heaved and groaned as we struggled on. "Al . . . most . . . there!"

I grasped for every bit of strength. The trees were close, but they tilted sideways.

"Jack, don't give up now! Just a few more steps!"

Annabella propped me up and the trees were straight again.

"Almost . . . there . . . now. There!" Annabella gasped for breath. "We made it!"

"Made it," I mumbled. The trees turned all the way upside down as I crumpled to the ground. I heard Annabella calling my name, but the sound was very small and far away, and then it was gone altogether.

When I woke, it was still daylight. My leg was still swollen and it still hurt like a thousand beestings, but now I could bend it slightly. I grabbed on to a branch and pulled myself up. Everything blurred and swirled, and I had to sit back down again.

Where was Annabella? I didn't see her anywhere. My chest started to pound. I shouldn't have fallen asleep! The pixies could have gotten her. "Bells?" I called.

Something rustled in the branches, and I crouched down, fearing another pixie attack. Now I understood why Bruno was so scared of them.

"You're awake!" chirped Annabella. She climbed down from her perch. Leaves stuck to her back, and her skirt was torn and muddied. Her feet were bare and her hair was so tangled she looked wild enough to be a pixie. In her hands she held a rope braided out of giant blades of brown grass.

"What's that for?"

"Oh. I was bored while you slept. I thought it might

be useful for something. I don't know." She coiled it up, slung it over her shoulder, and looked down at her feet.

"I lost my shoes in the pond," she said wiggling her toes. "But I sort of like it."

My left foot was bare, too. The swelling had gone down, so instead of a ball, it looked like a loaf of rising bread dough. I kicked off my other shoe. Now we were both barefoot, ragged, and dirty.

I looked at the sky. The sun was straight overhead.

"How long did I sleep?"

"An hour, maybe two."

My stomach growled. I hadn't eaten for a full day.

"I'm hungry, too," said Annabella, "but I waited for you before I ate."

"That's silly," I grumbled. "Besides, there's a famine, remember? We'll have to do without food until the castle."

"There must be *some* food. What do the animals eat?"

"Worms, flies, beetles . . . little girls."

Annabella sighed. "What a pity. I was hoping the pixie bite might have knocked some sense into you. Here." Annabella pulled a giant bean out of her apron.

"Ick! I don't want beans!"

"I suppose I could find you a worm. Or did you say you preferred beetles?"

"Har, har," I said. "I'll just wait. There's lots of good food in the castle."

"Jack, you're injured and hungry. Eat." She waved the bean in my face. It was bloated from being in the foul swamp water. I closed my eyes and grimaced, but my stomach screamed at me, so I took the bean. I nibbled it. Ech! As if beans weren't bad enough, this one had the added flavors of swamp and toad. I forced down a few bites, just enough to lessen the pangs of hunger.

"Let's go," I said.

"Jack, your leg—"

"I'm fine." I broke a long stick off the bush and used it like a crutch, dragging my injured leg on the muddy ground. Every step hurt like an axe chopping at my leg, but I had to keep going.

We kept moving, slipping on the mud and tripping over dead branches and rotting leaves.

"So the famine . . . ," said Annabella. "That's why the giants took our crops?"

I nodded. "Tom says it's a curse."

"Who's Tom?"

"A boy who lives in the castle kitchen. He's loads of fun, but not very much help when you need it."

"So a lot like you?" Annabella said with a smirk.

I threw the rest of the bean at her head. "Anyway, he says the giant land is under some kind of curse and that's why there's a famine."

"A curse," Annabella mused. "Well, we'll just have to break it," as though that were as simple as snapping a twig with two fingers.

I told Annabella about my adventures so far, from getting chased by a cat to falling in the pudding to stowing away in a shoe. She chuckled and gasped and yelped in all the right places, and I almost felt like Papa, telling the stories of Grandpa Jack. The only difference was that Grandpa Jack probably would have conquered a few giants by now, and I hadn't come even close. I'd only managed to not *get* killed—and that hadn't been easy.

"His name is King Barf?!" Annabella laughed when I told her about the giant king.

"He has lots of gold. Oceans of it. And a pet hen that lays golden eggs whenever he wants."

"Real gold?"

"Yes. All the king has to do is say 'Lay!' and the hen lays a golden egg as big as a barrel!"

"That's funny, isn't it?"

"What is?"

"Well, it seems like in a famine, regular eggs would serve the king better."

"But gold can buy lots of food," I argued.

"Not if there isn't anything to buy. Not if nothing is growing."

I started to protest and then stopped. What Annabella said was so simple and true. When I saw the king's gold, I figured he could buy anything he wanted, but you can't buy food that's not there. You can't buy food that isn't growing. That's why they were stealing it from us. But what could we do about it? If there was a curse on the land, how could we stop it?

My leg was throbbing now. I was short of breath and soaked with sweat.

"Maybe we'd better stop and rest again," said Annabella.

"No. We've wasted too much time already." There

was so far to go. We weren't even halfway up the hill, and I couldn't stop imagining all the things that could have happened to Papa since he'd left in the king's shoe.

I gritted my teeth and pushed on. Annabella amused herself by racing ahead and climbing the brown stalks of dead flowers while I hobbled to catch up. She sat atop one such stalk, arranging her skirt so it looked like a blossom.

"What a poor land this is," she declared. "It's not just the food—*everything* has stopped growing. The trees, the grass, even the flowers. It must be a terrible famine if flowers cannot grow. What do you think is wrong with this place?" she asked.

"I told you. There's a curse."

"But what *kind* of curse?"

"Maybe a pixie curse," I said. "They're probably destroying all the crops with their screeching voices and venomous fangs."

"Don't be mean, Jack. I'm sure it's not the pixies."

A gust of wind blew, and Annabella swayed on her stem. Dried leaves flew up in the wind and rustled around, so I didn't hear anyone approaching. I didn't hear any footsteps until a giant foot crashed down, right in front of me. It wore a familiar shoe, freshly stitched and polished from the cobbler's shop.

Martha! Oh, what luck! I'd be back in the kitchen in a wink! But luck was not on my side that day. I forgot about my log-leg and fell flat on my face when I took a step. But Martha had seen Annabella.

"Oh, a flower!" Martha exclaimed. "I haven't seen a

buttercup in ages. I do hope this is a good omen." She bent lower to sniff the blossom, which was really Annabella. "Oh! Oh my, what's this?" I buried my head in my hands as Martha plucked the "flower" and lifted it up. She squealed with delight. "An elf! A beautiful girl! Oh, how I have wished and wished for a little girl, and here you are, born right out of a flower. This is a good omen indeed!"

Annabella shrieked as Martha started to walk away.

"Martha, wait!" I called after her. "It's me, Jack—I mean Tim! Wait for me!" But my voice was lost to the wind, and soon I could no longer see them.

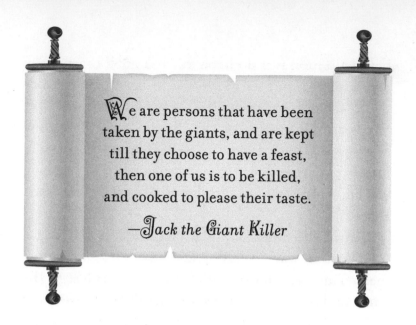

We are persons that have been
taken by the giants, and are kept
till they choose to have a feast,
then one of us is to be killed,
and cooked to please their taste.

—*Jack the Giant Killer*

CHAPTER SEVENTEEN
King Barf's Ambassadors

Martha's footsteps led the way to the road, and I soon caught sight of the familiar procession of giants, animals, and wagons.

I hobbled as fast as my sore leg would carry me and hid beneath a dry leaf on the edge of the road. A skirt brushed past and I successfully grabbed hold of it, but almost immediately the woman looked down and caught sight of me. "Nasty pixie, get off!" She shook her skirt so violently, I was flung into the middle of the road. I dodged a gnome and grabbed ahold of a boot, but there was no buckle or laces to hold on to, so with each footfall

I slid down and down some more until I was back in the mud.

A wagon was coming. I waited until it was about to pass, and then I leaped onto the wheel. I clung to a spoke as the wheel carried me up and around. I got a little queasy but moved steadily up the hill.

The wagon stopped near the castle, with me upside down at the top. I slid down the spoke to the hub and hopped to the ground.

Eeeaaagghhhh! I kept forgetting about my log-leg.

The castle grounds were bustling with life. A gnome ran past shouting out a message for Bart the blacksmith, and then another went the other way with a message for Frieda. Lords and ladies assembled in their finest gowns and robes embroidered with gold. In another part of the courtyard, workers and peasants were gathered. Many of them craned their necks and whispered excitedly. Perhaps there was to be a royal ball, or an important visitor coming. Curious, I hobbled between skirts and feet and hooves.

"I hope they got a good haul this time," said a giant woman. "I've had nothing but gruel these past weeks. We'll have to eat the last of the chickens soon if we can't find anything else."

"Someone tried to buy our goat for a sack of gold," said another woman, and her companion laughed as though that were the most ridiculous thing she'd ever heard.

"I said to him, 'Do I look daft? What use is gold to me?' I chased him from the door, but the goat's not giving milk anymore, so it seems we must sell her or eat her."

"Eat her quick before someone steals her," said a third woman. "We got all our chickens stolen, and now there's no meat but the worms and beetles in the ground. I'm ashamed to say I've taken to eating 'em like a common troll!" The woman sniffled a bit.

"There, there, Fran. Don't you cry. There's no shame in that. But laws! My belly aches for a bit of meat and potatoes."

"Even them tiny potatoes," said the first woman. "No one but the king and his men know where to find 'em."

"I don't care what size they are, so long as I can eat 'em."

"Look! It's coming!" someone shouted as a wagon approached, pulled by two sallow horses. Cheers erupted from the crowd. The wagon was stacked high with bulging sacks and crates and baskets, and hungry giants swarmed forward, tugging at the canvas that covered its contents. They pushed and shoved, and their squabbling was so loud I had to cover my ears.

The driver of the wagon stood and cracked a whip. He scowled at the crowd, and I recognized him at once. It was none other than the queen's brother Frederick. Bruno was there, too, slouched down with his head in his hands—the perfect picture of misery. They were both covered in dirt, so it was clear enough where they'd been.

"Give us food!" cried a woman. "I need grain and potatoes!"

"My cows have stopped giving milk! Give me cows!"

"My chickens no longer lay eggs! I need chickens!"

And then a hundred voices were crying out at once.

They crowded the wagon like a pack of hungry wolves, until Frederick again cracked his whip and drove them back.

"I am Frederick, ambassador of King Barf—er, Bartholomew."

A few people in the crowd snickered at his slip of the king's nickname, but Frederick boomed over them.

"If you want food, you must pay hogage—"

"Homage," mumbled Bruno.

"That's what I said, you must pay hordage to the king, who in his noble greatness will give you sullinance."

"Sustenance," corrected Bruno again.

"—sorcerance in this time of great greed, I mean need. Come to the Golden Court tomorrow morn—"

"Tomorrow?!" cried the woman who had been eating worms and beetles.

"But we're hungry *now!*" other voices rose in protest.

Frederick cracked his whip again and they quieted. "Come tomorrow morning and bring your tribute of gold to His Majesty King Bartholomew Archibald Reginald Fife!"

Angry shouts rang out again. Frederick cracked his whip and the wagon moved onward—but not before I could climb onto the wheel. I allowed the first turn to carry me up to the wagon bed, and I hopped onto a ledge as the wagon entered the inner wall of the castle. The gate closed on the angry mob, leaving them to press against the bars, begging and crying for food like hungry children.

I tumbled into the cart atop a wooden crate filled

with sheep. They were baaing hysterically and running into the wooden slats. I could hear other animals, too— clucking chickens, snorting pigs, and lowing cattle. There were turkeys, geese, and goats, all caged in barn-sized crates stacked on top of each other, or penned inside of actual barns that had been ripped out of the ground. And all around were mountains of onions, cabbages, carrots, beets, radishes, pumpkins, squash, wheat, and barley, and other plants and foods I couldn't even name. They must have robbed a hundred villages.

In one corner of the wagon there looked to be an entire apple orchard, ripped right up by the roots. It would take a dozen elves just to harvest the apples. And speaking of elves . . .

A metal birdcage contained hundreds of men, women, and children. They clung to the bars as the wagon bumped and rattled along, looking lost and frightened beyond speech. They probably thought they were about to be eaten—chopped into a stew or a pie, or even roasted whole. Was this how Papa had come to this world? Caged like an animal headed to the slaughter?

I climbed down from the crate and worked my way toward them through hills of potatoes and squash. A little girl about Annabella's age spotted me and pointed.

"Look!" she said. "There's a boy! He's not locked up!"

The prisoners all gathered close to the bars, their faces lighting up with the faintest hope.

"Boy!" called a man. "Can you free us? Can you get us out of here?"

Grandpa Jack had been known to free the prisoners of giants, but this cage had no door.

"How did you get in?" I asked.

"Up there." A man pointed to the top of the cage, where a big metal plate was latched down. "We've all tried to climb up, but none could get more than a few feet."

"I'm good at climbing." I tried to pull myself up on the bars and then yelped as pain shot down my leg. Stupid pixies!

Well, if I couldn't climb, surely I could break the bars. I reached for my axe, but it wasn't there. I tried to remember the last time I had it. The pixies. I must have dropped it when they attacked me.

The wagon lurched to a stop.

"We're doomed," said a woman. "We're going to be eaten!"

"No, you're not," I said, trying to calm them. "I've been in here, and no one will eat you." I recounted to them what Tom had told me when I'd arrived.

"You mean . . . we're their slaves?" asked a man.

"In a way," I said. "It's complicated."

"I want to go home," whimpered the girl, and she buried her face in her mother's lap.

"There is no more home," said a man. "They've taken everything from us, including ourselves."

The back of the wagon was opened, and servants began unloading the crates and baskets. I could hear Frederick directing them where everything should go, which was mainly to the kitchen, of course.

The people inside the cage whimpered and clung together.

"Everything will be all right." I tried to sound brave and reassuring, like a hero should. "We'll beat the giants."

"Will we?" said a man. "I don't see how."

Suddenly two giant hands reached into the wagon and picked up the cage full of people. I crouched low in a basket of pumpkins and peeked through a knothole in the side of the wagon. Frederick swung the cage in front of his face.

"Bwahahahaha!" He laughed maniacally and made ghoulish faces at the elves, who screamed and rattled the bars.

Bruno approached from around the cart. "Hand him over," he demanded.

"Who?" Frederick lowered the cage.

"*You* know who. Sir Bluberys."

Frederick scratched his head as though confused. "Sir Bluberys? I don't know what you're talking about. Oh! You mean your dolly."

"My knight!" said Bruno. "You said you'd give him back after the raid."

Frederick grinned malevolently. "You know, Bruno, you're really getting too big to play with dolls. I thought it was for the best to . . . *relocate* your friend."

"What did you do with him, Frederick! What did you do!" Bruno lunged, and Frederick jumped back, swinging the cage wildly about. The elves screamed and slammed against each other and then tumbled in the other direction as Bruno lunged again. Frederick merely laughed and shoved his brother. Bruno stumbled and splashed in a puddle.

"You said you'd give him back." Bruno sniffled, wiping mud and tears from his face. "You promised."

"Stop your sniveling, you big baby. All elves are the property of the king. You're lucky I didn't tell on you. And won't His Goldness be pleased to see *these* elves!" Frederick leered into the cage. The elves yelped and clung to one another.

"What is to be done with us, giant?" said a man. "What does this king have planned?"

"He's going to eat you and grind your bones to bread! Bwahahahaha!"

The elves broke into sobs as Frederick carried them away. And Bruno trailed after him with muddy tears streaming down his face.

I watched all this from a basket of pumpkins, too small and weak to do anything about it.

Oh, monster! are you there?
It will not be long before
I shall take you fast by the beard.

—*Jack the Giant Killer*

CHAPTER EIGHTEEN

Tales of Tails

"Look at my three beautiful children—Tom Thumb, Tim Thumb, and now tiny Thumbelina." Martha clapped her hands together. "I've never felt so happy in my life!"

Martha had not stopped chattering from the moment I'd arrived. My disappearance had been totally forgotten in the excitement over Annabella . . . or Thumbelina, as Martha called her.

Martha picked all three of us up and squeezed us to her chest. Annabella looked at me as though pleading for me to save her. I just smiled. And then Martha plopped us into the washbasin.

"So dirty!" she said, dousing us with sudsy water. "And we'll have to make you new clothes. Tim, dear, your pants are torn to bits. Did you get in a fight with the pixies?"

After we were half drowned, Martha pulled us out of the water and dried us off, then she went to her sewing basket and pulled out some pants and a shirt and shoes for me. I would have been grateful, seeing as my own clothes were practically falling off, except the pants were red on one side and yellow on the other, and the shirt looked like it had been knit out of dried grass and dyed purple, probably with berry juice. It smelled kind of fruity. And the shoes . . . well, they had *bells* on the twirly tips.

"You look like a jester," said Tom.

"I'll never be able to sneak around in these." I took a few steps and the bells jingled.

"I think that's the point," said Tom.

Annabella giggled. "We can call you Tinkle Toes."

"Ha. Ha. Let's see what she dresses you in."

"Thumbelina, I have just the thing for you!" Martha pulled out three little dresses, as if she'd been waiting for an elf girl to dress like a doll. There was a blue dress trimmed with lace and one with green polka dots. Annabella picked a frilly pink one with six flounces and a sash that tied into a humongous bow at the back.

Once she was dressed she did a twirl, and Martha clapped her hands and wiped a tear from her eye. "Aren't you precious? We must celebrate! I'll get the cheese!"

Martha brought the block of cheese from the

cupboard and sliced off big chunks for each of us. "Eat up, Thumbelina. You are so tiny, I'm afraid you might disappear. Now, I must think what to cook for the king tonight. The puddings have not sat well with him of late. I'd roast some chickens, but he was so upset last time. I suppose it reminded him of that silly hen he carries around...."

Martha popped a chunk of cheese into her mouth and began gathering ingredients from the baskets and buckets—potatoes and onions, beets and radishes. "Perhaps a stew will do," she mused.

"I guess you didn't find your papa, then," said Tom.

"No," I said.

"I'm sorry." Tom looked down and shuffled his feet. I could tell he wasn't just apologizing about Papa, but for the things he said to me before I left.

"It's okay," I said. "We'll find him. He got away from the cobbler in one of the king's shoes."

"That's not good," said Tom. "What if King Barf squished him with his big toe?"

"Our papa is smart," said Annabella. "I'm sure he's fine."

"You're right. He probably got out of the shoe. I just hope Rufus didn't eat him."

"Who's Rufus?" asked Annabella.

"That's Rufus." Tom pointed to where the orange beast sat on his haunches beside the table, his big yellow eyes fixed on some elves cracking chestnuts. His tail flipped back and forth.

"Oh, what a sweet kitty!" cooed Annabella. She went

right to the edge of the table and called out. "Rufus! Here, kitty, kitty! C'mere, kitty!" Rufus turned his attention to Annabella. He dipped his head and stalked forward.

"That's a good kitty. Come on!"

"Bells, I wouldn't—"

The cat sprang up and swiped a giant paw at Annabella, who shrieked and stumbled back. Tom and I fell over laughing. Annabella glared at us, but it was hard to take her seriously in that frilly pink dress. Rufus sprang up once more, but this time Annabella looked him square in the face and hissed like a rabid alley cat. Rufus mewled and ran back to the fireplace, his ears pressed down flat. Tom and I looked at each other. Neither one of us was laughing now.

"Well done, flower girl," said Tom. "Nobody's ever been able to tame Rufus, not even Martha."

"I have a way with animals," said Annabella. "At home I could always get the sheep to follow me. Jack never could."

That was true, but so what? At least I didn't scream at the sight of snakes and grasshoppers.

"So how do we get out of the kitchen to find Papa?" Annabella asked.

"We could ride mice," I suggested.

"I don't know a way to the king's chambers through the walls," said Tom. "Martha could send a gnome to someone in the castle."

"We can't wait around for that," I said.

Suddenly Tom snapped his fingers. "I've got it! Rufus!

He'll be much faster than mice, and we can go wherever we want without being noticed. Nobody pays any mind to a cat."

"What are you talking about?" I asked.

"I mean we should *ride* on Rufus! It'll be an adventure!"

"Are you *trying* to get eaten again?"

"We'll sit on the back of his neck where he can't reach!"

"You're crazy," I said.

"I think it could work," said Annabella.

"You're not serious, are you?" I asked. "Bells, that cat just tried to eat you!"

"It's all right, Tinkle Toes," said Annabella, smirking. "I understand if you're afraid. Tom and I can ride him, and you can stay here with Martha. We'll be back with Papa before you know it."

I glared and flung off the ridiculous shoes. "Fine. You want to ride the cat? We can ride the cat."

Tom whooped and grinned. "Now, we just need to get something to lure Rufus and distract him. If only we had a rope . . ."

"Like this?" Annabella whipped out her braided-grass rope from an inner pocket beneath one of her flounces.

"Fantastic!" said Tom. "Well done, blossom head. Now we just need to tie it to the end of something. Jack, can you go get one of Martha's knitting needles from her sewing basket?"

I sulked all the way to the sewing basket, thinking this was a terrible idea. When I got back, Annabella was fraying and tangling the end of her rope, and Tom was telling Annabella about one of his adventures. She laughed. I started to feel this burning in my stomach. I wished Annabella had just stayed home with Mama.

"I have the needle," I interrupted them.

"Good!" said Tom. "Let's get going."

Tom tied the rope to the end of the knitting needle, and we gathered at the edge of the table. Annabella lowered the tangled end of the rope and gently swayed it back and forth. Rufus stared at it for a few seconds, his ears and tail twitching. He stalked toward it like a hunter on the prowl. Annabella bounced the rope, and Rufus followed it with rapt attention. She let it rest, and Rufus came in for a sniff. She led the big cat until he was in position right alongside the table.

"On three," said Tom. "One . . . two . . . three!"

Tom and Annabella jumped, landing neatly on Rufus's back, but I held back. Jumping from high places had never been one of my favorite things. I much preferred climbing.

"Jack! Jump!" Annabella shouted. "He's starting to move!"

Rufus pawed at the grass rope Annabella was dangling in his face, getting farther away from the table.

It was now or never, and I wasn't about to let Annabella face the giants without me! I jumped, but my leg was still weak, so I didn't push off hard enough. I fell fast, but the cat was not beneath me.

"Jack!" Annabella screamed. Rufus shifted back just enough, and I landed on his tail.

If there is a place you don't ever want to be, it is on the end of a giant cat's tail. Rufus turned and hissed, baring his dagger teeth. Then he began to chase his tail and therefore me. I held on to his fur for dear life as I went around and around, first one way and then the other. The pots and pans and food and fire all turned to a streaky blur.

Somehow, as I was being whipped around and nearly clawed or gnawed to death, all I could think was that this beast of a cat was punishing me on behalf of all the mice and toads and crickets and spiders—all the small animals I had ever used for pranks. I was sorry! So sorry! Let me live!

"Oh, Rufus, you silly cat," I heard Martha say. She apparently did not notice the three silly children clinging to his fur. "Get out from under my feet and go chase some mice!" She pushed Rufus out the kitchen door, which momentarily caused him to stop chasing his tail.

"Jack!" shouted Annabella. "Climb up here!"

Climb? I knew how to climb. If only I could remember how. I was so dizzy, I barely knew my own name. I grabbed a clump of Rufus's fur and pulled myself upward, then grabbed another. Finally I reached the neck, where Rufus couldn't see or bite us. The world was still spinning, and my insides felt all tangled up like tree roots.

"That was amazing!" said Tom. "Was it fun? Did it feel like you were spinning inside a tornado?"

I took deep breaths. "It felt like a giant cat was chasing me while I was hanging on to his tail."

"You look a little green," said Tom.

"I think he's going to be sick," said Annabella.

"Try not to be sick in the fur," said Tom. "We don't want Rufus to give himself a bath while we're up here."

"I'm fine," I said. "I just have to catch my breath."

Rufus meowed and stalked aimlessly, as though he wasn't sure what to do next.

"Let's go catfishing," said Tom. "Flower girl, toss the line!"

"Aye, sir!" shouted Annabella, and she flung the knitting needle forward so her grass rope flew out in front of Rufus. Rufus shot into the air, and we all lurched forward, clinging to the fur.

Away we went, flying down the corridors. Once Rufus showed signs of slowing down, we pulled in the rope and flung it out again, and Rufus chased it like a mouse—or me.

Once my dizziness subsided, I had to admit that cats were magnificent as far as rides go. Rufus was perfectly still one moment, and then he'd spring to a run in the next. Then he'd jump and land so lightly, we barely felt the force of it at all. Cats are a very unpredictable, unboring way to travel.

It also allowed us to search the castle in plain sight. A cat is a creature that has the right to roam wherever he pleases, since his sole purpose is to catch mice, and mice could be anywhere and everywhere. We went through the dining hall, which was empty except for a servant dusting the great golden chandelier and a few pixies buzzing in her face.

"Pixies!" Annabella exclaimed.

"Don't call their attention here!" I hissed, but the servant took care of them by whacking them with a cloth. They fluttered down to the ground.

"Oh, how horrid! The poor creatures!"

"Annabella thinks the pixies are sweet." I rolled my eyes at Tom.

Tom shrugged. "She tamed Rufus. Maybe she can handle pixies."

I scowled, annoyed that he would take her side.

We went down another corridor and entered the great hall. The ceilings were so high, I half expected to see clouds up there. Servants polished the gold floors and a great golden staircase. I thought I saw some elves polishing right along with the servants, but then they flew off and I realized they were more pixies.

"Let's go up the stairs," Annabella suggested. "I bet that's where the royal chambers are."

"Yeah," said Tom. "Then we can slide down the banister on the way back!"

We launched the rope up the golden staircase, and Rufus bounded up faster than a galloping steed. I loved giant cats!

But when we reached the top of the staircase, Rufus was done. Annabella whipped out the rope again and again, but the cat just meowed pitifully and would not move farther.

"Lazy cat!" shouted Annabella. She tried to spur him on like a horse, and then she tugged at his fur with all her might, but Rufus didn't respond.

He sauntered to a golden chair against the wall, leaped onto the cushioned seat, and curled up in a great furry ball.

"I guess he's tired," I said.

Annabella started walking down Rufus's back.

"Where are you going?" I asked.

"Well, we're not going to find Papa here, are we?"

She had a point, so we slid down Rufus's tail. He was asleep now, and he didn't so much as twitch a whisker as we slid down the chair legs and tiptoed down the corridor. We kept to the walls and hid whenever we heard footsteps or voices.

We came to a door and slipped beneath the crack to see what was inside. There wasn't much, except a wolf-skin rug with fur so long, it came to our waists, and we trudged through it like a furry field. The wolf's head was stuffed and resting on the floor with its jaws open wide.

"It looks like it might swallow us whole," Annabella said, a little nervous.

"Better than biting you in two," said Tom.

The second chamber was filled with all sorts of treasures that looked dusty and forgotten. There were paintings of old nobles, piles of furniture, books, vases, and other valuable ornaments of silver and brass and finely carved wood.

"This must be where they store all the nongold things," said Tom. "I've heard about this. King Barf hates anything that isn't gold, but of course he would never get rid of treasure."

We searched several more chambers and found

nothing. Looking for Papa was like searching for a single wheat kernel in fifty acres of wheat, impossible, but finally we found something promising.

"These doors are gold," I said, digging my fingernail into them. "Pure gold."

"This has to be King Barf's chamber!" said Tom.

Yes! My heart ballooned and then deflated in a moment. "How can we get in?" The door came all the way to the floor, no more than a sliver of space. The king had taken extra precautions, probably to keep pixies out.

"Maybe there will be a way to get in through the next room?" Annabella suggested.

"Yes," said Tom. "A secret passageway. Castles are full of secret passages."

We went on to the next door, which we could slide beneath. Annabella and I chattered about all the things we would do when we found Papa.

"He'll swing me up in the air," said Annabella.

"He'll wrestle me onto the ground," I said.

"He'll tell us a story about giants."

"And we'll tell *him* a story about giants, only we'll be in it!"

"And you'll go home?" asked Tom.

"Yes!" said Annabella, beaming.

"And the giants will never bother you again and everything will be perfect?" There was a hint of scorn in his voice.

Annabella and I glanced at each other.

Tom heaved a sigh. "This is stupid. I'm going back to Martha."

"But you said you would help us," said Annabella. "You know this castle better than we do."

Tom shrugged. "This isn't any fun, and I'm hungry."

"Is that all you care about? Fun and food?"

"So what? You can't live without food, and if it isn't fun, what's the point?"

"To find our papa!" shouted Annabella.

"Don't you get it? Even if you found your papa and made it home, the giants would snatch you again on their next raid, or maybe they'd take your mama. Then what will you do? Go after her, too? You're wasting your time."

I'd seen this side of Tom once before, and I didn't like it. Worse, Annabella was crying now. She hiccupped with every breath. I glared at Tom. "Go back to Martha already. You don't care about finding our papa."

"Why should I? He's not *my* papa!"

"It's a good thing he isn't. You'd probably just let the giants have your papa and go eat a giant block of cheese to celebrate."

Before I knew what was happening, I was on my back. Tom punched me in the gut and followed up with two blows to the face. I growled and rolled on top of Tom to punch him back. He scratched at my face and pulled my hair.

"Jack! Tom! Stop!" Annabella tugged at my arm. "Stop it! Stop it right now!"

But we didn't listen to Annabella. We kept punching and growling and scratching like two wild animals, until something else stopped us.

"Fee! Fee! Fum!"

Tom and I froze, our hands still at each others' throats. We looked up. There was the giant baby, Prince Archie, on hands and knees. His fat face was just above us. A thread of saliva dropped down from his mouth and slimed my arm. He bounced and panted like an excited puppy, and then he slapped a chubby hand around all three of us, squishing us together like wads of dough.

"Fee! Fie! Fo! Fum!" he sang.

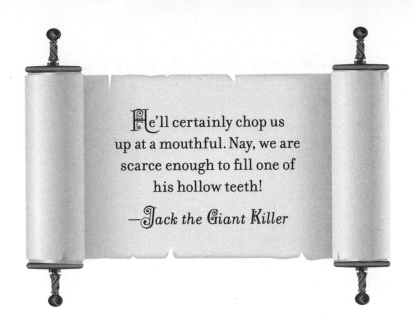

He'll certainly chop us
up at a mouthful. Nay, we are
scarce enough to fill one of
his hollow teeth!

—*Jack the Giant Killer*

CHAPTER NINETEEN
Queen Opal

I took a moment to curse Great-Grandpa Jack's stories and their lack of certain details. Here I was in the presence of a giant *baby* and I was barely able to breathe, let alone chop off his fingers or nose or head. And what kind of monster chops up a baby anyhow?

But apparently the baby was not opposed to the idea of chopping us up. He raised us to his mouth where it smelled of soap and sour milk. Annabella screamed, which made the baby flinch and cry.

"Archie?" said a woman's voice. "What do you have there? Pixies! No, Archie, NO! Give them to Mama, now!" We were ripped from the baby's clutches and dangled by our feet in the giant queen's face. Queen Opal.

"Oh! You're not pixies, are you?" she said. "You must be elves." She brought us even closer to her face, so all I could see was my upside-down reflection in the black center of her eye. "I've never seen one this close before. Do you bite?"

"No, Your Majesty," said Annabella.

"Do you steal? The king says elves are thieves. Did you little demons come to steal my baby?" The queen held us at a giant arm's length, as though we reeked of lies and evil deeds.

"Please, Your Highness, er, Majesty," I stuttered. I had never addressed royalty before. "We are not here to steal anything, least of all a giant baby."

The queen eyed us warily. "You have no wish for a baby?"

We all shook our heads. "We only want to get back what was stolen from us."

The queen put us down on her dressing table. "And what was that?"

"Our papa," said Annabella.

"Your papa!" She sounded genuinely surprised. "Well, that's rich. If my father were carried off by trolls, I wouldn't search for him a moment. I would celebrate!"

Annabella gasped in horror. I raised my eyebrows, and even Tom seemed a little shocked.

"Oh, you think I'm despicable for saying such a thing," said the queen. "But you would despise your father, too, if he cursed you and told lies about you and ordered you about like a common dog."

"Your *papa* cursed you?" asked Annabella, and I knew she was thinking about the princesses in Papa's tales—they were always getting spells and curses put on them, but usually by evil wizards and witches, not their own fathers.

"When I was only six, my father gave me a potion to make me beautiful. He said that beauty would fetch me a rich husband. The potion did work, of course. I am quite beautiful, perhaps the most beautiful in all The Kingdom, but what my father didn't tell me was that the beauty potion contained frog tongue. It was the frog tongue that did it, I'm sure."

"What did the frog tongue do?" I asked.

"It gave me a horrendous craving. I can't . . . oh, it's too awful! I can't stop eating flies!" And just like that, she snatched up a dead fly from a jeweled candy dish on the dressing table and popped it in her mouth. She closed her eyes, and something like relief washed over her face.

"I can't stand the taste of anything else," she went on. "Bread tastes like soap to me. Even a sugar cube turns to ash in my mouth. And to make matters worse, whenever I get nervous or upset, my tongue flicks out like a frog's. See? I'm doing it now just thinking about it." The queen flicked out her tongue a few times.

"But he didn't know, did he?" said Annabella. "Maybe he just wanted you to be pretty so you would be happy."

"I used to think that," said the queen. "And perhaps

if it had been his only act against me, I would have gone on thinking it. I did become a queen, after all. But you see, the king did not marry me for my beauty. He married me because he thought I could spin straw into gold." The queen shivered as though remembering something unpleasant.

"Can you?" I asked.

"No," she replied. "My father lied to the king. I don't know what made him say it. I *could* spin, but nothing out of the ordinary—flax and wool and such."

"What did you do?" Tom asked. He was now sitting on the edge of a silver brush, his face in his chin. Apparently this was no longer boring to him.

"I cried," said the queen. "I thought I would be put to death for my father's lies, until a little man appeared, a boy really. A very strange boy. He said he could spin the straw into gold for me, and he did. He spun all the straw into gold, and I was so happy because not only would I live, but now I was rich! The king was so happy, he said he would make me his queen, and I thought we would live happily ever after, just like a princess in a tale." She shuddered and popped another fly into her mouth. "I was a fool. A fool for ever trusting my father. A fool for believing the king would love me more than his gold, and a fool for allowing that demon to spin the gold. He turned out to be the worst of all, because in exchange for spinning the straw into gold, he made me promise him my firstborn child."

"Your firstborn child? You mean the demon wanted *him*?" Tom pointed to the baby prince crawling all over the floor. He was blowing raspberries and sending great globs of spit all over.

"Yes, he wanted Archie. No doubt he wished to eat him!" She licked her lips, snatched another dead fly, and ate it. "I know it's terrible! But I didn't know anything about babies. I didn't even have one then, so I thought, What difference does it make? I can have more children and it won't ever matter. But it did matter! It did! Archie, forgive me!" The queen lifted her child and held him tight, sobbing into his neck.

The giant baby continued to blow raspberries, only this time the globs of spit came down on us like rain. A slobber shower. Tom ducked behind the brush. Annabella took shelter in a carved wooden box, and I covered myself with a giant lacey handkerchief, until the queen snatched it off me to blow her nose.

"I'm sorry," said the queen, wiping her tears. "It's just that somehow you little ones bring me back to that time when Archie was taken, and I thought I'd never get him back. When I felt so afraid and so . . . so small."

It seemed a strange thing for a giant to say, but I guess no matter how big you are, there's always someone or something bigger than you. Even giants must feel small from time to time.

"So how did you get your baby back?" I asked.

"I guessed his name."

"The baby's name?"

"No, the demon's name. It was some kind of talisman, I think, and when I said it aloud, it destroyed him and Archie was safe."

"Wow," said Tom. "I wonder if he's still around some-where. What's his name?"

"I do not speak it," said the queen sharply. "Do elves not know the power of a name? If saying his name made him disappear, what if saying his name again would bring him back? And if he did come back, the king would surely bargain away Archie in return for more gold. And then I would die of misery, for Archie is the only person in the world who truly loves me."

"Surely not the *only* person," said Annabella. "You're the queen and you're so beautiful."

"I used to think being beautiful would make people love me. I thought the king loved me. But he doesn't. He loves only gold, and when he discovered I could no longer give him any, he cast me off like an old shoe and found another way to get what he wants. Oh how I hate gold! If I could destroy it all, I would!"

I noticed for the first time that there was not a bit of gold in the entire chamber. The blankets and tapestries were blue with silver tassels, and all the furniture was plain wood without a single gold ornament. The table we were sitting on had lots of jars and bottles, the carved wooden box, and a few jewels, but no gold.

The queen loathed gold because it stirred painful memories. She understood what it meant to have people you love taken away from you.

"Your Majesty," I said, "we love our papa, and he got taken from us. With your help we'd have a better chance of finding him. Won't you help us?"

"I don't see how I can."

"I think you could," I said. "You see, my papa escaped the cobbler's shop in a shoe. A golden shoe—"

"Well, it wasn't mine! The only person in the world who's fool enough to wear a gold shoe is— Oh . . . I see. You're talking about the king, aren't you?" The queen's face fell. "Oh, dear."

"What is it?" Annabella asked.

"Oh, nothing. . . . Only . . ."

"Yes?" I asked.

"Well, a day or two ago I heard the servants talking about an elf who was caught stealing the king's gold—"

"Our papa would never steal!" said Annabella, indignant.

"Of course not. It's just that . . . the king found an elf inside his wardrobe . . ."

We all fell silent. My stomach plummeted.

"What happened to him?" I asked.

"I don't know. That's all I heard."

"Then you must ask the king!" I said. "We must go to him at once and tell him to give our papa back! He'll listen to you, won't he?"

"Oh, no. The king doesn't care what I have to say. I'm afraid it might be too late."

Annabella gave a strangled sob.

Too late. I swallowed the words like sharp knives and they cut me all the way down.

"Your Highness," said Tom, "with all due respect, you don't know that it's too late. You could at least ask him what he did with the elf, couldn't you?" I stared at Tom. Was he mocking me again? I didn't think so. He seemed in earnest.

"Oh, no," said the queen. "No, oh, no, no, no. I'd have to go to the Golden Court to see His Royal Majesty, and I cannot abide it. Gold, gold, everywhere you look. The sight of it nearly gives me a rash. See? I am starting to itch just thinking of it." She scratched at her neck and arms, and her tongue flicked out several times.

"All you'd have to do is ask him," I pleaded.

"No, no. I couldn't!" The queen was wringing her hands now, working herself into a real tizzy. "You don't understand! I could make things worse for both of us! The king could suspect something. He could lock me up, or take away Archie! I couldn't bear it!"

"Your Majesty, please," I said. "Think what we have lost—someone we love more than anything. You know what that's like, don't you? Remember how you felt when Archie was taken? How would you feel if an ogre tore through the ceiling and snatched him right out of your arms again?"

The queen's lower lip trembled. She flicked out her tongue and then burst into tears. "Oh, I can't bear it! Archie!" She hugged the giant baby and kissed his chubby cheeks again and again.

"Fee, fee!" The baby reached his pudgy hand out, and we all ducked. The queen's tears at last subsided. "Very well, elves. I understand your pain all too well. I will take you to the king."

"Oh, thank you, Your Majesty!" Annabella fell to her

knees and wrapped her arms around the queen's pinky finger.

"Yes, thank you," I said. I started to feel my heart rise back into my chest.

"But it will be very dangerous," the queen warned. "You must stay hidden. If you are seen, you will most certainly be mistaken for pixies and smashed on the spot!" We nodded vigorously. "I will ask the king about your father, but you must understand that I can do nothing more to help you. Please do not ask me to do more."

"We won't," I promised. "We can manage on our own from there."

The queen sighed and popped three more flies into her mouth. "Now I must change. It displeases the king enough that I never wear gold to dine. He'll be furious if I enter his Golden Court in anything but gold."

The queen set Archie on the floor with a silver rattle, then went to change her gown, leaving us to discuss our plan.

"Should we speak to the king directly?" Annabella asked. "Perhaps if he knew our plight, he would take pity on us, like the queen."

"Not likely," I said. "From all I've seen, the queen is right about him. We'd best stay hidden. Hopefully the king will reveal where Papa is. If not, we should follow him and try to get inside his chambers."

"Yeah," said Tom. "We can hang on to the hem of his robes."

I glared at Tom. "I thought you were going back to Martha to eat cheese."

Tom's cheeks reddened, and he mumbled something about wanting to see the Golden Court. I shrugged him off. He could come if he wanted, but I wouldn't mind if he got spotted as a pixie and swatted away.

The queen emerged from behind her screen dressed in a gown of pure gold with a high collar, embroidered bodice, gaping sleeves that dipped to the floor, and the skirt full and trailing at the back like a golden river.

"How beautiful she is!" said Annabella.

"You could look like that, too," I said. "You just have to be okay with fly suppers and a frog tongue. Maybe Gusta has a son you can marry."

"Har har," said Annabella.

When the queen caught sight of herself in the mirror, she covered her eyes as though she had seen a monster. She scooped up her baby protectively. "Don't worry, Archie, I won't let anyone harm you again! Never ever!"

"Fum!" said the baby, and he tugged on his mother's long braid. The queen then put a gold romper and cap on Archie. I wondered what King Barf would do if they showed up to the court in anything but gold.

"Now, little elves, I think the best way to keep you hidden in the court will be inside my crown." She took a set of keys from a drawer in the table and unlocked a chest. She pulled out a box and unlocked that, and then unlocked another box and finally pulled out a crown made of gold filigree. It had five points that were high enough to cover us. "It feels like I'm wearing a curse," said the queen, and she shivered as she placed the crown upon her head. She then lifted us up, and we kneeled behind the three middle gold points. The filigree had enough holes that we could see through, but the giants wouldn't see us.

"Now, take care, little elves! I hope you do not come to regret asking for my help."

With Archie still in her arms, the queen exited her chamber and glided down the grand golden staircase. Servants, lords, and ladies stopped to bow as she passed. There were stares and whispers. Clearly the queen did not get out much.

She made several turns and walked down many long corridors. I would never remember the way, but hopefully it wouldn't matter. We were getting closer to Papa—I could feel it.

What heavy news can come to me? I am a giant with three heads and can fight five hundred men, and make them fly before me.

—*Jack the Giant Killer*

CHAPTER TWENTY
The Golden Court

The queen took a deep breath and knocked softly on a giant golden door. It swung open.

The Golden Court was just what you'd expect: golden. The walls were gold, the floors and ceilings were gold, and the tapestries and draperies were woven in gold brocade. The mirrors and the window frames, the tables and chairs and vases, were all gleaming gold, and a golden chandelier hung from the ceiling like an upside-down tree, lit with a hundred twinkling candles. Gold dust must have been mixed into the wax, because the candles were gold, too.

Sentries dressed in gold livery stood at attention by the door with gold spears crossed to bar entrance. They lifted the spears to let us pass and then slashed them back into position.

There was music playing, a harp and a lute. It took me a moment to see who was playing them because the musicians' gold outfits made them blend in with the rest of the room.

Gold statues lined the walls of the court. There was King Barf perched atop a rearing stallion. King Barf dressed in full armor with a sword raised and ready to strike. King Barf holding sacks of gold coins, tossing them to bowing beggars. Obviously these were not true likenesses. The statues also made the king look taller and stronger than he actually was. The sculptor probably guessed that the king would not be pleased with an exact representation.

The real King Barf sat upon a golden throne on a dais. I nearly mistook him for a statue, since he was covered head to foot in gold. But then he sneezed and his brown hen—quite drab among all the gold—clucked.

The hen looked scrawnier than the last time I'd seen her, but the king still held her in his lap and petted her as though she were the most precious thing in the world.

A pixie with purple hair and wings fluttered up to the hen, chirping excitedly.

"Servant!" shouted the king. "Remove the pixie!"

A servant rushed forward and smacked at the pixie with a gold paddle while the hen squawked and flapped hysterically. The pixie dodged the first few thrashes until finally the servant smacked her squarely from behind. Annabella gasped softly beside me. The pixie shrieked and fell down. She tried desperately to flap her damaged wings, but to no avail. The servant scooped up the pixie and flung her out the window.

The king comforted the hen with gentle strokes. "There, there my Treasure. I won't let those nasty pixies harm you."

The queen approached the dais.

"What are you doing here?" The king seemed annoyed. "Why have you brought that . . . that *creature* into my court?"

Annabella gasped beside me. "Has he seen us?" she whispered.

"We can jump now if he has," said Tom. "We can slide down the queen's gown and make a run for it."

"No," I said, remembering how the king had spoken of his son at supper. "He's talking about the baby."

The queen sat down on the smaller throne next to the king and held Prince Archie on her lap. "I thought our son should know how a kingdom is ruled," she said, "since it will be his kingdom one day."

"That won't be necessary," said King Barf, sneering at the baby. "I've decided I shall never die."

"How will you manage that?"

"Magician will see to it."

Kessler the magician was juggling three golden eggs and singing a song about marrying a bird. His fingers on his left hand were still carrots, though two of them had been nibbled down to normal size.

"All magic comes with a price," said the queen. "Even gold."

"Aha! I knew it!" shouted the king. "You are jealous of my gold. Jealous that you can no longer make your own."

"No! I want nothing to do with your gold," said the queen.

"You lie!"

The queen trembled. She seemed to have forgotten why she had come at all. I tapped her on the head to remind her that we were here. That seemed to help.

"I only wanted to ask a question," said the queen. "You see, I heard talk about some elves—"

There was a knock at a door, a different one than we had come through.

"Your Goldness!" said the magician. "It is your loyal subjects, come to bring you more gold!"

"Well, what are you waiting for? Let them in, you fools!"

The guards opened the doors, and a stream of people came into the court. Some looked to be nobility and some ragged peasants, but even the lowliest among them had some gold stitched or embroidered on their clothing in honor of the king. They all carried sacks and baskets full of gold—gold coins, gold trinkets and chains, gold boxes and statues and tea sets. The guards sorted the people according to who had the most gold.

The first to approach the king was a nobleman wearing blue velvet robes with gold embroidery and a poufy golden hat. He snapped his fingers, and two servants brought forth sacks of gold. They dropped them at the king's feet and some coins spilled out. The king smiled.

"Very good. Next!"

"But—but, Your Highness," stammered the man.

"Your *Goldness*," corrected the magician.

"Your Goldness. Some food, perhaps? I've eaten nothing but watery gruel for *months*."

"Whatever for? You look rich to me," said the king.

"I am," said the man. "I mean I think I am, but in all my acres of land—"

"You mean *my* land," said the king.

"Yes, of course, Your Goldness. In all the acres of *your* land that I oversee, I can't grow a single stalk of kale."

"What is kale?" asked the king.

"You know," said the farmer. "A leafy green vegetable."

"Oh, how horrid!" The king shuddered. "Why do people eat *leaves*? And green ones, too. It's disgusting!"

"Well, in any case, the kale is dead," said the man. "Shriveled up as though poisoned!"

The king sighed in relief. "Well, of course it's dead! This is a *golden* kingdom! Not a green one. Plant something gold next time."

"But might we have some food, Your Goldness? To tide us over in these difficult times?"

The king gave a long-suffering sigh. "Very well. Magician, the food."

The magician brought forth a sack and swung it around his head a few times before he dumped it at the man's feet. A good amount of food spilled out of the sack, but not giant food. The man bent down and picked up a handful of tiny potatoes. He stared at them.

"Th-thank you, Your Majesty," said the man as his servants scooped every bit of spilled food back into the sack.

"Next!" bellowed the king.

Another giant stepped forward, this one dressed in breeches that were cinched at the waist with rope, as though he'd recently lost weight. He bowed low and placed a golden urn at the king's feet. "Your Goldness, I have just come from my fields—"

"You mean *my* fields," said the king. "Unless of course, they're *green.*"

"Of course, Your Goldness. Your fields. In the spring I planted wheat and barley, as I do every year. The grass sprouted and grew tall and turned golden."

"Oh good, very good. Go on," said the king.

"When I went to harvest the wheat, I noticed the strangest thing. There were no seeds, no wheat kernels at all!"

"You must have a pest problem," said the king. "Pixies, probably."

"But I haven't seen any pixies in ages," said the giant. "They've all come here, where the real gold is."

"Yes, the pests!" growled the king. "I shall purge my kingdom of them all." He found a pixie fluttering near his hand and flicked it toward the giant, who dodged it as the pixie went sailing past.

"It seems," said the farmer, "as though my wheat somehow . . . disappeared."

"Ooh! Magic!" said the magician. "I can make things disappear! Once I disappeared my own head!" He took a bite of his pinky carrot finger.

"How did you get it back?" asked the farmer.

"I didn't! It's lost! Hehehehahahahaaaa!"

"Next!" said the king, sending the farmer on his way with a sack of food.

Person after person came to the king, each with an offering of gold and all with similar problems. Their crops had failed, or even disappeared. One farmer said he sowed seed for melons and they never sprouted, and when he dug in the dirt, the seeds were gone.

The king did not seem very concerned. He simply advised each of his subjects to eliminate pixies and green things of all kinds. Frederick and Bruno would then give them a basket of food, which contained a whole winter's worth of food for me but very little for the giants. One man picked up a good-sized pumpkin between his thumb and forefinger and squeezed it so it squirted in his eye.

Finally a woman approached carrying not an offering of gold but a simple earthen pot, and in the pot was a young sapling, tender and green. She bowed low before the king and held out the plant with trembling hands.

"What is that?" said the king with a sneer.

"Your Goldness, I have guarded and cared for this young sapling in the hope that it might one day bear fruit to feed my family, but we have no other food. I beg of you to take this young tree, and give me food in return so that I may eat and not die."

"Who let her in?" the king demanded of his guards. "How dare you bring me such an offering!" The king knocked the plant out of the woman's arms so it crashed to the floor. The woman stared at it in horror.

"Out! Out!" shouted the king. "Leave me in peace! All of you!"

The guards immediately herded the people toward the exit, pointing spears at them to force them out, then slammed the doors.

The king let out an enormous sigh. "That was awful. I need something to refresh me. Let's make more gold! Treasure, lay!"

Bergeek!

The hen froze up for several seconds and finally released an egg. The king slipped it into his pocket. "Lay! Lay! Lay!"

The hen laid three more eggs, though it seemed to cause her great pain.

"Jack, look!" said Annabella. She pointed down at the king's feet, where the sapling lay. The tender green leaves were browning and shriveling before our very eyes. Finally it was nothing more than a dried-up stalk in a heap of dirt.

"Lay!" the king commanded, and with a pitiful cluck the hen gave one final egg and then flopped unconscious in his lap. "What is wrong with this creature?" spat the king. "She used to give much more gold."

"Oh, we just need to feed her some magic," said Kessler. "Magic makes the gold!"

"Then feed her," said the king. "I want to turn this

entire palace into gold, Magician! The entire kingdom! If I am to be the Golden King, then I need a Golden Kingdom to rule, and therefore I must have more gold!"

"Jack, do you think . . . ," whispered Annabella. "Do you think all the king's gold has something to do with the famine?"

"How could it?" said Tom. "It's just gold. Not poison."

"But didn't you just see that plant shrivel up and die?" said Annabella. "And right while the king was making the hen lay eggs."

"Coincidence," said Tom.

"Or not," I said. As much as I didn't like to admit it, Annabella could be onto something. But what was I supposed to do—kill the king's pet chicken? Somehow I didn't think that would induce him to tell us where Papa was.

"I think the queen has forgotten us again." I rapped on her head to get her attention. She started and then said to the king, "I heard that you found an elf in your stocking drawer. That must have upset you."

"Yes, the little thief was trying to steal my gold. I took care of him."

"In what way?" said the queen.

I held my breath.

"Why I threw him in the— STOP him!" The king was pointing at Archie. "He's eating my gold!" The baby prince was crawling around in the pile of gold offerings, sucking on a coin like a pacifier.

"No, Archie!" cried the queen. She bent down, which made her crown slide forward precariously.

"Treason!" shouted the king. "Hang the thief!"

"You can't hang your own son!" exclaimed the queen. "He's just a baby!" The prince started to crawl away, and the queen scrambled after him, as did several servants.

"I think we'd better go now," said Tom as we bounced around in the crown.

"But he didn't say what he did with Papa!" I shouted.

"If the king sees us, we'll be smashed like pixies!"

Suddenly the queen stumbled. We lurched violently, and then the crown flew off her head. I clung to the gold filigree as it spun in the air.

"Oh, my crown!" The air rushed in my ears and all I could see was a gold blur. I crashed on a heap of coins and slid down in an avalanche of gold. I came to a stop at the golden urn, directly under the king's feet.

"Pixie!" shouted the king. He lifted his foot and tried to stomp on me. I rolled and ran. "Pixies! Kill the pixies!"

There was a flurry of movement and the sounds of crashing gold.

A paddle swung down at me. I rolled and narrowly missed getting smashed.

"Kill the little monsters! Snatch them by the wings! Don't let the thieves get away!" shouted the king.

I ran, tripping over gold coins and chains.

"Jack!" Annabella called.

"Run, Bells! Find a hole! Hide where they can't get you!"

"We can't hide when they've already seen us!" shouted Tom. "We have to get *away*."

I ran as fast as I could, dodging feet and swatters

and giant hands. I crawled under a table and someone tipped it over. I ran behind the curtains and they were torn from the wall. A hole, where was a mousehole? I just needed a crack, someplace where I could get away.

"Stop!" shouted the queen. "Oh, stop! They aren't pixies! They're just elves!"

"They're stealing my gold!" said the king. "Slice them in two! Crush their bones!"

The magician took a golden axe off the wall and swung it wildly. It cracked down on the golden floor, and sparks flew.

Annabella, where was Annabella? Had she managed to dodge the axe? I looked behind me.

"Annabella? Annabella!"

There she was, dashing toward the door, but the servants were gaining. At the last possible moment, a couple of real pixies, orange and red, flew in the faces of the servants. The giants were distracted just long enough for Annabella to get out of the way, until another pixie swooped down and carried her out of harm's way.

"Kill the blasted pixies!" shouted the king. "Don't let them get away!"

The pixies spiraled upward around the chandelier before disappearing in a crevice.

I gaped upward. I had stopped moving without realizing it, completely forgetting where I was. A moment later a giant gold swatter knocked me flat on my back. My head cracked against the floor, and the whole room turned white.

"No wings," said a voice very close to me. "It's an elf."

"So is this one!" said another voice.

"Give them here," said the king. The servant brought me to the king. The other brought Tom, and the king wrapped his beefy hands around us so only our heads and feet poked out. I kicked and struggled, but the king tightened his grip. I could hardly breathe.

King Barf brought us to his red, puffy face and sneered. "Thieves! Villains! No one steals my gold and gets away with it!"

"But they're only children!" pleaded the queen. "Don't hurt them! Give them to me. I'll . . . I'll give them to Archie for toys."

Prince Archie bounced in the queen's arms and reached toward us. "Fee, fee!"

"No," said the king in a cold voice. "There is only one thing I do with elves who dare to steal my gold."

"We don't want your gold," I managed to say. "I just want my papa back!"

The king scoffed. "Excuses will not soften your punishment."

He dropped us inside a box and shut the lid. I couldn't see anything, not even my hand in front of my face, but I could tell we were moving. The king was taking us somewhere, and I was sure it was nowhere good. Tom whimpered and cried for Martha. There was nothing I could say to comfort him. I had no comfort for myself.

I felt the jolts and bumps of moving up stairs. Then I heard the clings and clicks of a door unlocking—or a dungeon. Finally, the lid of the box was raised.

I couldn't see much except the ceiling, which was

gold. There was a gold fireplace, too, and the king lifted us out of the box and walked toward it.

"Oh no," said Tom. "Oh no, oh no, oh no!"

Tendrils of smoke rose from the grate, as though a fire was just getting started. All it needed was some kindling to coax out the flames.

We were the kindling.

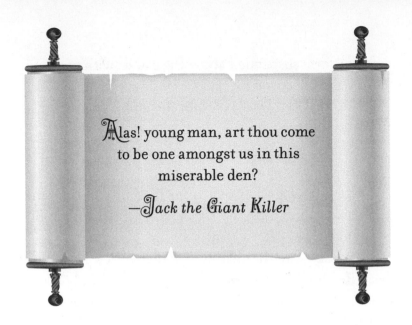

Alas! young man, art thou come
to be one amongst us in this
miserable den?

—Jack the Giant Killer

CHAPTER TWENTY-ONE
Into the Fireplace

The king turned a crank, and the grate of the fireplace split apart to reveal a dark, smoking cavern.

"No!" cried Tom. "Don't put me in there! I'm sorry! I'm sorry! I won't touch your gold ever again. Just take me back to the kitchen! Martha needs me to milk the cows!"

"Oh, but if you like gold, you'll love it down here." The king pulled a golden egg out of his robes and dropped it into the hole. There was a thud and a crack and something that sounded like the echo of voices.

"Now it's your turn," said King Barf. The king set us

on a platform suspended above the cavern with ropes on both sides. He turned a crank and down we went. Daylight was replaced by the glow of fire and it grew warmer as we went down.

"Oh no," said Tom. "Oh no, oh no, oh no! He's going to roast us! He's *eating* us!"

When we were just feet from the bottom, the king took hold of the rope and shook it violently. Tom and I were both flung off the platform.

I shook away the dizziness and then felt scorching heat. Red-hot flames blazed right next to my head. "Ooh, hee, haaaa . . . HOT!" I scrambled away, but there were more flames. Fire everywhere. Tom was huddled down with his head between his knees, rocking back and forth.

"Careful there now," said a voice. I looked up and saw a man, not a giant. He had a grizzly beard, and his face was covered in soot and ash. He grabbed our collars and pulled Tom and me away from the flames. "You don't want to melt, now do you?"

Tom ran back to the platform and tried to climb one of the ropes, but yelped as soon as he took hold of it. The ropes were heavily barbed.

"There's no climbing out of here, boy," said the man. "There's no way out at all."

We were in a cavernous dungeon as big as the castle kitchen. When the shock wore off I realized that the fires we had landed near were actually inside ovens. Another man was now removing a pot from one of them. He poured a shimmering soup into a wide, shallow tray, then lowered the pot into a water barrel. A puff of white steam billowed up, causing him to disappear for a moment.

In the center of the dungeon was a mountain of golden eggs. People were climbing all over it like ants on a sugar hill. They had axes and chisels, and they pounded on the eggs like miners. Surrounding the pile of eggs were shanties, hastily thrown together with broken boards and branches and dirty rags. It was a dismal sight.

"Is Martha here?" Tom asked. He must have thought we were in some back room of the kitchen. He was looking around as though any moment Martha would swoop down and feed him some cheese like a little mouse.

"Can't say that I know," said the man. "Not too many women down here."

"What about Henry?" I said. "That's my papa. He could have come here today, even just a few hours ago."

"I'm not much for names. And there're lots of us here."

I looked at the men working. "What are they doing?" I asked.

"We elves of the dungeon must make the giant king's gold into coin," said the man. "That's the punishment for stealing. He'll make you repay him a hundred times what you would have taken."

"Did you steal the king's gold?" I asked.

"I sure tried," said the man. "I thought it would be easy, seeing as the king has mountains of the stuff, but

that ogre can smell a thief from a mile away. I don't need
to tell you. You're here. I guess we all got what we wanted
in the end. More gold than we could ever hope to steal."
He laughed bitterly and went back to his work.

I looked up to where King Barf had lowered us
through the hole. There were just a few shafts of light
coming through the grate of the fireplace, but otherwise
the cavern was dim and depressing. The walls were hard
dirt, high and smooth, not at all good for climbing. We
were well and truly trapped.

I searched for Papa all over. It was not an easy thing.
Firstly, the dungeons were a dangerous place to navi-
gate, between the fiery ovens and hot vats of gold, and
hammers, chisels, and pickaxes crashing down everywhere. Secondly, everyone looked the same—sooty and
weary and miserable. But hope kept me going. He had
to be here.

"I want to go back to Martha," said Tom, collapsing
against an egg.

"We'll find a way out," I said. "I've been in worse fixes."

"Really? You think we'll just climb out of here?"
Tom's voice was thick with bitterness. "You think all
these people stay here because they want to?"

"Well, it might take some time, but when I find
Papa—"

Tom scoffed. "Your papa. Searching for your papa is

what got us here in the first place! If you had just listened to me, we wouldn't be here."

"Tom, you don't understa—"

"No, *you* don't understand. We were fine in the kitchen with Martha. We had all the food and fun we wanted."

I felt my face getting hot. "I didn't *make* you come with me! You thought this would be one of your grand adventures, like getting eaten by a cow."

"That was a cow," said Tom. "This is a dungeon. This is *King Barf.* You think you can beat a giant? You can't. You're too small. You're never going to find your papa, and we're never going to get out of here." His eyes were wet and shining.

I didn't know if I wanted to hit him or start crying myself, but I didn't get the chance to do either one, because a man stepped forward, axe in hand.

"You boys need to get to work if you want to eat," he said. "Get a cart now and start gathering gold. Take it to the fires."

Tom turned his back on me and did as the man said. He grabbed a cart and started hurling chunks of gold into it like he wanted to shatter them into a million pieces.

I stared after him. I felt a hardness in my throat, almost choking me.

You can't beat giants.

You're never going to find Papa.

You're never going to get out.

"Better get to work, boy," warned the man. "No one takes kindly to shirkers here. We don't get food until the king gets his gold."

I picked up one of the rickety old carts and mindlessly gathered chunks of gold, but really I just kept looking for Papa. I thought I saw him on the egg mountain, and then by an oven, and then pushing a cart like me. He was everywhere, and nowhere.

It was so hot. Before long I was soaked in sweat and my throat felt like coals, hot and dry. The only water to drink was the same water used to cool off the gold, so not only was it warm, it had a metallic taste that clung to my mouth. It didn't refresh me very much, and I was so hungry. When would we get food?

If only these eggs were real. Well, they were real in a way. They came out of a real hen. They were just really *gold*. But lots of food is golden. Wheat. Bread. Pies. Pears. Peaches. Gold can be good food for eating. King Barf eats it.

I lifted a piece. It was smooth and shiny like a glazed bun. Delicious. I opened my mouth to take a bite.

"Tut, tut, sonny. I wouldn't do that if I were you," said a man. I dropped the gold and whipped around.

"I didn't . . . I wasn't . . . ," I stammered.

The man laughed. "Don't worry. We've all tried to eat it at one point or another, but you'll wind up with a broken tooth, or at least a bad, bad stomachache."

I took a closer look at the man. He seemed familiar. He was tall and thin and bald, except for his face, which was scruffy with a beard and a curling mustache. "Do I know you?" I asked.

"Of course, of course," he said. "We all know each other in this place, don't we?" His mustache bounced and wiggled like butterfly antennae.

"Baker Baker?" His eyes widened. Yes, it was him! And there was his bakery! A little crushed and cracked in spots, but the same bakery that used to stand in the village, all full of pies and sticky buns. What I wouldn't give for some Nutty-Nutty bread.

"Do I know you?" asked Baker Baker.

"I'm Jack. I live on a farm near your bakery."

"Jack . . ." He twisted his mustache. "Yes, yes, I remember. The rascally boy. Do you still have a farm, then?"

"Not really. I mean our house is still there, and some of the barn, but the giants took everything else."

"I still have a bakery, but I never bake bread anymore, only gold." He sighed. "Gold, gold, gold."

"Have you seen my father?" I asked.

"Your father?"

"Henry. He used to sell you wheat." I hoped that would spark his memory, but he just twisted his mustache some more, befuddled. "Henry . . . he could be here, but I don't know. Not much time for visiting in this dull, dull dungeon. All we do is work, work, work. What does it matter if there's a Henry or a Jack or . . ."

". . . Or a Baker Baker?" I asked.

"Right, right, exactly. It doesn't matter. We're all just here, baking like bread." Baker Baker slid a pot of gold into the oven where he used to bake bread. The front wall of his house had been torn open, so he didn't have to go inside. I guessed there wasn't really an inside or outside here anyway. Just trapped.

We heard shouting down the path and turned to see.

"Melt! Melt! Melt!" someone chanted in a loud voice. "Keep your fires going, lads! Chop! Chop! Chop those eggs! Keep the gold coming! Come, soldiers! Do not slacken your pace! We must hasten the work!"

There, of all people, was Sir Bluberys. His rusty armor was blackened with soot, and his mule looked more tired and swaybacked than ever. He plodded along the well-trodden paths of the encampment, issuing commands and shouts of encouragement.

"Very good! Faster now. More fuel for the fire!"

People scowled as he passed.

"Fool!" muttered Baker Baker. "Thinks he's Lord of the Dungeon. Rides around on that mutt of a mule telling everyone what to do and never lifting a finger except to eat."

"When *do* we eat?" I asked.

"Soon, I hope. We've made lots and lots of gold today. The king just throws the food down when he comes to collect his gold."

Baker Baker took out the pot of gold and poured it into one of the molds.

I glanced up at the dungeon ceiling. It was dark now, no light glowed through the grate. People were slowing down on their work. They stopped chopping the eggs. A few fires were doused. The coins were being rolled and stacked in towers on the platform. People looked upward expectantly, waiting for food. I imagined melons and berries raining down. I'd catch them on my tongue.

I saw Tom, but he wouldn't meet my eyes. He stood with another boy who looked like he had been here a long time. He was scrawny, his clothes were torn and sooty, and his eyes looked lifeless. Is that what fate had in store for me and Tom?

The dungeon grew silent with anticipation. My neck grew sore from craning. Stomachs rumbled. And then . . .

Boom, boom, BOOM!

The cavern shook. The gold coins clinked together in their towers. The grate creaked open.

"Your gold, Your Goldness!" shouted an elf, and the king turned a crank that caused the platform full of gold to rise.

I wondered if I could get onto the platform and sneak out by hiding in the gold. I could tell Tom had the same idea, because he stepped forward, but his new friend pulled him back and whispered something in his ear. Tom's face fell. I guessed it wasn't a good idea. It had probably been tried before without success.

We all remained still and silent as we listened to the king inspect the gold. He counted the coins, sniffed them, and spoke to them softly. It reminded me of Miss Lettie, singing to her cabbages.

"Oh yes, aren't you a pretty one? Oh, you have a spot

there—I'll shine you up good as new. Beautiful, lovely, perfect. Mine, mine, mine."

Finally the king held a sack over the hole. The whole dungeon took a collective breath.

"It's coming, it's coming," said Baker Baker, and his stomach growled. Twice.

"Your reward, my elves," said the king. He poured out the contents of the sack, and it rained. It rained grapes and apples and cheese, chunks of bread, scraps of potatoes and onions. Everyone dove for the food, ravenous and beastly as wolves.

I snatched a chunk of bread and an onion and shoved them into my pockets. I caught a bit of cheese that fell down, but after that, every time I tried to grab something, someone else snatched it away. Two men fought over a potato. Another group was arguing over a chunk of cheese, each person with his hands on a side of it. I spotted Tom and his new friend just shoveling food into their mouths as soon as they picked it up. You didn't have to fight over food that was already eaten.

The food was nearly gone when I spotted an apple on the ground, shiny and red. No one seemed to notice it. Quick as a jackrabbit, I dove for the apple and collided with another body. We rolled over each other, each grasping to get the apple, which kept tumbling out of reach as we fought for it. Just when I thought I had it, the man pinned my arms behind me, but I wasn't going to lose this battle. The apple was rolling toward me, so I opened my mouth and sank my teeth into it.

The man started laughing and released me. "Well

then, I guess you win," he said, helping me up. "You know you remind me of my—"

The man stopped talking. I looked at him and the apple fell out of my mouth and bounced and rolled in the dirt. In two seconds someone else came and snatched it off the ground, but I didn't move. I just stared at the man right in front of me. He was thin and dirty, his hair long and unkempt, and a scruffy beard covered half his face. But his eyes were exactly the same. Brown and warm, like rich earth baking in the sun.

"Papa," I whispered.

"Jack," whispered the man.

"Papa!" I shouted.

"Jack!" shouted the man.

It was Papa. It was *Papa*! He opened his arms and I crashed into him and we fell to the ground laughing, and maybe crying just a little.

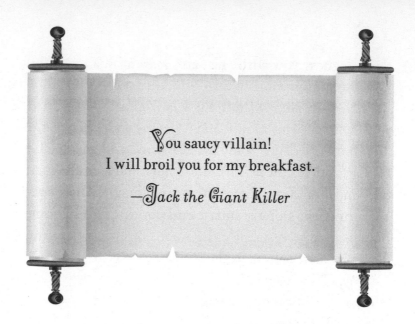

You saucy villain!
I will broil you for my breakfast.
—Jack the Giant Killer

CHAPTER TWENTY-TWO
Egg-Quake and Food Drought

After we stopped laughing and wiped the muddy tears from our faces, Papa and I shared our meal. Between us we had a celebratory feast of bread and cheese and grapes and onion. I couldn't stop smiling.

"Where are your mama and sister?" asked Papa. "Are they safe?"

"Mama is at home. Annabella was, too, until she followed me up the beanstalk."

"Beanstalk?" Papa scrunched his face in confusion, and I remembered that he didn't know anything about Jaber's giant beans, so I told him about how I'd gotten here and how Annabella had come up, too. "But she got away," I assured him. I left out the details of exactly how she got away. The fact that she was here at all seemed to worry Papa enough. For Annabella's sake, I hoped the pixies were as sweet as she believed.

"Oh, Bells. I hope she's all right."

"She'll be okay," I said. "I never thought I'd say this, but Annabella's pretty smart. Smarter than me in some ways."

Papa chuckled. "She takes after your mama. She could always outsmart me and I wouldn't catch on until the next day. She must be worried sick, your poor mama."

"Do you think we'll ever see them again?"

"I hope so," said Papa. "I didn't think I would see any of you again, but now I've got you, so I have to believe there's a way."

Suddenly I saw Tom peering out from behind an egg. He stared at Papa and me.

"Tom!" I said. "I found my papa! This is him! Isn't that amazing? We found him after all!"

I thought this would make Tom happy, or at least get him to forgive me a little, but Tom didn't even smile. His eyes got all shiny and his chin started to tremble. He dropped the food in his arms and ran away. Within a minute it was gone, snatched up by other hungry workers.

"He doesn't seem too pleased that you found me," said Papa.

"He's mad at me," I said. "It's my fault he's here. He was helping me search for you when we got caught, but

I don't know why he wouldn't at least be happy that I found you."

Papa gave me a pat on the back. "Sometimes people have things going on inside them that we don't understand."

I rested my head on his shoulder. I understood enough. Tom didn't have a papa and he was afraid. We had been captured by giants, and enslaved in a deep, dark dungeon full of smoke and fire, but in that moment I felt so light, I could almost float above it all.

I had found Papa. We'd find a way out of here, too. We'd find a way home.

"To work, Jack," said Papa when morning came.

The words filled me with happiness, because they came from Papa. I felt I could work a thousand years in this pit, as long as he was by my side.

Papa whistled as he raised an axe and cracked it down on the egg.

"I lost your axe," I told him. "I brought it to fight the giants, and then I lost it fighting pixies."

"That's all right. There are plenty of axes here." Papa chopped on the egg again, so it split clean in half. I hadn't paid much attention yesterday, but the eggs were actually hollow, the gold shells about as thick as my arm. Something fell out of the hollow middle of the egg and rolled right to my feet. I picked it up. It was dark brown, a smooth oval shape about the size of a regular egg from Below.

"What's this?" I asked Papa.

"Just the stone that comes out of the eggs—you know, like a yolk. Look there."

He pointed to another man who was splitting open an egg. He pounded with a hammer and a chisel and finally cracked it in half. The "yolk" rolled out of the bottom. Another worker picked it up and tossed it into a fire, where is sizzled and smoked.

I turned the yolk over in my hand. "Can we eat them?"

Papa shrugged. "Go ahead and try it."

I looked at him, unsure, but he smiled and waved me on. I sniffed at the yolk and pressed my fingernail into it. It made sense. You don't eat eggshells. You eat the gooey stuff inside.

I sank my teeth in and then quickly spat it out. Blech! The yolk was dry and bitter, like green wood. It tasted like poison. I spat again and again, trying to get the disgusting taste out of my mouth.

Papa laughed. "Bitter, huh? We've all tried it. I even tried to roast them, but that only made it worse. We just use them for firewood. They smoke a bit, but they burn all right. Just toss them in the oven when you find them."

I tossed it in the oven right away, glad to be rid of it. What a disgusting egg yolk! I couldn't get the taste out of my mouth for the rest of the day, and the metallic water only made it worse.

Papa went on chopping gold, and I gathered it and took it to the fires. I noticed more and more of the yolks. They were all a little different—all shades of brown and black, some as big as melons and others no bigger than my pinky nail. Occasionally I'd slip a nice round one into my pocket with my sling. They'd be good for target practice sometime. Maybe I could throw one at Tom and he'd think it was funny and we could go back to having fun together like we used to. This place could use a good prank to liven things up.

But the next time I saw Tom, I noticed how dark and glazed his eyes were and I slid my sling back inside my pocket. What was I thinking? Pulling a prank was all fun and laughs when times were good, but when things were tough, it was just spitting in someone's eye, kicking a man while he's down, and I couldn't imagine that would feel very fun.

In the dungeons the weather was always hot. It hailed gold and rained food, though never enough of the latter.

"It seems like the more golden eggs we get, the less food we eat," said Papa. "Is there any food left?"

This reminded me of what we had seen in the Golden Court. I told Papa how that plant had shriveled up after King Barf made the hen lay golden eggs.

"Do you think that could have something to do with the giant famine?"

Papa paused and sat on the edge of the egg he was taking apart. It was cut in half now, and the yolk rolled lazily away, like it too was tired. "Could be. On a farm, you only reap what you sow. You can't get something from nothing."

"So what's the something the hen is making into gold?" I asked. "Could it somehow be taking from all the growing things? Growing is powerful, isn't it?"

"Very powerful," said Papa. "From one tiny seed you can grow a tree as big as the giants. Now that's magic, if you ask me."

The days blended together, and so did our brains, like melted cheese, hot and gooey. It was hard to not think of food. I wouldn't have minded some of Martha's cheese. I would have liked to swim in a pudding, or bean soup. Even Papa couldn't help but talk of food.

"You're skinny as a beanpole, son," he said. What I wouldn't have given for some beans. Green anything sounded good. Leaves and grass and maybe even fuzzy green caterpillars. Giant juicy ones.

One evening, after a long hot day of work, the king opened the grate. He lowered the platform and took the gold coins as usual. Then he lifted a bulging sack above the dungeons. We opened our mouths and held out our arms, but it wasn't food that rained down.

"Egg-quake!" someone shouted.

Eggs crashed down like boulders. They tumbled

down the egg mountain, creating an avalanche. Everyone ran and ducked for cover.

"In here, Jack!" Papa flipped the hollow half of the egg on top of me, closing me in like a baby bird while eggs crashed and clattered over the dungeons. When the egg-quake was over, Papa lifted the eggshell off me. The mountain of golden eggs had been well replenished, and dozens of eggs wobbled and spun all around the dungeon, but no food had come down.

We all looked up, waiting for more, but nothing came. The king replaced the grate and went away.

We dragged through the next day's work as though we had great chains about our ankles. I gathered gold. I drank water to fill my empty belly. By the end of the day I could barely move the cart. We gathered all the gold. It wasn't as much as usual, but the king had to feed us. We wouldn't be able to make his gold if we didn't eat.

Boom, boom, BOOM!

The king arrived. He removed the grate and lowered the platform. Slowly, we lifted the gold and the king raised it up. He counted it. He ran through his usual ritual of sniffing and murmuring to it.

We all waited, parched and wilting, for the food to rain down.

Finally, the king made it rain bread and cheese. Moldy bread. Moldy cheese. The food shower stopped far too soon, and we looked up, waiting for more. All that work, practically starving, and this was our reward?

"Hey! Hey!" shouted Baker Baker. "Where's the rest? This isn't enough to feed a chicken's chick!"

"Be grateful," the king said. "You made very little gold for me today."

Baker Baker balled up his fists and turned red all over. Something in him seemed to snap. His patience. His hope. His sanity? "Grateful? *Grateful?* You steal from us and enslave us, and we're supposed to be grateful? You're nothing but a lazy, lying, thieving, stupid tyrant!"

Angrily, the king shot down a pair of fire tongs and snatched up Baker Baker. King Barf lifted him up to the top of the grate and dangled him upside down.

"I am your king!" he shouted. "Everything you have is *mine.* Everything you see is *mine.* The gold you make for me is *mine,* and whatever I choose to give to you, that is *mine,* too. When you are not grateful, it makes me angry." He tore the food from the baker's arms and then let him go with the tongs so he tumbled down the mountain of eggs and landed in a heap at the bottom. King Barf threw the food into one of the fires, and everyone watched it sizzle and melt and turn to ash.

"Who's next?" asked the king, whipping the tongs in the air. "Who dares to speak against me, your king?"

No one said a word. No one breathed. It was one of those moments when Grandpa Jack would have stood up and fought the king: When all was lost. When no one else would. I was supposed to be Jack the Great, but I didn't feel that way now. I was just another elf, doing whatever King Barf told me to, because I didn't want to get crushed or roasted.

I, Jack, the weak and lowly, could not vanquish the villainous giant.

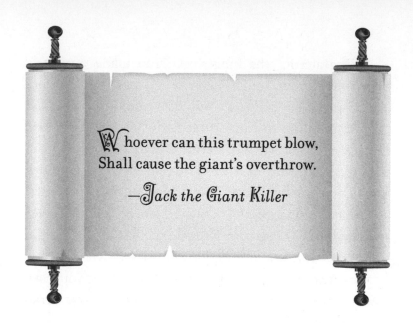

Whoever can this trumpet blow,
Shall cause the giant's overthrow.

—*Jack the Giant Killer*

CHAPTER TWENTY-THREE
The Overlooked Thing

"Papa?"

"Hmmm?" Papa was leaning against an egg, half awake. There was just a faint glow from the fires and most people were asleep, but I could not rest.

"Will you tell me a story about giants? One where they get beaten."

"They always get beaten," said Papa.

"Tell me."

Papa spoke with his eyes closed.

"Once there was a giant with two heads, named Thunderdell. He wanted revenge for all the giants Jack had killed.

"Let him come!" Papa spoke in his valiant Jack voice. "I have a tool to pick his teeth!"

But Jack used his wits. The castle was surrounded by a moat, over which lay a drawbridge. Jack ordered his men to cut through the ropes of the bridge until they were just about to snap. He brandished his sword of sharpness, and at length, the giant came.

"Art thou the villain who killed my kinsmen? Then I will tear thee with my teeth, suck thy blood, and grind thy bones to powder."

"You'll have to catch me first," said Jack, and he ran onto the bridge. The giant followed after him, swinging his club. But when the giant reached the middle of the bridge, his great weight caused it to collapse, and he tumbled headlong into the moat.

Jack laughed at him. The giant roared, but he could not get out of the moat to take his revenge. Jack wrapped the giant's two heads with rope and chopped them clean off with his sword. The end."

The story was supposed to make me feel better, but it didn't. I felt hollow and frustrated.

"Papa?"

"Hmmmm?"

"Why did everything come so easy for him?" I asked.

"Who?"

"Grandpa Jack. Everything just . . . came to him,

like when he escaped the tower room out the window with the rope, or tricked the giant with a lie, and when he chopped off the giants' heads with a swoop of his sword."

"Maybe it wasn't as easy as it sounds in the stories," said Papa. "Action takes more effort than words."

"But we've seen the giants now. We know how big they are. Do you really think he cut off a giant's head? A *two-headed* giant? Even cutting off a nose seems impossible." I thought of how Martha had plucked my axe right out of my hands.

Papa looked thoughtful. "It was a long time ago," he said. "I heard the stories from my papa, and he heard them from his, and he from his, and so on and so on. It's hard to know where things got exaggerated or details got left out."

"Like how the giants live in the sky?"

"Yes, that," said Papa.

"And how much effort it takes to travel from one place to the next when you are as small as a mouse?" He nodded. "And about giant snakes and toads and spiders, and how maybe not all giants are terrible?"

"Yes, all those things, but the important parts are there. Jack really had to fight the giants, and he really beat them. And there was nothing so great about Jack, not more than anyone else. He wasn't a knight or a soldier. He was a common man, a poor farm boy, just like you. But the thing that made Jack different was that he saw the small things, the things other people didn't notice. Maybe the way he beat the giants seems easy in the stories, but if it was so easy, how come no one else did what Jack did? How come no one else could beat all those giants?"

I thought about it long into the night. It gnawed at my brain. I was supposed to be like my seven-greats-grandpa Jack. I was supposed to know what to do, but I didn't know anything, and I couldn't shed the feeling that I had overlooked something, but I didn't know what it could be.

There had to be something that could defeat King Barf, something that could get us out of this dungeon, if only it would show itself to me. Where was my rope? My sword of sharpness? Where was my magic?

I could really use some right now.

I woke to a strange sound, like a moaning wind, but there was no wind in the dungeon. Someone was crying. I looked around. Papa was fast asleep, snoring lightly. Everyone else was sleeping, too. Perhaps I had imagined it. I lay back down.

Then I heard it again. A soft moaning, barely more than a sniffle. I sat up and followed the noise until I came upon someone curled up in the half shell of an egg.

"Tom?" I whispered.

He stopped crying right away.

"Tom, are you all right?"

Nothing.

"Tom, I'm really sorry that I got us trapped here. It's

awful and miserable and you'd rather be with Martha, where there's more fun and food."

Tom turned over and wiped his sleeve across his face. "You think I'm crying over cheese?"

"Well, Martha would, wouldn't she?" I tried to laugh a little, to help lighten the mood.

"You don't know anything." Tom sat up, and in the dim light I could just see the glisten of tears on his cheeks and the shadow of his scowl. "Did you know I used to have a papa, too? I did." In fact, I had wondered about this. "The same giant took us together, but my papa got thrown from the giant's pocket. I grabbed onto his hand, but I couldn't hold on, and he . . . he fell. He fell a really long way, and I wasn't big enough or strong enough to save him." Tom's chin quivered, and tears created little rivers through the soot caked on his face.

This was the thing inside Tom I didn't understand. Tom had lost his papa, too. All this time I had been searching for my papa, and I thought Tom just didn't care. I thought he only wanted to have fun and eat, but really he was trying to ease the pain that could not be mended. He knew his papa was gone and could not be found.

"It's not your fault," I said. "It was the giant."

"Maybe," said Tom. "Maybe it's not your fault we're here in this dungeon."

We were silent for a time and I decided I was tired of the dungeon. I was tired of being tossed and bossed around by a giant. I wanted to do something. I didn't know what, but I was resolved.

"Tom," I said. "Let's defeat the giants. Let's conquer King Barf."

In the morning I took Tom over to Papa, who was dividing what was left of our food into two small piles.

"Papa, this is Tom," I said. "He helped me search for you."

Papa shook Tom's hand. "Thank you for looking for me, Tom. I'm glad I was found."

Tom smiled and looked down at his feet, just a little uncertain.

"Let's have breakfast!" said Papa, and he divided the food to make a third portion for Tom. None of us had much to eat, but I didn't mind because I was so glad to have Tom talking to me again.

Work was even better with Papa *and* Tom. We raced back and forth from the gold to the ovens, and then we gave each other rides in the carts. Once I lost control and crashed Tom and the cart into an egg, which shifted and upset the whole mountain of eggs.

"Egg-quake!" I shouted, and everyone ran for cover. Tom and I hid beneath one of the carts as the eggs tumbled and spun. When everything settled, an old man yelled at us, "You hooligans can't just run all over the place and crash into things!"

"Sorry, sir," I said. "We just lost control of the cart." Tom clamped his hand over his mouth to hold in a laugh.

"You think it's funny, do you? You could have knocked me into a fire! You could have killed me!"

The smile faded right off Tom's face.

"Hey, it wasn't his fault," I said. "We were just trying to have some fun."

"This is no place for fun," grumbled the man.

"Come on, boys," said Papa. "Back to work."

We picked up our carts and started gathering gold. I picked up a few more of the yolks, and that gave me an idea.

"Tom," I whispered, "want to try some target practice?" I pulled my sling out of my pocket.

"What are we going to throw?" he asked.

"These." I placed one of the yolks in my sling.

Tom brightened right up. "Terrific!"

We ran to a far side of the dungeon, which served as a kind of graveyard for broken carts and barrels. Tom had never used a sling before, so I decided we'd start by throwing yolks at the wall to get a feel for it; then we could move on to simple targets like carts and eggs. I took out my sling and showed Tom how to put the stone in the center. I swung it around and around, gathering speed.

"The faster you get it going, the harder it will fly." I released the yolk and let it fly hard and fast into the dirt wall, where it stuck.

"Amazing!" said Tom. "Let me try."

Tom took the sling from me and loaded it. He was just starting to swing it around when suddenly—*snap! thwack! froosh!*—something burst through the wall.

"Snake!" Tom shouted, diving for cover among the broken carts.

Right where I had thrown the yolk, a giant green snake was shooting through the wall. It curled and slithered toward us.

"I'll shoot it!" said Tom. Frantically, he shot and missed by several feet. The snake kept uncoiling out of the wall, growing bigger and bigger, as though it had no beginning or end. A moment later—*crack! shwip! fwip!*—another snake burst out of the wall. They started to twist around each other and rise up.

"Tom . . . ," I said, realization dawning. "Those aren't snakes. . . ."

"What are they then?"

Little buds swelled on the ends, and then they lengthened and branched out and more buds formed. Leaves unfurled and spread.

"They're . . . *plants!*" I said.

The green vines were growing out of the wall, faster than any plant I'd ever seen. Faster than the beanstalk even. It was some kind of magic.

The plants swelled and split and twisted. They rose right up to the dungeon grate, where they finally slowed to a stop.

Tom and I gaped at each other. I pulled another yolk out of my pocket and examined it closely. How would I view this stone if it were much smaller? It was a *seed*.

I looked back toward the pile of golden eggs. More seeds were strewn about in the dirt. There was one as big as my head, white and almond shaped, probably a pumpkin or a squash. A man walked by and chucked it into the fire, which smoked and sputtered. I winced. How could we have missed it? It seemed so obvious to me now. The magic to make the gold was drawing power from growing things. The hen sucked up that growing power to make golden eggs, and inside each egg, some power remained in the form of a seed. A seed that sprouted and grew with incredible speed once planted.

"Do it again," said Tom.

My hands trembled as I loaded another seed into my sling. I swung it around and around and let it fly. The seed buried itself in the dirt wall, and almost immediately a green stem burst out and swelled and split and spread. This one didn't grow up, it grew out. It grew around our feet and crawled up and over the carts and toward the pile of golden eggs and everyone else.

People stopped what they were doing and shouted and backed away as the vines reached them. Giant leaves unfurled, and green globes swelled to the size of my head, and then bigger and bigger until they weighed heavy on the vine. The green globes were now as tall as me and as wide as I was tall. They began to blush and redden.

"They're giant tomatoes!" said Tom.

Everyone crawled over the vines and leaves to look at the giant tomatoes. Someone bit into one. "Food!" he shouted, and suddenly everyone started to devour the tomatoes.

"Jack!" called Papa, running toward me. When he saw me next to the giant tomato, he dropped his pickaxe. "Jack, are you all right? What happened?"

"Papa!" I shouted. "The yolks in the eggs! They're seeds, Papa! They're seeds!"

"What?!"

I ran around until I found another seed, a bean-shaped one as large as my hand. It was smaller than Jaber's beans and a little richer in color. Perhaps the magic made them a little different, but still, I should have known or at least suspected.

"Watch!" I told Papa. I slipped the bean into my pocket and started to climb the egg mountain as high as I could get. Everyone was still devouring the tomatoes, eating them right off the vine. They didn't know yet that there was more. So much more.

I put the bean into my sling. I swung it around and around, faster and faster, and then I threw it down to the ground.

Papa yelped and jumped back as the bean sprouted and shot up like a green fountain. It swelled and twisted and grew up against the wall of the dungeon, higher and higher. It pushed through the grate and grew out of the dungeon.

I hopped down from the pile of eggs to Papa, and we both stared up at the giant beanstalk.

Papa wiped his brow and just kept staring up. "Well, son, I think you found what we've all been overlooking."

I wrapped my arms around Papa. "We're going home."

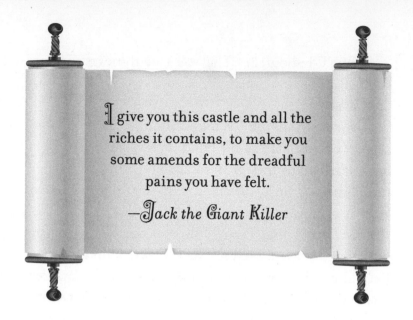

I give you this castle and all the
riches it contains, to make you
some amends for the dreadful
pains you have felt.

—Jack the Giant Killer

CHAPTER TWENTY-FOUR
Escape Plan[t]s

I t was decided that we would leave that very night, before King Barf could discover the plants and ruin our
best chance of escape. But first we had to grow more seeds.

Everyone went to work, gathering what seeds were
strewn around that hadn't been burned, and cracking
open eggs to get more. We worked harder than we ever
had, knowing that this was our chance at escape, and
since we now had plenty of food, the work was easier.

Once we had gathered as many seeds as possible,
we sorted them into piles and tried to determine what
was what.

"That's tomato," I said, since I'd just grown one.

"And that's a wheat kernel," said Papa. "Why didn't I see it before?"

"You're not used to seeing giant ones," I said. "And I think these ones are a little different. They have magic in them. That's why they grow so fast."

"Those are onion seeds," said Baker Baker, pointing to some pointy black ones. "And those look to be carrots."

"Save those," said Papa. "They won't help us get out of here, but they can feed us well later."

"Wouldn't I love a giant carrot!" said Baker Baker. "I could make a carroty carrot cake. Oh! And that's a cherry pit." He pointed to a seed the size of a melon. "I could make cherry pies, cherry tarts, cherry puffs . . ."

"We can't grow a cherry tree here," said Papa. "It would take over the entire dungeon and give us away."

Baker Baker sighed. "Well, one can dream," he said, and he placed the giant cherry pit into his pocket.

We identified at least thirty different varieties of seeds, and looking at them all in their piles, I felt as though we'd discovered a great treasure. We would plant the ones that grew tall, and leave behind the ones that grew like roots, or into trees.

"What do we do once we escape the dungeon?" someone asked. "How do we get out of the castle?"

"Does anyone know where we are?" I asked. "I didn't see anything except the fireplace when the king brought us here."

"Same for me," said Baker Baker.

"Me too."

"Have no fear, lads!" said Sir Bluberys. "I know exactly where we are!" He pushed through the crowd on his mule, kicking and scattering seeds. A few people groaned, but they leaned in to hear his answer anyway.

"I saw gold when I was brought here," said Sir Bluberys. "Therefore we are in the treasury!"

Tom slapped his forehead. "Sir Bluberys, practically the entire palace is made of gold! We could be anywhere! We could be in the stables, for all we know, or the bathroom."

"No, I am quite sure," said Sir Bluberys. "I have traveled the giant world extensively. We are in the royal treasury."

"It doesn't matter," I said. "No matter where we are, we should be able to slip out beneath doors or through the cracks of the wall. The hard part is getting out of the dungeon."

We left it at that and got to work sowing seeds. At first I threw the seeds into the dirt. The force of my sling made the plants burst and grow almost instantly, but the roots didn't take a deep hold in the ground that way. Since we needed the plants to be sturdy for climbing, we decided it was best to dig holes for planting.

So we dug into the hard earthen floor of the dungeon, pounding out holes with chisels and hammers and axes, and placing the seeds inside. We replaced the dirt, watered the ground, and waited. They didn't grow as quickly that way, but the roots grew deep and strong, and the leaves and vines crept steadily upward.

Just for fun, I shot more seeds with my sling, and

Tom took a few turns, too. It was as if the force of the seeds hitting the earth made the magic within them explode. The plants had been imprisoned, and once they were set free, they shot out and stretched and grew, reveling in their freedom.

We grew them up along the walls, creating webs of flowers and grass, cornstalks and beanstalks, tomatoes and berries. They spread over the floor and crawled up the walls, transforming our sooty dungeon into a sea of green. They crawled up and over the edge of the dungeon. We grew a blackberry bush, and none of us could help ourselves: we pulled down the giant berries and devoured them, letting the juice drip down our faces and fingers down to our chins and chests.

"You look like you ate a person," said Tom, wiping the juice off his mouth.

"You too," I said, and we both smiled, showing our blackberry-stained teeth.

Something else interesting happened as we grew the seeds. The gold disappeared. It shimmered and dispersed like clouds after a storm, leaving behind a subtle metallic vapor. I guessed gold that's made by magic couldn't remain gold once the magic is reversed. I imagined the look on King Barf's face when he came here and discovered all his gold had been replaced by tomatoes and onions and berries. He ought to be pleased, but more likely he'd explode.

When all the eggs had been split open, and the dungeon was webbed with vines and branches, we prepared to go.

Papa turned to me. "Jack, you discovered the seeds. You found our escape. You should go first."

Everyone nodded in agreement, including Tom, who pushed me toward the wall of green webs. "You'll come up right after me?" I asked.

"Right behind you," said Papa.

I nodded, then I grabbed ahold of a cornstalk and began to climb.

When I reached the top, I stayed hidden in the corn leaves and peered into the dark space before me. The chamber beyond the grate was larger than the dungeon and filled with shadowy objects as big as mountains. Only a sliver of moonlight shone through the curtains and spilled onto the floor like a frozen river.

Something growled. I shrank back into the leaves. The growling continued, a steady rumble occasionally broken by a harsh snort. There must be some dog or beast set to guard us. Slowly, I rose from hiding and looked out in the direction of the noise. I saw no movement. The sound seemed to be coming from a huge rectangular structure set at the center of the chamber. Then there came an altogether different sound.

Bok, bok. Bok, bok. A chicken?

"Quiet, Treasure . . . ," a sleepy voice mumbled.

Bergeek!

Treasure! We were in the royal bedchamber. The

king and his golden hen were in bed. This was way worse than a dog. If we woke the king, it would all be over.

The plants rustled behind me, and Papa and Tom emerged over the edge, breathing loud and hard. I placed my hands to my lips and nodded toward the king. "King Barf . . . ," I whispered. "We're in his bedchamber."

"He snores like a bear!" said Tom.

"Shhh!" I hissed at Tom. "The snoring might cover the sound of our escape if we're quiet."

"You boys search for a way out," whispered Papa. "I'm going back to help the others."

We nodded and scurried off to begin our search. The chamber had several large windows, but they were high and hard to reach. I figured there had to be an easier way out—a mousehole, or a crack beneath a door. But then I remembered how the doors went all the way to the floor, leaving barely a crack big enough to fit my arm through. We searched all the corners and crevices for a mousehole, but every nook and cranny was smoothed with solid gold. There wasn't even a hole big enough for a mouse from my world. We had escaped into a second dungeon.

"I guess we can try the windows," I suggested. "Look, the table is just close enough. If we climb up the table leg, we can grow more plants on the outside and climb down."

"We can swing down like monkeys," said Tom.

We went back to the fireplace. A good fifty people had now reached the top, and more and more were on

the way, climbing beanstalks and cornstalks and tomatoes. Sir Bluberys rose out of the dungeon atop his mule.
The mule's legs were splayed in a very awkward way. They
were being lifted by a slow-growing artichoke.

"Fear not, peasants!" shouted Sir Bluberys. "I am
come to lead the charge!"

The mule bellowed, and they both crashed to the
hearth with a clanging clatter of metal and angry bel-
lows.

"Do not be alarmed!" said Sir Bluberys. "'Tis only a
scratch! Where is the foe? I shall vanquish him with my
blade and valor!"

"*Shhhhhhh!* Sir Bluberys, you must be quiet!" I hissed.

"Oh. Right," he whisper-yelled. "A noble knight must
know how to practice stealth." He tiptoed around with
huge exaggerated steps while his armor creaked and
clacked on the golden tiles of the hearth.

The hen clucked and flapped her wings. "What was
that?" Sir Bluberys cried, looking left and then right.
"Show yourself, you fearsome beast. En garde!" His voice
rang out across the entire chamber.

"Sir Bluberys, *shhhhh!* You'll wake the king."

"The king? You mean my noble liege has come to protect us? Lead me to him. I am his ever faithful servant!"

"No, no." I slapped my hand against my forehead.
"Not *our* king! The giant king!"

"Giant! I have slain many a giant! Fear not! I shall
vanquish the foe! I shall—"

Baker Baker stepped forward and punched Sir Bluberys square in the face—twice. The blabbering knight

fell straight back and crashed to the floor. The hen clucked again. King Barf snorted and stopped snoring altogether. We held our breath.

"Lay . . . ," yawned the king.

Bergeek! There was the sound of rustling feathers, and then the king smacked his lips and began snoring again.

We all glanced at Sir Bluberys, who lay motionless on the floor. "Well done, Baker Baker," Papa said quietly.

"I've been wanting to do that for a while now," the baker admitted.

As if in agreement, the mule blew a big raspberry and kicked Sir Bluberys with one of its hooves.

"Now what?" said Papa.

"There's no way out except the window," I told them. Then I shared my idea about growing more plants to climb out.

"Great idea, Jack," said Papa. "Let's go see what can be done."

But my grand plan was not to be. With great effort we were able to reach the window and pry it open. Except below us there was not dirt, but flowing water. The king's window overlooked the castle moat, and the seeds merely floated away when we threw them down.

"We could jump," said Tom. "There's a chance we'll get swallowed by a fish, but they're usually easy to escape."

Papa and I both stared at Tom.

"Didn't I ever tell you about the time I got swallowed by a fish?"

"No," I said. "But this isn't really the ti—"

"It was amazing!" gushed Tom. "The fish was caught

and taken to the castle kitchen. Then Martha slit open the belly to gut it, and there I was!"

"That's disgusting," I said.

"Amazing," Tom repeated.

"Night is almost over," Papa cut us off. "Whatever we do, we need to hurry, before the king wakes."

He was right. The sky was no longer black but deep purple. Behind his heavy bed curtains, there was a good chance the king would sleep beyond sunrise, but we couldn't take any chances. Any moment he could waken, and we'd be back where we started.

"Look up there," said Tom. He pointed to the stars twinkling in the night sky. I was about to say that now was not the time for stargazing, but then I saw what he was really pointing at. Some of them were zipping around, like comets gone wild. They were getting closer and closer and closer.

"Oh no," I said. "Not *them*."

"Who's that?" asked Papa.

"Pixies!" burst Tom. "Get inside! Shut the window *now*."

We tried to close the window, but it was much harder to pull it shut than push it open, and the pixies were too fast. They streamed in the window by the dozen, chirping and squeaking and chanting over the gold in the chamber—all except one, who rushed straight at me and shoved me to the ground.

"Jack!" she squealed.

"Annabella?"

"I knew I'd find you! I knew it! The pixies knew just

where you were, and we've been searching and searching for a way to get inside and we did it!" The green-haired pixie prince who'd been carrying Annabella fluttered down next to her and chirped. When he saw me, he sneered. I flinched and backed away.

"Bells?" Papa stepped forward. Annabella released me and turned. Her whole being lit up.

"Papa!" Annabella threw herself at Papa, and he picked her up and swung her around. The green pixie squealed in protest.

"It's all right, Saakt. This is my papa."

The pixie squeaked and Annabella laughed.

"What did he say?" asked Papa.

"He says I must look like my mother."

"That she does," said Papa, smiling. "And speaking of your mother, I would like to get home before her heart bursts with worry."

"The pixies will help," said Annabella. "They can fly us home."

"But, Bells," I protested, "it isn't safe. Remember how they attacked us before?"

"I remember how they attacked *you*, after you went at them with Papa's axe."

At this the green pixie pulled out an axe and swung it at my face. I backed away. "Hey! That's mine!"

"*Eets tein sot!*" he squeaked.

"He says it's his now," said Annabella. "You can't be trusted."

"*I* can't be trusted? What about *him*?"

"The pixies saved me from the king, and I've been

with them this whole time. They brought me to their big nest, Grand Pixie Palace, in the woods, and they fed me nectar and honey and let me sit on a golden throne, and I slept in a walnut shell! And they've been helping me search for you every day."

"Bells, I'm glad you found us," I said. "But we can't just ride out of here on pixies. It's too dangerous." My leg was starting to ache just thinking about it.

"We can!" Annabella tugged on my arm. "They're my friends."

"No, Annabella."

"Why don't you trust me?" said Annabella.

"Because you're too small!" I burst.

Annabella scowled at me. "Small doesn't mean I'm wrong, Jack. It doesn't mean I can't help."

I looked at the pixies, now all over the chamber, gleefully pawing and dancing all over the king's gold.

"Jack," said Papa "maybe we should trust your sister? Have faith in the little things?"

I wrestled with this in my head. I didn't want to be rescued by pixies. Also, I had to admit that I didn't want to be rescued by Annabella. I was supposed to be the hero. Jack the great. But maybe part of being great was knowing when to step aside and let someone else take the lead, even if they were smaller than you.

Annabella looked at me pleadingly. I smiled.

"Wow, Bells."

"What?"

"I think you're growing before my eyes."

She looked down at herself. "Really?"

"Really. Can the pixies fly us now?" I asked.

Annabella beamed. "Of course they can!"

She whistled, and the pixies arose from all over the royal bedchamber and converged in a tight diamond formation. I couldn't believe the power my sister held over them—more than their attraction to gold. They flew in a circle faster and faster until they spiraled down like a tornado, squeaking and chirping.

"Bells, tell them to be quiet!"

"I can't just tell them to be quiet. They're excited!"

The pixies began to pick people up one by one, sweeping them off the ground by their arms and legs or clothes. Baker Baker was picked up on either side by two pixies with wasp wings. He became rigid as a board and looked utterly terrified as he was lifted off the ground. Four pixies each took a limb of Sir Bluberys's unconscious body, and another four pixies lifted his mule and flew them out the window.

Papa watched all this and scratched his head as though he were not certain of the whole endeavor, especially when a pixie with yellow hair and blue moth wings grabbed him by the shirt and lifted him off the ground. He hung in the air, flailing his arms and legs like he had no idea how to use them.

"It's all right, Papa!" said Annabella. "It's perfectly safe!" Before Papa could respond, the pixie flew him out into the sky, now pale pink and getting brighter every moment.

With the sun, the king would wake. He would find us gone and much of his gold, too. It would fill him with rage, of course, but would it stop him? Perhaps he would not come after us, but surely the king would find other elves to make his gold, other slaves. The hen would keep laying, the crops would keep dying, and nothing would change. It wasn't enough just to escape. Someone needed to stop the king before his gold obsession destroyed not one but two worlds.

The green pixie took hold of Annabella's arm and lifted her up, and a pixie with orange hair took Tom. A blue pixie grasped my arm, but I pulled away.

"Don't be afraid, Jack! They won't bite you!" Annabella called.

"My sling!" I called back. "I forgot it." I patted my pockets as though searching for it. "Go on ahead! I'll catch up!"

"Hurry!" cautioned Annabella, and she and Tom flew out the window. Soon they were nothing more than specks against the rising sun, now blossoming over the dusty horizon. The rays stretched through the windows, glistening against the gold. There wasn't much time.

I had not lost my sling, of course. But I had gotten an idea.

The pixie looked at me expectantly. She jerked her head toward the window.

"I can't fly out now," I told her. "I have a hen to steal."

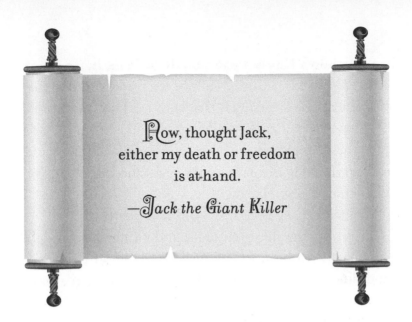

Now, thought Jack,
either my death or freedom
is at hand.

—*Jack the Giant Killer*

CHAPTER TWENTY-FIVE
Stealing Treasure

I had to steal the golden hen. I guess I'd always known it would come to this, one way or another. Ever since I'd seen that hen lay one of her golden eggs, ever since I'd known it was the magic that was sapping all the power and life from the land, I'd known that somehow it would have to be stopped. I couldn't stop the king's greed or the magician's insanity, but I could take the golden hen, and I could put the giant seeds back in the ground and things would start to grow again. Maybe then the king would start to see that the land—and all that could grow out of it—was more precious than gold.

Stealing a hen is a particularly difficult business, almost impossible. I'd tried it once for a joke on Miss Lettie Nettle. The difficulty is that hens are highly excitable. You have to be stealthy—silent as a shadow. You have to take the hen without its noticing. So what did it take to steal a giant hen that lays golden eggs? I had absolutely no idea—maybe just a barrel of luck and a bushel of crazy—and chicken bait, of course, but I had plenty of that.

I ran to the dungeon grate and climbed down just enough to reach an ear of corn. I peeled off the husks and dug into the giant kernels, working them free from the cob. The kernels were as big as my hands. I made a pile of them on the edge of the hearth and then climbed back up the cornstalk. The blue pixie squeaked at me and hovered over the corn.

"Shoo!" I waved her away. But the pixie didn't budge, and I didn't dare do anything to anger her and risk another pixie bite. I gathered as many corn kernels as I could hold and laid a trail from the king's bed to the window on the other side of the room. I hoped the hen was as hungry as she looked.

After I had placed a dozen kernels along the floor, I slid one into each of my pockets and began to climb the posts of the king's bed. The posts were smooth and slick, and they shook with the king's snoring, so I slid down a foot for every two I climbed. Soon my hands became slick with sweat, and I slid all the way back to the floor.

The pixie came closer and suddenly I found myself picked up by the seat of my pants and lifted into the air.

No! I wasn't ready to be rescued yet! But to my surprise, the pixie carried me through the bed curtains and hovered above the sleeping king and the hen.

"Hey, thanks," I whispered. "Uh . . . can you lower me down, please?" Very slowly, we drifted down like a feather floating in a breeze. It would be sunrise by the time we reached the hen. "Faster!" I said, and with an angry squeak, the pixie dropped me the rest of the way. I landed with a soft *flump* on King Barf's pillow.

With a smug smile, the pixie landed gently on top of the hen.

Cluck.

I held my breath and listened. The king was still snoring, but we needed to get out of here fast!

I pulled out a kernel of corn and held it up to the hen's enormous beak. She stretched her neck and, after a few moments of inspection, snatched it out of my hands and gobbled it up.

"Good girl, Treasure," I whispered. "Come on. There's more." I held out another kernel and then backed away. The hen followed, hesitantly at first, and then faster until suddenly she hit the end of her chain.

The chain! Snakes and toads, I'd forgotten about the chain. I stumbled over the pillows and blankets until I found it, but then the king mumbled, "Good girl, Treasure. Lay."

The hen suddenly went rigid. She trembled as she expelled her golden egg, and the king clutched it in his hand and turned over in his sleep, pulling the chain, the chicken, and me with it.

I waited for the king and the hen to settle. Then I took hold of the chain and followed it toward King Barf.

The end of the chain was attached to a golden band on the king's wrist, but the link was not so tight that it could not be unlinked—especially with my tiny elf hands. Very slowly, I unhooked it from the king's wrist. With a gentle tug, I led the hen toward the edge of the bed. She followed me with a curious cluck. The pixie lured her along as well with one of the corn kernels.

I parted the bed curtains. Golden rays of light were seeping through the open window.

I hoisted myself onto the hen's back. We'd be riding from here on out.

"Look down, Treasure," I said. "See the corn? Go get it!"

The hen swiveled her head in confusion, until finally her eyes locked onto the trail of corn below.

Bergeek!

I held tight to Treasure's feathers as she jolted forward and we landed with a heavy thud. Chickens are not the most graceful of birds. Treasure pecked at the corn and followed the trail right to the window, just as I had planned. But when we reached the table, she had no interest in going *up*. The pixie buzzed in front of her face and then rose quickly to the window and back down again. The hen clucked but did not move.

"Treasure?" said the king sleepily.

Oh no! The hen went rigid at the sound of the king's voice, probably expecting a command. "We have to go *now!*" I said, and I dug into the hen's pinfeathers and tugged with all my might. Treasure squawked and flapped her wings wildly and with a jerky motion rose up to the windowsill.

"Treasure?" The king opened his bed curtains and shielded his eyes from the bright light, but as they adjusted, his pink face grew red and his eyes widened with surprise when he saw me.

"Thief!" shouted the king. He jumped out of bed and stumbled after us, reaching for Treasure.

"Go!" I shouted. "Go! Go! Go!" I yanked more feathers, and the pixie grabbed the back end of the hen and flapped her own wings. The hen squawked and tipped out the window, just as the king's fists came crashing down on the sill.

"No!" he screamed. "Treasure! Come back!"

The hen beat her wings in desperation, as did the pixie. We were barely able to move beyond the moat and land at a bumpy run. The king's screams rang in our ears. "Guards! Guards! They stole my hen! They stole my Treasure!"

"Come on, Treasure!" I shouted. "Run! Fly!"

The hen did move, but not nearly fast enough. The pixie tugged and pulled but couldn't lift her, and finally she abandoned us, flying beyond the castle gates and down the hill.

"Wait!" I shouted. "Don't leave us!" So much for trusting the pixies.

There were shouts and crashes from the palace, and I knew the king and his men would soon be upon us.

"Treasure, do you want the king to get you? Move!"

Bergeek! The hen flapped her wings and scuttled forward. We were nearly to the gates when a swarm of pixies appeared. They dipped down, surrounded the hen, and picked her up entirely, led by the pixie I thought had abandoned me. She grabbed me by the back of my pants and lifted me up, up, up and away. A second later, the castle doors burst open and the king spilled out in his gold nightdress, followed closely by a dozen soldiers, groggy and disheveled, holding spears and axes and swords.

"That's my hen!" raged the king. "That's my Treasure! Don't let them get away!"

But what could they do? They couldn't fly. I laughed as the pixies flew us over the castle and out of sight of King Barf and his giant tantrum.

Tom and Annabella were waiting for me at the beanstalk. It looked as though the rest of the elves, including Papa, had already gone down Below. Annabella waved as the pixies lowered us to the ground.

"Jack, what—"

"I couldn't leave her," I said. "King Barf will never stop taking from us as long as he has Treasure."

"What are you going to do with her?" asked Tom.

"Bring her home."

"Mama is going to faint," said Annabella.

"Probably." I smiled as I imagined the look on Mama's face when she saw a chicken the size of her kitchen.

The pixies were buzzing around the hen, squeaking

and chattering, like they knew exactly what she was capable of and wanted in on the gold just as much as the king.

"King Barf's going to come after her," said Tom.

"But they won't know where to look," I said. "I don't think they'll find—"

Boom.

The earth began to vibrate, and a deep rumbling grew louder and louder. Up on the hill, a dozen or more soldiers on horses stormed down the road, including Frederick and Bruno, the magician, and King Barf leading the charge. He was still in his golden nightdress, a crown thrust hastily over his nightcap. I would have laughed if I hadn't been so terrified.

The hen squawked in distress and started to peck furiously at the ground, like she could sense it was her only escape.

"Get on the hen!" I told Tom and Annabella, and we all climbed up her wings and sat on her back. Saakt squeaked and fluttered in front of Annabella.

"Won't you come with us?" she asked.

The green pixie squeaked some more and looked unhappily at the hole.

"Oh, yes. Too much dirt. I understand. I hope to come back someday, if I can. Will you try to stop the king from coming after us?"

The green pixie stood tall and raised his hand in a kind of salute. He squeaked at the other pixies, and they all rose up in a flurry and shot after the king and his men.

"Go down, Treasure!" I kicked at the hen like a horse. At first she just squawked and flapped her wings, but then she stumbled forward enough that we fell through the hole and plummeted toward earth.

"She's not flying!" Annabella shouted.

Indeed she wasn't. The bird was limp and lifeless as a chicken supper. Was she dead? I could see people below, gathered around the beanstalk. I could see our house. I could see the hard ground getting closer and closer.

"Pull her feathers!" I shouted. We yanked hard, which roused the bird to frenzied flight. She flapped her wings just enough to catch the air before we hit the earth. The hen landed with a bounce and a crash, and we tumbled from the tail and rolled onto green grass— normal grass that came in tiny blades beneath our feet. Treasure squawked and flapped around as though her head had just been chopped off. The men from the dungeon had gathered in our fields and were now dodging Treasure's haphazard jerking and flapping.

Tom, Annabella, and I stood up and shook away our dizziness. We plucked the giant feathers from our clothing and hair. We looked around, disoriented from our sudden fall and the change of worlds. The sun was setting here, as it had been rising in the giant world, and everything was so . . . small. We looked at one another with shocked faces.

"I thought we were dead meat," I said.

"I've never been more terrified in my entire life!" said Annabella.

We looked at Tom, who was very pale and still teetering, but he smiled and said, "That was *amazing!*" We all had to laugh at that.

"Well, well. You certainly brought home a big pet," said Baker Baker. He and all the rest were gaping up at the hen, which was eagerly pecking in the ground for bugs and worms and seeds.

"Jack!" someone called. "Annabella!" It was Papa. He was moving toward us from the house—which was now completely covered with vines and leaves from the giant beanstalk—and with him was Mama. She was limping as fast as she could on her injured foot, leaning heavily on Papa's arm.

"Mama!" Annabella shouted, and ran. I ran too. It was only a matter of weeks since we'd left, but it felt like years and years. Annabella and I both reached Mama at the same time, and Mama grabbed us both and squeezed us hard, harder than Martha, even. I always knew Mama loved me, even when I was naughty, but now I knew she loved me so much it actually hurt—both of us.

"I thought you were gone. I thought I'd never see you again, you naughty, naughty children!" Tears rolled down her cheeks.

"We're home, Mama," said Annabella.

"Home," I said, wiping a tear from my eye before anyone saw.

Cluck, cluck, bergeek!

Mama looked up and shoved us behind her to protect us.

"Don't worry," said Annabella. "She's really a very friendly hen, and she'll be able to catch all the mice around the farm!"

"A hen . . . ," said Mama. She twisted at her apron, unable to take her eyes off Treasure. "Well, I suppose it's better than a giant spider or . . . or a toad."

Annabella looked at me and giggled. It felt so good to have everything back in its rightful place and size, but then I saw Tom standing alone with his hands in his pockets, kicking his feet in the dirt. I pried myself from Mama's arms and waved for Tom to come over. He walked toward us with his eyes on the ground and his shoulders up around his ears.

"Mama, this is Tom. Tom Thumb." He smiled at the name.

"Hello, Tom," said Mama. Tom opened his mouth to reply, but just at that moment, the sky rumbled and then—

Boom.

Boom.

The giant beanstalk quivered. The earth trembled. The sky creaked and groaned.

BOOM!

Mama grabbed me and Annabella. People ran and screamed as dirt began to sprinkle down. Great globs of earth hurtled from the sky and exploded on the ground.

"They're coming," I said. "King Barf is coming."

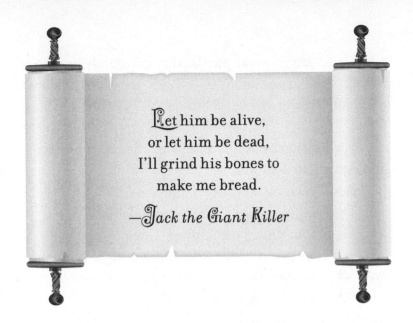

Let him be alive,
or let him be dead,
I'll grind his bones to
make me bread.

—*Jack the Giant Killer*

CHAPTER TWENTY-SIX

Jack vs. King Barf

Bergeek! The hen flapped her wings and ran in circles, molting brown feathers. She knew her master was coming for her.

BOOM! CRACK!

The sky split open wider than ever before. More dirt poured down like a cloudburst.

"Run!" shouted Papa. "Take cover! Don't let the giants see you!"

People ran this way and that, like sheep with no shepherd. They ran into the trees, crouched down behind rocks, and jumped into the Giant Feet Ponds. Even Sir Bluberys hunkered down in a ditch. He didn't seem so eager for battle anymore. His black eye had left him chastened.

Papa ran toward the house with Mama in his arms, and Annabella followed.

"Jack!" Papa called. "Come on!"

"The hen!" I shouted. "I have to hide her!"

"There's no time, Jack! Hurry!"

But I couldn't just leave her in plain sight. I dug into my pockets and pulled out another piece of corn.

"Come on, Treasure," I coaxed. She followed me toward the torn-up barn. The roof was gone, and it was mostly in shambles, but maybe that was all the better. I could hide her in plain sight in a pile of straw and lumber.

"Good girl." I tossed the corn into a pile of hay. Treasure squawked and dug her beak into the pile. I went outside again and looked up.

Ropes were dropping down from the sky—not just one or two, but dozens and dozens. The giants began to descend one after the other. Soldiers with shields and swords landed—

Boom! Boom! BOOM!

—on the ground. The earth shook so violently, my stiff legs buckled beneath me.

After the soldiers, Frederick and Bruno came down, followed by the magician. He climbed down halfway, then did a flip and landed on his bottom.

And then came the biggest dirt shower of all. With a

crash and a roar, King Barf lowered himself down in his gold nightdress and a crown over his nightcap.

BOOM!

The hen squawked and flapped, sending bits of straw everywhere.

"Treasure! Where is my Treasure?"

Boom, boom, Boom!

The king stomped all over, tearing up bushes and trees, exposing all the people hiding beneath them. They screamed and scattered, but King Barf stomped down his foot and they were half buried in a wave of dirt. He snatched someone up and lifted him by a leg. It was Baker Baker.

"Where is my Treasure! Where is the thief who took my golden hen?"

"I don't know! I don't know! I'm just the Baker Baker!" Everyone began to flee and find other hiding places.

"Catch them!" said the king. "Squeeze them until they give me back my Treasure!"

The giants stomped around, scooping up the escaped prisoners. The magician picked up three men and juggled them. Sir Bluberys tried to escape around the other side of the house, but his mule brayed loudly.

"Sir Bluberys!" shouted Bruno, and he bounded toward him, but Frederick tripped his brother and snatched up Sir Bluberys for himself.

"Give him here!" Bruno chased after Frederick. They nearly crushed a dozen people.

I watched all this from the remains of the barn, quietly moving straw and broken boards to keep Treasure covered. If anyone searched here, it would look like a jumble of ruins.

"Treasure!" shouted the king. "Where is my Treasure! Where is she!"

Bergeek! The hen flapped her wings, upsetting the boards and straw. I jumped onto her back and tried to calm her.

"Treasure, quiet!" I hissed. "Lay down!"

The hen seized up. She squawked and released a golden egg.

Oh no. I said the magic word!

A golden egg rolled out of the barn. I winced as it wobbled to a stop right at the magician's toes. He bent down and picked it up. "Your Goldness! Look at this! A golden egg! They have them here, too!" He waved the egg in the air.

The king snatched the egg out of his hand and sniffed it. "Still warm," he muttered, then he sniffed the air.

"Quiet!" shouted the king. "Be still!"

The world became quiet and still; even the hen seemed to hold her breath.

"Treasure, lay!" King Barf commanded.

The hen trembled as though trying to resist, but she could not disobey. She laid another egg, and again it rolled out of the barn. It came to a stop at the king's heel. He whipped around and picked up the egg, searching all around to see where it had come from.

"Lay!" he commanded again, and again the hen obeyed.

"Over there!" called the magician. "In that pile of sticks!"

Boom, boom, boom!

A great shadow loomed over us, and in an instant the jumbled remains of the barn were ripped apart so that the hen and I were fully exposed to King Barf.

Bergeek! The hen went berserk.

"Treasure!" the king exclaimed, like a child who has found a missing favorite toy. Then he saw me. "And the thief!"

There was no time to flee, no place to hide. King Barf snatched the hen in one hand and me in the other. Up we both went.

"Don't you worry," the king cooed to the hen. "You're safe, and I'll never let anyone take you again. Now, lay!" The hen froze, trembled, and expelled a golden egg into the king's hand.

"Lay! Lay! Lay!" It was as if the king were checking to make sure the magic still worked. And it did. The beanstalk was fading before my very eyes from green to brown. The leaves curled and the bean pods shriveled. Didn't they see? Couldn't any of the giants see?

The king lifted me to his lumpy pink face. "You will pay for stealing my Treasure."

"Your Majesty, please!" I said. "I meant no harm. I only took your hen to save your kingdom from destruction!"

"You steal *my* gold to save *my* kingdom?" the king

scoffed. "Did you hear that? The elf says he stole my hen, my golden hen, to save us!" The king laughed, and so did the magician and the giant soldiers. It felt like the whole world was laughing at me.

"No, I promise! You must listen! Your hen, the golden eggs . . . the magic is killing all the growing things. Don't you see? The magic is making your land poor."

"Poor? Ha!" said King Barf. "My hen has made me rich! The richest king in the world!"

"But the magic . . . the hen has to get the power to make gold from somewhere, and she's getting it from the earth. Every time the hen lays an egg, you kill something growing—don't you see? Look at the beanstalk!" I pointed to the brown stalks, the withering leaves. "It was green just a moment ago, before you made more golden eggs."

There was a shifting among the other giants. Mutters and whispers. They were beginning to see.

"Of course!" said the magician, clapping his hands. "Your Goldness, I remember now! When I made the golden hen, I called for all the powers in the *earth* to make her gold! Oh, goody—now we can make a whole flock of golden hens, and golden geese and pigeons and peacocks . . ."

"Yes!" said the king. "We shall, Magician."

"But, Your Majesty," said a soldier, "if this elf speaks the truth, then this hen and her golden eggs are the cause of the famine."

"And so what?" said the king. "What is a beanstalk to my gold? Nothing but a nasty little weed."

"Your Goldness," I said, carefully, a plan sprouting in my brain, "I've never liked beans myself, but at least they can feed you. Can your gold do that?"

"Of course it can! My gold has always fed me well. I'm the richest king there ever was."

"So you need nothing besides gold?"

"Nothing!"

"Very well, then," I said. "Eat it."

"Eat what?" said the king.

"Your gold. If gold is all you need, if the gold makes you so rich, then you should eat it."

The king stared for a moment, and then he laughed a high, mirthless laugh. "What an amusing little thief! Shall I eat you as well?"

"Are you afraid, giant, to eat your gold? If you can't eat your gold, then you will starve, because soon that's all that will be left in the worlds Above and Below. Just gold. If gold is all you need, then prove it. Eat some. Eat one of your golden eggs."

"Ha! Why not? It's an *egg*, after all." The king turned me over to one of his soldiers. He picked up a golden egg, polished it on his nightgown like an apple, and popped it into his mouth. He crunched down once, twice, three times and swallowed. He looked at me and smiled. "Delicious! I think I'll have another."

He ate another egg, and another. He gorged himself on golden eggs until there were none left, and still he was not done.

"Lay!" he commanded the hen.

The hen obeyed, and the king ate another egg.

"Lay! Lay! Lay!"

The hen laid three more eggs, and with each egg, the land faded. A tree collapsed. Flowers and shrubs shriveled. The brown beanstalk started to fall from the sky, coiling like a giant snake until the final stretch of it crashed to the earth and dust billowed out in a cloud.

"Gold is good for me." King Barf patted his stomach and belched. He snatched me from the soldier's hand and brought me back to his face. His breath was metallic and foul. "Now I will grind your bones, you little thief!"

His hand squeezed me tight. My breath grew short. My vision blurred, and my bones groaned with the enormous pressure. Any second now and they would crack, snap, and crumble.

King Barf froze. The villainous smile left his face, and his nose started to twitch. He sniffed. His eyes crossed.

"Eeh! Aye! Oh! Uhhh . . . ahhh-CHOOGAA!"

Leaves exploded out of the king's nose. Vines crawled down his mouth and chin and spread over his cheeks, so he looked like he had a green beard. The king went cross-eyed looking at the plant, and then he ripped it out of his nose. He roared in pain and then gazed at the plant in wonder. "What is this?" he said.

The magician clapped his hands together and jumped up and down. "Ooh! Well done, Your Majesty! What marvelous magic! Do it again!"

The king kept hold of me, but he dropped the golden hen and clutched at his stomach. He staggered sideways and groaned in pain.

"What's going on? What is this! I've been poisoned!"

Suddenly a vine shot out of his ear. It branched out in three directions, and buds formed on each branch. King Barf reached up and pulled but only managed to snap off a leaf. The king roared and threw it down, but then another vine exploded out of his nose, and several more from his mouth. He coughed and choked and tore at the vines and leaves, but they just kept coming. The vines twisted down and wrapped around the king's legs. Pods formed and swelled on the vines. Green beans.

The beanstalks wrapped around his ankles. His face went from white to pink to red and then to blue. His dark eyes met mine, wide and frightened, and then angry like a mad dog's. He roared through the plants and squeezed me tighter, until a vine coiled right around his hand, forcing his fist to release me. I dangled from a vine a hundred feet above the ground as the king staggered and swayed and, finally overcome by green growing things, crashed to the earth.

I held on tight as the vines continued to grow, thrashing and roiling like a terrific storm. Dozens of beanstalks twisted and knotted themselves around King Barf, until he was consumed by the tangle of stalks. The vines wound around each other and rose up into the air. They crashed through the Blue, and dirt showered down in a torrent. The earth tilted and trembled. It felt as though the sky were falling, until at last it stopped.

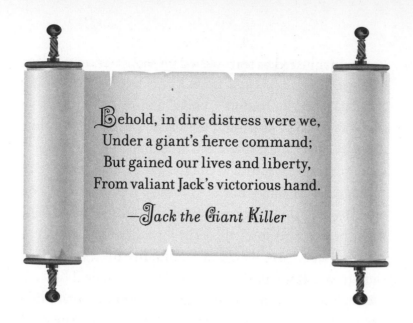

Behold, in dire distress were we,
Under a giant's fierce command;
But gained our lives and liberty,
From valiant Jack's victorious hand.

—*Jack the Giant Killer*

CHAPTER TWENTY-SEVEN

Growing Up and Down

Above and Below, the whole world was still and silent. Everyone, giant and small, stared at the tangle of beanstalks that had been King Barf. I shook the dirt from my hair and climbed through the vines and branches and leaves. When I emerged from the plants, everyone stared at me.

"Jack!" shouted Papa. He burst from the crowd and ran to me. He picked me up in his arms and held me tight, tighter than King Barf even, but I felt so safe, I didn't care that I couldn't breathe.

"You did it," said Papa. "You conquered the giant."

My vision blurred as tears welled up in my eyes and rolled down my cheeks.

There was a crashing sound of metal. Papa and I came apart and I wiped my eyes. The giant soldiers were all dropping their swords and axes and shields. One of them stepped forward and kneeled down before me. "What is your name, boy?" he asked gently.

"Jack," I said in a trembling voice.

The giant scooped me up in his hand and raised me high for all to see. "Hail, Jack! Conqueror of King Bartholomew Archibald Reginald Fife!"

"Hail, Jack!" the other giants cheered, except Frederick. He shoved between the soldiers, still holding Sir Bluberys in his hand.

"So what?" spat Frederick. "So the king was fool enough to fall for elf tricks. They're still littler than us! They're still our slaves!"

Suddenly Bruno came hurtling at Frederick like a battering ram. Sir Bluberys went flying out of Frederick's hand, and Papa and I rushed to help him up while Bruno grabbed a sword and pointed it at Frederick's neck.

"Being bigger does *not* make you in charge!" Bruno shouted.

Frederick gulped as the sword got closer and closer to his neck. I guessed Bruno had been teased and bossed one too many times.

"That's right, lad!" shouted Sir Bluberys as he staggered to his feet. "Stand your ground!"

Frederick slowly backed away toward the ropes. Bruno gestured with his sword, and Frederick scuttled up like a frightened beetle. He disappeared beyond the Blue, a sprinkling of dirt falling in his wake.

The news of King Barf's defeat spread quickly. Queen Opal commanded that all elves be returned to their homes and compensated for any food or animals that had been taken.

Over the next few weeks our village was returned piece by piece. Baker Baker's bakery was extracted from the dungeon and replaced in the village, as were the cobbler's shop and the mill. Widow Francis requested that she be given the shoe she had lived in at the cobbler's because her children preferred it. And the children brought home Milky White's calf, George. Widow Francis tried to return him to us, but Papa refused. He said those kids loved George more than Horace loved his pig, Cindy.

Miss Lettie Nettle settled for one giant cabbage in exchange for her stolen field, and even though we did not have a village festival, everyone agreed it would have taken the prize in vegetables.

The queen appointed Bruno as Ambassador to the Elves and Frederick as his lowly assistant in charge of manure distribution. And plenty of manure was needed, because the crops were growing again, both Above and Below.

I told Bruno about the dungeon beneath the king's fireplace and the seeds that were inside the golden eggs. Since the magic contained in the seeds made them grow very fast, the giants were able to build up enough stores to last them through the winter. We also had enough of the giant seeds from the golden eggs to grow our own food. Tom, Annabella, and I spent a day at target practice, throwing giant seeds all over the fields surrounding the giant beanstalk that had grown out of King Barf. We grew giant tomato vines, berry bushes, and pumpkins as big as carriages. We called it Barf Gardens.

"It doesn't sound very appetizing," Mama complained one day as she was harvesting a squash.

"But it's *funny*," I said. "And besides, the garden grew so fast, it's almost like the ground barfed it up."

Mama rolled her eyes and shook her head.

"Jack's right, Mama," Annabella chimed in. "And it will always remind us how something as horrid and sour as King Barf can be turned into something sweet and delicious." She took a bite out of a strawberry as big as herself.

"Like sour milk turns into cheese," muttered Tom, looking up toward the sky. I knew he was missing Martha and giant cheese and his sugar bowl. He probably missed getting swallowed every now and then. No one said he had to stay, but something seemed to keep him here.

When winter came, the giant world was closed to us. The beanstalk still stretched to the sky, but even if we could reach the top in the driving rain and snow, we suspected the Blue was frozen, and surely above all the dirt were miles of snow. I didn't really care to dig through that. So we waited patiently for spring. We sat by the fire and told stories. We told the tales of Grandpa Jack, and we told true stories of our own adventures.

Our friends and neighbors brought back endless stories from the giant world, many of them sad and dreary but some of them funny, like one about a giant who secretly dropped elves into his children's pockets, so whenever the children were naughty, the elves would whisper things to scare the children! We all laughed at that one. If I had been one of the elves in a child's pocket, I probably would have just helped her be naughtier.

Really, I wasn't very naughty anymore. Not *very*. Except when there's snow, it's so easy to just pack it in your hands and peg your little sister. . . .

"Jack!" Annabella screamed. She ran away, and I thought she was going to tattle—same old Annabella—but a minute later there was a load of snow going down my back. I yelped and did a dance to get the snow and cold out of my shirt, and Annabella just stood there laughing. Then Tom threw a snowball at my butt, and we had an epic snow battle. We built forts and threw snowballs and wrestled in the snow, until Tom suddenly froze up like a snowman. He didn't move, even when I hit him with a snowball as big as his head.

"Tom?" I tapped his shoulder, but he just kept staring off into the distance.

"Do you think he turned to ice somehow? Like a spell?" asked Annabella.

Tom's eyes widened, and I followed his gaze. There was Jaber the tinker, hobbling down the road, leading a cow in one hand and pulling a cart with the other. He sang:

> Tommy boy, Tommy boy,
> Full of lies and mischief.
> Tommy boy, Tommy boy,
> Angerin' the mistress . . .

Tom continued to stare. I guessed he was staring at Jaber's wooden leg. "That's Jaber," I said. "He's the one who gave me the beans to get to the giant world."

"Jack traded our milking cow for them," said Annabella. "Mama was furious."

"Well, it was worth it, wasn't it? We got Papa back."

Tom mumbled something, too quiet for me to hear. Something about Papa.

"Yes," I said uncertainly. "Jaber helped me find Papa."

Tom just kept staring, and Jaber's eyes were now fixed on Tom, too. He also seemed to have frozen where he stood.

"Jack," whispered Annabella, "do you think Jaber could be Tom's—"

"Papa!" shouted Tom, and he burst into a run.

Jaber let go of the cow and the cart, and he ran as fast as he could on his wooden leg.

Of course! Why hadn't I realized it before? Tom was Tommy, the boy Jaber was always singing about. And that story Jaber told, about the man and his son who had been taken by the giant, that was Tom and Jaber.

Jaber had been dropped, his leg broken so badly it had to be removed, and Tom had been taken up to the giant world without him.

As soon as they reached each other, they fell down in the snow. They laughed and cried and hugged one another so tight, I didn't think even giants could tear them apart.

And so Jaber and Tom stayed with us that winter. We were cozy in the house, and sometimes I think we drove Mama a little crazy, but if we ever got in her way, she took delight in whacking us on the head with giant beans. She stacked them all neatly in the cellar, and though I still did not think they were the most delicious food in the world, I ate them because I grew them and growing is a magical thing.

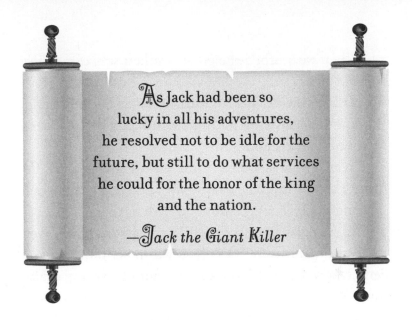

As Jack had been so
lucky in all his adventures,
he resolved not to be idle for the
future, but still to do what services
he could for the honor of the king
and the nation.

—*Jack the Giant Killer*

EPILOGUE

Great

"**H**urry, Jack! Climb faster!" Annabella shouted down the beanstalk.

"I'm coming," I huffed. I was out of climbing practice. I had done very little all winter, and the distance to the Blue seemed greater than I remembered. I looked down. Our village looked like nothing more than a few blocks and sticks, with little bugs crawling all around them. So small, and yet it was my whole world.

At last we reached the Blue. It felt cold and moist, like it was thawing from winter. We found the edges of a seam, pulled it apart, and got a dirt shower.

When we reached the giant world, it was completely transformed. Everything was alive and green and growing. The grass was thick and reached over our heads, the flowers were budding and blossoming, and the butterflies, and beetles, and birds—

"Watch out!" shouted Tom. We all had to duck beneath the beanstalk as a crow swooped down and tried to snatch us.

Yes, the giant world was still a dangerous place, even when the giants were friendly. It was probably *more* dangerous now that the land was green and growing again. More snakes and toads and other menacing creatures.

Mum Martha cried tears of joy when we popped out of the mousehole into her kitchen, and we all had a giant slab of cheese to celebrate—cheese she made herself from a giant cow. Tom wanted to try to milk it, but I didn't think that was the best idea.

News of our arrival spread quickly, and a giant feast was given in our honor. Queen Opal sat at the head of the table, wearing a green gown and a crown of yellow roses, not a stitch of gold on her or in sight. The golden place settings had been exchanged for silver and pewter and crystal, the linens for creamy silks and rich red velvets. Apparently Queen Opal had been working hard to remove all the gold from the palace. It wasn't worth so much anymore.

Prince Archie was next to the queen. He had grown twice as big since the winter. And he had learned to walk. He ran around the table banging everything with a silver spoon, singing, "Fee! Fie! Fo! Fum!"

"He's probably the most dangerous giant in all The Kingdom," I said.

"But the cutest," said Annabella.

"Cute can be very deceiving," said Tom. "Speaking of which, here come the pixies." A swarm of pixies flew through the window and shot straight toward us.

"Get some dirt!" I shouted, and hid behind a goblet.

"Don't be ridiculous," said Annabella. "I asked the queen to invite them."

"And she said yes?"

"Of course," said Annabella. "She thought it was a grand idea. They're helping her remove all the gold from the palace."

The pixies descended upon us in all their color and sparkle. They were delighted to see Annabella, and the green pixie prince brought her a crown, delicately woven with strands of gold.

"Oh, thank you, Saakt!" she said. "I shall wear it always."

"Does this mean I have to call you Princess Annabella?" I teased.

The green pixie snapped at me in a shrill voice, showing his razor-sharp teeth. I backed away slowly. I could feel my old bite scar throbbing.

Annabella smirked. "Saakt says you're to call me *Queen* Annabella."

Snakes and toads! I do not like pixies at all.

But that didn't matter. I liked the giants, and the giants loved me. Martha had cooked up a storm of pies and stews and cakes. There were mountains of giant berries and potatoes and bread. There was a roasted chicken, but it wasn't Treasure, for she had become Bruno's pet. After a few months of no one commanding her to lay, the magic faded from her, and she went back to laying regular eggs, though the shells were speckled with gold.

Tom sat next to Martha, and I sat next to Bruno. Sir Bluberys was still with him, now clad in shining armor with a sword and shield. Sir Bluberys even had a real horse to be his noble steed, though it still bucked him off.

Kessler the magician sat next to Bruno and Sir Bluberys, with two guards standing directly behind him. The queen had forbidden him to ever use magic again, and if he cast even the tiniest spell, the guards were to chop off his head. Kessler did not seem at all worried by this, because he believed his head was really a pumpkin.

"I think it's growing, don't you?" He patted his orange hair, which poufed out in a way that actually was quite pumpkin-like. "In the fall I will turn it into a pie!"

"He's barmy as a barnacle," said Sir Bluberys.

Someone tapped on a glass and everyone hushed.

Queen Opal stood. "I'd like to make a toast," she said. "To our little friends who helped us in The Kingdom's time of need."

"Hear, hear!" said a few.

"And to Jack"—the queen smiled down at me—"who showed us how to grow again."

"To Jack!"

"Jack!"

I blushed as everyone stood and raised their goblets.

"Jack," said Annabella, "they think you're great!"

"Yes, well, I knew that all along," said Tom, who was devouring a giant pie. "Knew it from the moment he catapulted off a spoon."

I tapped on a giant spoon. "Shall we do it again?"

"I get to go first!" shouted Annabella.

Life on the farm was quiet after all that adventure, but I didn't mind. I worked with Papa in the fields, planting and growing and harvesting giant food. It fed our village like royalty, and royalty came to see it—this giant garden in a little village. All kinds of people came from near and far. They offered us gold and silver and treasures just for one piece of giant food, but we didn't take it. Firstly, what good was gold and silver to us? We couldn't eat it. And secondly, we had more than enough, and it all kept growing, so we just shared as much as we could.

"Isn't she a sight, Jack?" Papa said as we looked out over our fields. For the first time I saw what he saw: oceans and mountains and rivers of treasure, all of it green and growing.

"She's great," I said.

Papa wrapped his arm around my shoulder. I was almost as tall as he was now. "You're great," he said.

I smiled. I felt great. And it wasn't because I had conquered a giant or become a hero. It wasn't because I had gone on a noble quest and had so many adventures. It was because of all the growing. It was the things growing up and down, in and out, and around and between us all. It was the things growing inside me. The growing was magic, and the growing made the whole world great.

THE END

AUTHOR'S NOTE

Fee, fie, fo, fum.
I smell the blood of an Englishman.
Be he alive, or be he dead,
I'll grind his bones to make my bread.

These words, spoken by a giant, appear in both "Jack and the Beanstalk" and "Jack the Giant Killer," English folktales collected by the folklorist and historian Joseph Jacobs. These "Jack" tales share many similarities—so many that for years I thought they were just slightly different versions of the same tale. But upon closer inspection, I came to realize that despite all their similarities, they are also wildly different.

When I began the process of writing *Jack*, I thought I would just stick with "Jack and the Beanstalk" for inspiration, but there was something about "Jack the Giant Killer" that kept poking me every now and then, refusing to leave me alone. Clearly he felt he deserved a role in the tale as well, as any self-respecting adventurer would. I just couldn't see where this Jack fit, exactly.

As I was thinking about these two Jacks and how they might be combined, I stumbled upon an old video of my great-grandfather shortly before he died, just a year before I was born. What a treasure! Here was my great-grandfather, ninety-two years old, telling hilarious tales of stealing eggs from the neighbors' chicken coop, getting expelled from school, and skipping work to meet girls at the state fair. He was a rogue and an adventurer, much like Jack. These stories of my great-grandfather felt a little like fairy tales.

I think it was this experience that led me to bring together both "Jack and the Beanstalk" and "Jack the Giant Killer" in a way that would honor their similarities *and* their differences. What if these Jacks were somehow related? I decided that my hero, Jack, had been named after his great-grandfather, the famed Jack the Giant Killer, or "Grandpa Jack." He would grow up on his adventurous tales of conquering giants and, as his namesake, believe he was destined to be a heroic giant killer himself and claim fame and riches. As his journey unfolds, Jack looks to the stories to guide him, to inform him of who he is, but he also learns to make his own path.

Jack is my ode to the stories of my great-grandfather, and to all my ancestors whose stories have been passed down to me from long, long ago. I feel deeply connected to them. Their stories have rooted me, and yet, like Jack, my own life story has grown in wildly different and unpredictable ways. I can't wait to see what unfolds next.

ACKNOWLEDGMENTS

This book was a huge undertaking for me. So big, it took a giant village to bring *Jack* to life, so it is only appropriate that I give giant thanks to all those involved in this story.

To my heroic editor, Katherine Harrison, whose insight, faith, and encouragement kept both this book and me from dying an untimely death. You saved our lives!

To the gorgeous team of copy editors, Renée Cafiero, Marianne Cohen, Artie Bennett, and Alison Kolani. You possess superpowers to make magic logical and logic magical.

Thanks to Jinna Shin, Katrina Damkoehler, and Heather Kelly for their beautiful design.

To my super agent, Michelle Andelman, who possesses great calm and good sense. I can always trust you to say what needs to be said.

To Kate Coursey, Peggy Eddleman, Janet Leftley, Jenilyn Tolley, Krista Van Dolzer, and Tamera Wissinger, my trusty critique partners with sharp eyes and big hearts.

To my girls (you know who you are), who helped raise my children, fed me good food, and lifted my spirits every day. Your friendship means the world to me.

To Dad, who always knows what to do, and to Mom, who always listens. And love and thanks to all my siblings, who are always a great source of inspiration, but Patrick takes the cake with this one. Thanks for the torture, brother. It's paying off.

To Whitney, Ty, and Topher, my biggest fans, always too happy to give Mom her writing time. (Quit sneaking snacks, little thieves!)

And finally to my husband, Scott. I could not wish for anything more. You have given me the world.

Do you have big eyes?

And a big snout?

AND BIG, SHARP TEETH?

All the better to gobble up
Liesl Shurtliff's next adventure:

RED

THE TRUE STORY OF
RED RIDING HOOD

COMING SOON TO A BOOKSTORE NEAR YOU